WOLF MATED

LUNA MARKED BOOK THREE

HEATHER RENEE

ISBN: 979-8476395171

Line Editing and Proofing: Jamie from Holmes Edits

Cover: Covers by Juan

Character Art: @kalynne_art on Instagram

DEDICATION

To Michelle.
Thank you for being my emotional support person.

CONTENTS

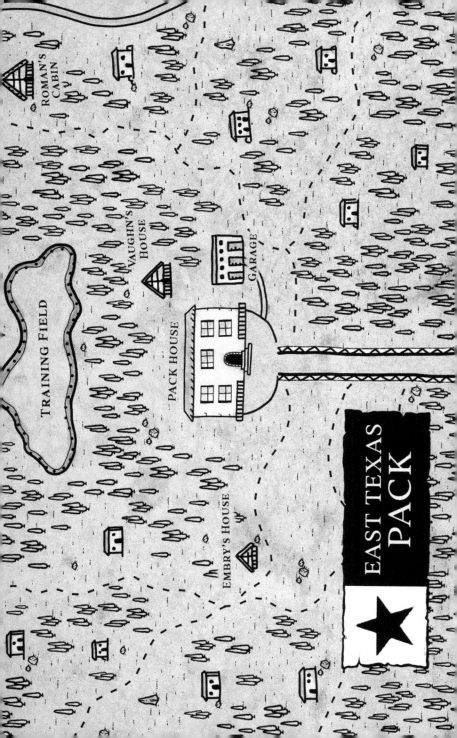

CAIT

Hungry and raging. That was how I'd felt the last couple of weeks as I healed from the poison Callista left me with before I killed her. There was a hunger brewing inside me for so many things that it had been hard to know where my focus needed to be.

I was convinced bonding with Roman was something that needed to happen sooner rather than later, but he wasn't as eager to seal the deal as I'd expected him to be.

Something I'd been obviously relentless about in many ways.

My palm is going to find your ass if you don't stop, Roman grumbled into my thoughts. The ability to mind speak had come and gone up until a few days ago. Once the perk finally decided to work consistently, it had completely changed my tactics.

Was that supposed to be a threat? Because I didn't hear one. Plus, I haven't done anything wrong to justify your tone, I replied sweetly.

I'd have to disagree. Picturing yourself naked in our bed while I'm in a meeting and sending those thoughts to me justifies quite a bit.

He closed the connection and got back to his conference call with the other pack alphas and betas. While I felt moderately bad for interrupting him, I'd needed the distraction from my thoughts of hunting down Kyle.

He'd killed Roman's father and needed to pay, yet none of our resources had been able to track the bastard down. That was where my raging came from. Kyle and Cohen had stuck their noses where they didn't belong, and people were dead. On top of that, the supernatural council had caught wind of my abilities.

To say that things were tense would be the understatement of the year.

There had been a one-month timeframe set for me to turn myself over to the council. Ten days of that time had passed, and as we inched closer to our looming deadline, my emotions were all over the place.

You need to be in control more than ever. Roman needs to stop being so obstinate, Adira complained. Her ire had moved on from my stupidity to Roman's, and it was great to not be the cause of her wrath.

Though, I understood where Roman was coming from. I'd been an idiot only mere weeks ago and rejected him. My change of heart had happened after life-altering events—you know, like dying a time or two —but that didn't mean my feelings weren't true. I'd just needed to have some sense knocked back into me before I truly understood.

All that didn't matter, though. There were consequences to my choices, and Roman's wants mattered just as much as mine. He needed to be certain I was confident in my decision, and I respected that. Even when the wait was driving me batshit crazy.

I'd meant it before when I agreed to push aside my fears and move forward. I was ready for whatever came next, and that included being bonded to Roman. I'd be as patient with him as he was with me.

"Hey, Asstie. You busy?" Embry called from the hallway.

I'd moved out of her cabin last week when I woke up one morning to find my clothes were no longer in my room.

Roman had added my belongings to what he'd already had for me and made things official. It was then that I knew I was ready to bond with him. The old me would have been pissed the hell off by him doing that on his own, but the complete opposite had happened.

My heart had melted into a puddle, and I'd eagerly accepted the movement of my stuff.

"Come on in," I replied back to Embry as the door was already opening. Her rose-gold hair was braided, and she had a backpack on. "Where are you going?"

My shoulders stiffened and fingers flexed as I awaited her answer.

"Vaughn and I are going to take the lead on the hunt for Kyle," she answered sheepishly.

I raised a brow. "By yourselves?"

"That's the plan."

My head shook. "I'm coming with you."

Embry wagged a finger at me. "I knew you'd say that, and no, you're not. You've been making progress by leaps and bounds, and you have your final test tomorrow that I'm beyond pissed I have to miss. Plus, we can't risk the council snatching you. Here, we have some protections. Out there? We have no leg to stand on if they find us."

The supernatural council was going to be the death of me. Possibly quite literally.

"How long are you two going to be gone?" I asked.

"No idea. However long it takes. I can't come back here and see Ramona's face if we fail. She'll take matters into her own hands if we don't bring results this trip. It's been hell keeping her here."

Oh, that I was already well aware of.

When Jack died, I'd been unconscious for the worst of it, but I'd seen the violent outbursts she still had two or three times a week. Her mate had been murdered, and she'd been forced to stay within the pack. Forcing an alpha female to do anything was not a pretty sight.

Roman had used his alpha power on her— something he'd very rarely used on anyone else. She'd refused to speak to him at first, but finally caved after the first five days.

Embry sat on my bed and took her backpack off. "How are things with you? Still being shut down?"

"I wouldn't say 'shut down' is the right way to describe things, but nothing has changed either." I sighed.

"I have some tips—"

I waved my hand as I joined her on the bed, crossing

4

my legs and facing her. "I'm good. I promise. Though, I wish we were going with you."

Vaughn strolled into the room as if he owned the place. "Hard pass, Witchy Wolf. We don't need the kind of attention you'll draw."

I laughed at his newest nickname for me. The beta was convinced I was part witch, given my inability to die—or stay dead, anyway.

Vaughn jumped onto the bed, nearly causing me to fall off with his momentum. "I thought you enjoyed the way I shook things up," I joked.

"Around here? Hell yes. Out there? Not so much. Plus, Roman would murder me," Vaughn answered.

"Yes, I would. I also might enjoy killing you for laying in the same bed as my mate," Roman said, standing in the open doorway with his arms crossed.

Vaughn held his hands up. "Easy there. I was just coming to get Embry."

Roman entered the room as Vaughn got up, grabbing Embry's bag and tossing it at her. "Time to go?" she asked.

"Yep. It's almost three," Vaughn confirmed while stroking his red beard. "If we leave now, we'll make our first stop just in time to grab dinner and go night hunting."

"Perfect." Embry turned to me, and I stood to hug her goodbye. "Be safe here, good luck tomorrow, and I'll let you know how things are looking out there," she said.

I nodded against her shoulder. "Don't do anything overly stupid without me, Asstie."

"Wouldn't dream of it." She moved back, joining Vaughn closer to the door and waving.

I blew her a kiss and then sent one to Vaughn for fun. Roman's chest rumbled next to me as they moved out of eyesight.

Turning toward him, I patted his chest. "How was your meeting?"

He picked me up by my elbows and tossed me back on the bed before stalking forward like the predator I enjoyed playing with. The rumble in his chest grew in volume, telling me his wolf was close to the surface. "It went as expected. I didn't give them all of the information, but enough that they've agreed to come here and meet you. Once they hear us out, I know they'll agree nobody has the right to demand another supernatural's presence without just cause."

"And I've given the Supernatural Council no reason, right?" I asked, because while I'd learned a lot recently, there would never be a day when I knew enough.

Roman settled his body over mine as I propped myself up on my elbows. "You most certainly have not given them any reason," he said before leaning in to kiss me.

Our lips met for the briefest of seconds while I sank my fingers into his hair and jerked him closer, causing us to fall back into the pillows.

"I missed you," I murmured against his cheek as he kissed down my neck.

"Not nearly as much as I missed you."

I no longer had any qualms about showing him affection. My wolf had made sure of that, and none of the other pack members seemed to bat an eye when they saw us together anymore. If only everything else wasn't so shitty, life would be great.

Roman pushed up, his eyes meeting mine, intense yet loving. "You've settled into the pack life this last week faster than I thought you would. How are you feeling about meeting the other alphas?"

When I first arrived in Texas and learned that wolf shifters were real, I'd been petrified of them, but I had no issues with meeting more. In fact, I could only think of reasons why it would be a good thing.

"They need confirmation of what they're potentially fighting for, and I'm happy to give that," I said.

He grinned. "You are the perfect mate."

I grabbed his ass cheeks. "Then, why don't we make it official?"

Roman's grin turned into a frown. "We won't be rushed. Everything is going to be perfect for us when it happens. Not convenient for everyone else."

I sighed and turned my head. We'd had the same discussion a dozen times now. He gripped my chin and turned me until I met his stare again. "The depth of my feelings for you is endless. You are mine for as long as I live. There will never be a lifetime when my soul doesn't find yours, now that we've met. We will know when it's right," he said, turning my heart into a heaping mound of emotion.

I didn't deserve him, but I quit telling him that after he withheld his touch from me after I said those thoughts out loud one too many times.

"Patience isn't really my thing," I replied with a grin.

"A lot of things aren't 'your thing', but you still manage to succeed at them, like the physical exercise part of your training. You're one of the fastest wolves in the pack. I'm eager to see what you can do during the next new moon," Roman said as he rolled off of me and stood next to the bed.

"No mid-afternoon foreplay?" I teased as I took his outstretched hand.

"Not today, Kitten. We need to go see my mom. I haven't told her that Vaughn and Embry left to hunt Kyle down. I wanted them gone before she knew."

Sadness slithered its way through me. I visited with Ramona at least twice a day and it never got easier. As a wolf shifter, we sensed high emotions, and her fury over Jack's death was potent, almost making it hard to breathe around her.

"I was with her this morning. She's not any better than yesterday," I said as I got out of bed and searched for my sandals.

"She won't be until we find Kyle. I never would have let Vaughn leave the pack otherwise," Roman said.

Vaughn ran what he called his Super Squad—a group of thirty wolves who were trained to protect our pack and run the perimeters daily, checking for anything unusual. The guards were spread thin with having to send some of them up north, where a good portion of the pack still was. For now, everyone was managing with the added workloads. We just had no idea how long that would last.

"They'll find Kyle soon and we'll have one less problem to worry about," I said as I took Roman's hand.

He led us into the hallway, and we made our way up to Ramona's room. I knocked once before we entered and heard glass breaking. Roman sighed and pushed the door all the way open.

"Mom?" he called out.

"What?" she snapped.

We followed her voice only to find her standing in the middle of the kitchen with shattered glass all around her.

It didn't always work, but I'd found the most success in getting Ramona to talk by using dry sarcasm.

"Didn't feel like doing the dishes today, huh?" I asked, ignoring her pointed glare.

"Something like that. What do the two of you want?" she asked with less bite than I expected. Then she grabbed another plate, and I didn't feel so confident.

Roman stepped closer, keeping his confidence. "I thought you'd want to know that Vaughn and Embry just left to join the search for Kyle."

The plate cracked within her hands, and I waited for it to break all over the floor. Instead, she threw the dish at Roman, narrowly missing his head.

"Get. Out." Her words held no emotion, but it was her eyes that broke my heart. They filled with unshed tears and wrath.

"Mom—"

She took a single step forward, claws extended. "I

9

said *out*. Or are you going to abuse your power some more and take over my private space as well?"

Her words made Roman flinch. They'd been a low blow and she'd have known that, but I couldn't see any regret written on her face.

Roman turned to walk out the door, and I met her gaze. "He's grieving as well. You shouldn't push him away."

"Until he lifts the ban on my ability to leave the pack, I'll treat him however I see fit. You of all people should understand why I'm furious about losing control. Oh, wait. I'd forgotten. You've fallen in line like the rest of them. Did Roman use his alpha power on you, too? Is that why you're so agreeable now?"

I'd thought Roman had left, but I'd been wrong.

"Enough," he roared. "You can take your anger out on me, but you won't disrespect Cait. I understand you're mad—"

She cut him off again, clearly not intimidated by his pissed-off tone. "Mad? You think I'm *mad*?" She let out a dark chuckle, eyes wide as she started to come unhinged. "Oh, dear son. I'm not mad. I'm a woman scorned, and if you don't let me out of this cage soon, you'll see a side of me you've never known existed."

Ramona was worse off than I'd yet to see her. Instead of allowing Roman to respond, I tugged on his arm until he willingly followed me out of the room. We safely made it to the bottom of the stairs before he stopped us.

"Am I doing the right thing keeping her here?" he

asked, voice rough with the sadness I knew consumed him deep down.

"For now? Yes, I believe so. She'd get herself killed out there with raging emotions like that. Once we have more information and she's had time to process more of the grief, then we should revisit the choice to keep her from leaving the pack."

Roman pulled me into his arms and squeezed me tight. "I can't believe he's really gone."

The anguish in his words nearly broke me, but I doubled my resolve and made a silent vow to be strong for him.

He'd been there for me, and it was my turn to be there for him.

Kyle would pay for what he'd taken from our pack. I wouldn't fully rest until we made sure of that.

2

CAIT

The following day, I braved my morning trip to see Ramona. She'd bolted her door the night before and skipped dinner, but I was hoping she would be reasonable enough to accept breakfast.

With a soft knock on the wooden frame, I held gooey cinnamon rolls in front of me, patiently waiting for her response.

Stomping feet sounded through the third-floor loft area she occupied, and when the locks disengaged, I breathed a sigh of relief.

The door cracked open, and she peeked through. "What?"

"I brought you a bribe." I pushed the plate closer to the door.

Ramona took one inhale and walked away from the entrance, but let the door fall open. I took that as my opportunity to follow after her.

The tornado of glass from the night before was gone,

but there were dark circles under her eyes that made my soul ache.

I hadn't officially bonded with Roman, so I didn't understand how she truly felt, but I could imagine the devastation. The thoughts didn't paint a pretty picture.

Ramona stood at her kitchen counter, and I set the sugar-coated goodies in front of her. "You can't bribe me into forgiving Roman," she said as her fingers itched closer to the food.

"I have no intention of doing that. Since I joined him in delivering the bad news, I thought maybe I needed to win you over again."

She shook her head. "Just don't come back with my son and I'll keep letting you in. But if you want me to be nicer, then get me off the pack lands."

"You know I can't do that," I sighed.

She leveled her powerful stare at me. "As alpha female, you can."

I raised a brow at her. "Explain."

"An alpha's mate is the only one who can veto them. You bond with Roman, and you can get me out of here."

There was a hole in her story. "Aren't you the alpha female until Roman and I make things official?"

"To the pack, yes. Power wise? Unfortunately, not." There was a tick in her jaw, and we were getting off track, so I grabbed plates and changed the subject.

"I can't help you and you know that, but I do have good news," I said as I served us each a cinnamon roll.

"Kyle is strung up a tree somewhere?" she asked.

"Not that I'm aware of, but I did convince Roman to

14

have Kyle brought back here so you can see his execution once he's found."

Ramona's lip lifted into a snarl. "If he's brought here alive, I'm killing him myself."

That didn't seem like an unreasonable request, and I'd make sure Roman honored it. His mother deserved that vengeance for her mate.

"Deal," I said.

She nodded stiffly and took an angry bite of the breakfast. We sat in comfortable silence until both of us finished eating and I stared at her until she met my gaze.

The depth of her hurt seared into me as I took in the shadows beneath her bloodshot eyes, along with the tear tracks staining her cheeks.

Ramona's soul had been torn in two when Jack died. The other half of her was off somewhere else, waiting to be reborn in hopes they'd find each other again. The knowledge of that was nothing short of heartbreaking.

"I don't need your sympathy," she deadpanned.

"I wasn't planning to give you any, so that's good."

She grunted. "Someone's gotten a backbone since they came back to life."

I had no reply to that. She was right. My first death had helped me move past my fears of accepting Roman, and the second one had lessened my give-a-damn. While I hoped there were no more episodes like that in my future, I couldn't complain much if I kept coming back a better person.

Or at least a better version of myself.

"It's more like acceptance," I said.

It's more than acceptance. You should be proud of all we've accomplished in the last two weeks, Adira said.

My wolf wasn't wrong. I was proud, but I didn't need to talk about myself with Ramona unless that was what she needed.

Revenge and time are all that will heal Ramona's broken soul, Adira added.

What if we don't get either of those things? I countered. There was a chance we might not ever find Kyle, and we needed Ramona whole before it was time to face the Supernatural Council. There would be no such thing as too much help when it came to dealing with the unknown of this world.

Adira didn't answer my mostly rhetorical question. Instead, I focused back on Ramona. "Care to go for a walk with me?"

She laughed. "Not a fucking chance."

I'd never heard her cuss, but the words rolled off her tongue naturally. "How about we play a game then?" I asked.

Ramona sighed heavily making her irritation known. "I appreciate what you're doing, Cait, but your efforts are wasted. Until my son understands what I need, I will stay up here where I can most feel Jack. What hurts me most is that when you were taken, I supported Roman. I encouraged him to do whatever it took to get you back. Now, when I need his support the most, he won't give it to me."

Her words were filled with a sorrow I'd yet to see from the strong alpha female, and I began to understand why she was acting the way she was. I'd

16

already told Roman we couldn't keep his mother locked up forever. Hearing how Ramona saw the situation, I had to find a way to help that still kept her safe like Roman wanted and needed. It was the least I could do for the woman who had supported me no matter what idiotic decisions I'd previously made.

"We're going to set this right," I vowed.

Ramona shook her head. "There is nothing right to set. There is only doing what needs to be done for the greater good of our kind."

Once an alpha female, always an alpha female. Ramona might be pissed the hell off, but I could see that no matter how furious she was, the pack would always come first. Killing Kyle wouldn't just bring her a minuscule amount of peace, it would also keep the pack safest from future threats.

I glanced at the clock on the wall. "I need to meet Roman. I'm taking my final training test I mentioned yesterday morning. Are you sure you don't want to come?"

"I'm sure, and I appreciate you coming by even after last night," she said, sounding more like herself than she had since losing Jack.

"There isn't a single thing you can do or say that will keep me from visiting you. You were there for me, and I have every intention of returning the favor."

She tried to smile, but the gesture didn't reach her eyes. "You're going to make a wonderful alpha female, Cait."

I wanted to hug her, but the counter still separated us, and I was sure she'd kept it that way for her own sanity. Instead, I reached a hand across and gripped her forearm. "Only because I'll have the best person to learn from."

Ramona nodded, and I took the opportunity to leave with things on a good note. As I closed the door behind me, I called out to Roman. *On my way. Be ready to have your ass kicked.*

His laughter echoed through my mind as I raced down the stairs. My training had included working with various pack members that specialized in certain fighting tactics like Muay Thai skills which were my favorite. While I had natural talent from my Luna Marked magic and the help of Adira, the other wolves had helped hone my skills in a way I hadn't thought would come for years.

As I moved through the pack house, shifters bowed their heads to me in a sign of respect. I smiled and waved, calling most of them by name. I'd worked hard to get to know as many as I could which was easier now, given half of the pack wasn't around.

Just as I stepped onto the porch Serene latched on to my arm. "Where do you think you're going?"

I sucked in a breath. "Are you trying to give me a heart attack?"

She grinned and released me. "Nope, but I could if you'd like."

"I'll pass. Were you headed to the pack house or looking for me?" I asked.

"For you or Roman. Beatrix needs my help with a young wolf pup out in LA. Given she came here when we needed her, I'm going to head there and see what kind of trouble I can stir up."

Serene was the absolute worst name for this woman. There was nothing calming about her, but that was what I enjoyed most when she wasn't trying to kill me.

"If we can do anything to help, let us know," I said.

She nodded, waving both hands in the air as she twirled back around and headed in the direction of her house.

Once Serene was out of sight, I leapt off the porch and shifted into my wolf form midair. When all four paws hit the ground, Adira shook out our long silky fur, and our tail sashayed back and forth as we ran swiftly toward the training area that held the obstacle course.

It was the last bit of training I hadn't completed. Once I was done with this, I would have a more normal schedule with the other wolves. I'd been excited for this moment for the last week of my expedited training.

Adira held our head up as we slowed down. She was a proud wolf, and it showed in everything she did. While we'd become more of the same being with our thoughts and actions, the pride she exuded I let her take all of the credit for.

We arrived at the main training field in record time to find Roman and Sam waiting for me. Sam had been playing a decent role in my newest training, but we still hadn't been able to talk much. Something told me she was still deciding my worth.

Adira thought the same and wanted to challenge Sam's wolf, but I held her off. Sam was not our enemy. She was protective of Roman, and I tried to be grateful for that fact. If the Supernatural Council did get their hands on me, he was going to need someone like her in his corner.

I shifted back to two legs. "Thanks for waiting for me."

"How was my mother?" Roman asked. He was wearing loose running pants and a fitted navy-blue tee that made his eyes stand out, a color he needed to wear more often.

"Better than I expected," I answered, leaving out any details for the time being. I didn't want to talk about Ramona's requests outside of our room. She deserved more respect than that.

Roman nodded. "Well, let's get started then. Today is the final challenge."

Sam's eyes moved over me. "Are you sure you're ready for this?"

I smiled in return. "I was ready days ago."

The obstacle course included rope contraptions, monster tires I had to manhandle, and concluded with a tower I had to get to the top of before Roman. On my own, the process was easy, but the course was meant to be competitive, and it would be Roman's job to make me fail. Though, he normally didn't handle this part for the rest of the shifters—that was part of Vaughn's role.

If I could make it past Roman and ring the bell at the top, then I was officially done. I had to do this.

"Being cocky is the number one reason most shifters get themselves killed," Sam said to me.

"I bet it's also how they get trapped in soul-sucking stones," I countered.

Roman tensed between us, but Sam just laughed. "Quite possibly."

I knew she wanted to like me.

Other wolves began to gather. They were all curious to know what I was capable of, and I didn't blame them. I'd have been, too, given I'd just showed up one day at the pack, rejected their way of life and then came back as some freaky wolf with abilities none of them had ever seen before.

Just for show, I stretched out my muscles, reaching for my toes, then up into the air. I was wearing tight black workout pants, a charcoal sports bra, and a loose t-shirt, but I didn't plan on playing fair. No, the shirt came off along with my shoes while Roman had his back to me and I stepped to his side.

"Beautiful day to kick your ass, isn't it?" I joked when he turned toward me again.

Heat filled his eyes as my lack of attire caused the distraction I was hoping for. "Where did your shirt go?"

"Back there with my shoes."

"And you have no shoes on because?" he asked, taking a step closer to me.

I tightened my ponytail and shrugged. "I feel closer to my energy this way."

That part was true. There was something to be said about laying in the grass and soaking in all that the earth had to offer.

He muttered something under his breath, and Sam joined us. "You have twenty minutes to ring the bell." She pointed to the top of the tower. "There are only three rules: no tampering with the structures, no physically striking each other, and no shifting. Understand?"

Roman and I both nodded.

Sam glanced at her watch. "Good. Your time starts... now."

I expected nothing less from Sam, so her lack of a heads up didn't surprise me. Running at top speeds, I arrived at the first obstacle and scaled up a knotted rope. Roman was right at my heels, but I ignored him.

At the top, there was a small platform made for one that Embry warned me to jump off quickly. Otherwise, Roman would have the opportunity to knock me back to the ground.

The balls of my feet barely touched the wood landing before I leaped toward the next rope. My fingers barely caught hold, and I had no time to recover before swinging my body back and forth. I needed momentum to get to the next section and ended up overcompensating. I flew over the wobbly, floating wooden steps and landed belly first halfway through the second section.

Roman growled from behind me when I almost fell the thirty feet back to dirt, but he clearly wasn't that worried, because he jumped over me, landing perfectly on the swinging step next to me.

He leaned down. "Need a hand, Kitten?"

"Not a chance." I had to do this on my own.

You can do this, Adira encouraged.

Everything had become so much easier when we got along better and her positivity boosted my energy, allowing me to get back on track with the course.

Roman was racing across the fragile bridge where one wrong move meant getting your legs tangled in a mess.

I quit paying attention to him and continued on. With one focused step at a time, I made my way forward and arrived at a loose rope wall that I needed to climb in order to get to the zipline that would take me to the monster tires.

Roman was already halfway to the top, but I still had time to catch up. This part was the easiest to get tangled in, according to Embry. I needed to act with precision and forethought, or I'd find myself caught in the spider's web.

Using all of my senses, I judged the tautness of each rope square. Not all were created equally, and only some of them would pave my way to finishing first.

Halfway up, I worried I was moving too slowly, spending too much time focusing and not enough of it acting on instinct. That was until I heard Roman.

"Son of a bitch," he muttered just loud enough for me to hear.

"I'd offer you a hand, but this kitten is all out of them." I winked and moved past him without an ounce of guilt.

My actions infuriated my mate more, causing him to get further tangled in the mess of ropes. I took the advantage and wasted no time going down the zip line.

At the bottom, I could see Roman continuing on, so I hurried to the tires. I had to move the six-foot-tall monster tire that weighed a bajillion pounds a total of one-hundred yards without rolling it.

This was where I had to work smarter, not harder.

I wasn't allowed to shift, but my powers didn't require me to be in wolf form in order to use them. Channeling my energy into my hands, I grabbed on to the nearest mountain of rubber, and any overflow of magic poured into the earth—my real reason for ditching my shoes.

He's gaining on us, Adira warned.

I didn't bother to look back. I buckled down and began the painstaking process of flipping the tire up and over, hoping to gain a bit of momentum with my consistent force.

Hope seemed futile as my muscles screamed at me, even with the added help of tapping into my energy.

This course was all about strength of the mind and body. Knowing what choices to make and when to make them. I hadn't been allowed to practice on it ahead of time, so Roman had a leg up on me there, but my mind was constantly evolving, thanks to my Luna Mark magic.

I could win this. I had to.

Otherwise, the training wheels weren't coming off anytime soon.

With those thoughts, I channeled the motivation needed to finish the task at hand.

ROMAN

I'd badly wanted Cait to lose. I wasn't ready for her to be unleashed on the world. Sure, that was selfish, but she was the most precious being in the world to me. The drive to keep her away from danger wasn't something I could make go away.

Except, the harder I tried to get ahead of her on the obstacle course, the worse things went for me. She was almost to the final tower, and I was tiring faster than ever before while still flipping a stupid tire.

I could use some help, I said to my wolf.

He was silent, which didn't bode well for me.

Are you seriously going to let her win? I asked.

This isn't my fight, he replied.

I was beginning to understand.

Have you been talking to her wolf somehow?

He grunted. *I wish. But I can sense her wants, and if she's capable of achieving them, then why not allow her to? We shouldn't be holding our mate back.*

While I didn't want to agree with him, he had a

point. Still, the overprotective alpha in me refused to quit trying.

With every bit of strength that I could muster on my own, I manhandled the tire down the field and got to the tower just as Cait was getting to the second level.

The tower itself wasn't complicated, but this part of the course was the whole reason two people competed at the same time.

I launched myself into the air, landing on the opposite side of the tower as Cait, and began to scale up. I could see her through the metal framing, but my view was obstructed by the contraptions at my disposal.

Racing to get even with her, I was finally able to get in a good position.

If you hurt her, I'll make you pay, my wolf warned.

Nothing here will harm a hair on her body.

Our mate's pride is just as important as her body, he replied.

His words slammed into my chest as they took hold of my thoughts. Cait and her wolf were extremely prideful. They thrived on being able to take care of themselves. Passing this test wasn't just about being able to go on more missions for Cait. No, it was also about showing herself and the other wolves that she was capable.

Damn it.

Still, I couldn't give Cait the win. That was just as bad as trying to sabotage her. I'd lost position when I'd let myself get distracted, but quickly caught up with her again. My wolf was helping me now that we were in agreement.

Cait needed to win, but she needed to be tested as well.

Using the tricks that I already knew about the tower, I rested against wood braces and reached into the middle. Three power lines ran up the middle, and if the right two crossed, it sent an electrical current through the metal.

The shock wouldn't hurt Cait, but it would certainly throw her off balance. If she was as good as she wanted to be, my actions wouldn't cause too big of a problem. Touching the lines together with a stick that kept me from getting zapped as well, my eyes darted up to watch Cait.

Her jaw clenched and grip tightened on the bars as her nerves responded to the shock waves. Cait's body glowed purple, and her eyes narrowed at me as she forced her grip off of the metal braces and onto objects the electrical current wouldn't travel through.

"You'll pay for that," she sneered.

"I have no doubt."

Racing further up, I began shoving braces through the tower, several of them jabbing Cait in the ribs and thighs, but she never once faltered. She kept pushing herself, even when I knew her body was battered.

Finally, we were only a couple of feet from the top and I pulled out the dirtiest trick on the tower. I hated to do it, but Cait needed to know she'd won fair and square, as did the rest of the pack watching.

There were ropes holding the top of the tower

together. With one yank, pieces of the side Cait was climbing began to fall off wherever she tried to grab hold.

"So much for no sabotaging," Cait sneered while doing whatever she could to find something solid to hold.

I'd broken no rules. This was part of the course. Just not public knowledge.

The only downside was that while I knew the trick existed, I'd never seen it played out. My dad had told me about it before I'd completed the course, and that was many years ago.

As parts of Cait's side kept coming apart beneath her weight, I began to regret my decision to push her so hard.

I opened my mouth to tell her to come around to the other side, but it was too late. Cait stumbled, her grip came loose, and she began to fall.

Shit, what had I done?

I moved to race around the tower and attempt to… I didn't know what I planned to do, but I couldn't stand there like an idiot when it was my fault she was about to fall almost fifty feet to the ground.

I'd barely made it two steps toward the other side when Cait screamed, but not a fearful one. No, this sound came deep from within—a warrior cry.

As I caught sight of her again, she had managed to grab hold of one of the beams I'd shoved at her previously and was drawing herself back up with only the strength of her arms since her legs couldn't reach the tower from her position.

"Come on, Cait. Don't give up now," I encouraged.

At this point, I was giving her the win by not moving forward, but not in a way that made her weak. No, if she could get back onto the tower after all that, then she showed skill few wolves around here had.

Cait made many more unnatural sounds, and I knew she was in massive amounts of pain, but not once did I see a glimmer of give-up in her eyes. She had zero intentions of letting the tower beat her, and it was in that moment that I knew.

Cait was everything to me. She was full of determination, kindness, bravery, and so much more that I never expected when I first found her. She was everything I didn't know I needed, and there was nothing in my life more important than her happiness.

My chest swelled with emotion. The need to claim her and tell her how much I loved her nearly drove me mad. I'd been pushing off bonding with her for many reasons, but we were both ready. I'd find the time soon to make sure we both finally got what we wanted.

For now, we had a challenge to finish, and my mate needed my full support.

Cait had finally gotten her body resting against the tower again, and I was done messing with her. She'd already won, and it was time for her to ring the bell at the top and make it official.

I moved so I could follow along with her to the end. Her face was scrunched, and she groaned with effort as she hoisted herself up the remaining sections. Gods, it was hard to only encourage her with words instead of physically helping.

"Three more steps, Kitten. Unleash those claws and finish this," I said.

She glared at me, and only replied with more grunts as she moved up another step.

Finally, we were at the platform, but Cait still had to haul herself over the edge and stand up on her own to reach the bell—all without using her wolf's power. Her eyes were filled with determination, but I knew she was weaker than she'd ever been.

I stayed on the tower, inching closer to her in case she wasn't able to get herself onto the platform.

"Move one more step and I will punch you in the balls," she muttered, causing me to grin.

"Yes, Mate."

Cait roared one last time and grabbed hold of the platform. Watching her dig deep and never once give up was a sight to behold. I hoped the pack could see what I saw from where they stood.

Cait was going to be a formidable female alpha.

As my mate threw herself onto the platform, her chest heaved and legs shook, making me worry she wouldn't be able to stand. I itched to join her, but she lifted her head and snarled at me before I could think twice about stepping in.

With trembling arms, she pushed herself up and grabbed on to the center pole that held the bell. More grumbles followed as she forced her body to finish the task.

When the bell finally rang, shouts from the ground sounded in chorus as everyone around cheered for her.

I grabbed Cait's waist as soon as she was done, and she fell against me, tears falling down her cheeks.

"I did it," she said, strong and proud.

"Yes, you did, Kitten. Just like I knew you would."

Our bond flared, and I channeled my energy into her. Cait still needed to grab hold of the rope that would allow us to zipline down to the ground. To truly finish the course, she had one last task to do. The easiest, yet hardest part.

"Can you stand yet?" I asked a minute later.

Her head nodded and she pushed away from me, muscles still quaking along her body, but there was a glow about her again that had been missing just moments before.

"Let's get back to the ground so I can spend the rest of the afternoon in that glorious tub of yours."

I grinned. "Of ours. Remember, what's mine is yours, Mate."

She nodded, a purple spark in her green eyes that made my chest tighten.

Cait grabbed hold of the bar attached to the zipline and lifted her feet while she was still on the platform, likely testing her own strength before jumping down. Smart move.

I found the secondary bar on the ground and waited for her to feel ready. She pushed off, and I quickly attached mine to follow right behind her.

Hug Cait as soon as she touches down. She might not be able to stand on her own, and I don't want her to fall in front of the pack, I said to Sam who wasn't much of a hugger, but this was important.

She immediately moved to catch Cait, arms open to do just as I asked. Cait's shoulders slumped as she fell into my cousin, and I knew I'd made the right call.

I jumped from the zipline before I got to the end, so I didn't crash into them, then took over for Sam. When I turned around with Cait, the present pack members had their heads bowed and were softly chanting "alpha female". The hum of their voices had my already elevated pride in Cait swelling even more.

Cait trembled next to me and brought her head up. "Thank you," she said confidently, moving her gaze to meet each of their lowered eyes.

The shifters nodded as she did, then moved on, offering more murmurs of their congratulations as they began to disperse.

The moment was brief, but impactful beyond words, and I hoped Cait understood the importance as well.

"Can we go home now?" Cait asked.

"Yes, we can." I picked her up without asking and turned to Sam. "Thank you."

She nodded at me and met Cait's gaze. "When you're recovered, let's talk."

Cait seemed surprised by the offer yet agreed to the request without hesitation as I began to turn toward the pack house.

My mate needed healing first, and I planned to make sure I played a very big role in making that happen.

4

CAIT

Ringing the bell at the top of that tower nearly killed me, but also proved just how far I could push myself. I'd thought that the echoing of the bell would be the most memorable part of the course, but it wasn't.

When I got to the bottom and Sam caught me, I didn't feel worthy, but as I heard the pack members chanting, a sense of rightness settled inside me.

I might have believed in their support already, but everything clicked into place the moment I turned around to face the shifters.

I was beaten, but not broken—exhausted, but energized.

My wolf healing had done a hell of a job getting me through the toughest parts of the course, but when I'd almost fallen, it had taken every ounce of power I had without shifting to get my ass to the top.

As Roman carried me back to the pack house, I gave

the tower a nod. Whoever had created that beast sure knew what they were doing.

I was sad Embry hadn't been there when I finished, but I hoped when we got back to the pack house that there would be word from either her or Vaughn about Kyle.

My best friend was smart, and she had killer intuition. If anyone was going to hunt that bastard down, I knew it could be her and the beta.

Even before we arrived home, I was starting to feel stronger again. Some of the wolves that had been watching were already back as well and standing in the yard.

That's Collin, Paul, and Jay, Roman said. He'd played a big role in helping me remember everyone's name, especially once I was able to communicate telepathically like everyone else.

"Good work today," Collin said to me.

"Thank you, Collin." I wiggled out of Roman's arms and moved to shake each of their hands. "Paul. Jay."

"Alpha female," they replied.

My greetings were stiff, but I was getting better. At least, I hoped.

Being an alpha's mate wasn't something I ever saw for myself, and figuring out how I was supposed to act wasn't easy. Roman consistently told me to just be myself, but I knew that wouldn't work. Not with this pack.

They needed to see me strong and resilient, especially after all of the loss we'd had.

Roman guided me into the house and picked me

back up again at the base of the stairs. I wanted to argue with him, but my muscles felt like wet noodles, and I was grateful for his assistance.

When we entered our room, I expected him to lay me on the bed, but instead, he carried me to the bathroom and set me on the counter.

Flashbacks to our first real night together hit me like a heatwave, but he shook his finger at me. "Don't get any ideas. You need to rest. Tonight, I'll treasure you."

I jutted my lower lip out. "What's wrong with now?"

He turned toward the bath, turning the water on, before glancing back and answering me. "I don't want to be the one doing all the work."

I barked out a laugh. "I think you deserve to after almost killing me back there."

Roman's face turned serious as he stepped back toward me, cradling my face in his hands. "I really didn't mean to do that."

"I know, but it was exactly what you should have done. I didn't want any passes because I'm your mate."

"I figured you'd think that way." He pressed his lips to mine before backing up and testing the water. "It's warm now."

I began unpeeling my sweaty clothes, and Roman took over for me after a few painful grunts slipped out. Once I was undressed, Roman helped me into the tub and then pulled the stool from the vanity over so he could sit with me.

"You're not going to join me?" I asked with a raised brow.

"As tempting as that is, you need to heal your muscles. I'm just here to speed up the process." He grabbed my hand and our connection flared. "We can have our fun tonight."

"But not *all* of the fun," I said.

Roman's lips thinned. "You're not making this easy on me."

"When have I made anything easy?" I teased.

"Never. I just don't want anything to be rushed. A lot has happened in the last month," he said, but I could tell something had changed for him. His words didn't hold the same resolve. I thought of pushing him on the subject, but he was right.

A lot had transpired in the last month, and I needed to remember that everything would happen when it was the right time. I was only torturing myself by torturing him.

I was meant to be with Roman, and I would be. I knew those words to be truer than anything else in the world. Unfortunately, I'd let fear keep me from accepting him in the beginning, and I'd began to worry that I'd passed that fear onto Roman.

He moved behind me, pushing my hair to the side and rubbing my shoulders as I sank further into the hot water. "Everything will find a way to work itself out. We may not like how things have gone so far, but it's all gone the way it needed to," Roman said, matching my previous thoughts.

I nodded, closing my eyes while his thumb pressed against a knot at the base of my neck. Tingles sparked along my skin as a wave of tiredness took over. As much as I wanted to continue our conversation, words were lost on me as Roman continued to massage the aches from my body.

Another moment would come around soon enough to try again.

///

I ENDED UP FALLING ASLEEP FOR SEVERAL HOURS, WAKING in the middle of the afternoon and remembering Sam wanted to finally have a private chat with me. We'd talked several times before, but never alone. I didn't think she hated me, but I knew she was leery.

After sending Roman away, I made my way to Sam's room and knocked on the door. She answered, looking as fierce as ever with her short blonde hair, bright blue eyes, and toned body she often had on display.

"Cait." She smirked.

"Hello Sam," I replied, waiting for her to invite me in.

"What's up?" she asked, still blocking her doorway.

I chuckled. "Not much. Just coming to see you like you asked. Now a bad time?"

She hummed, seeming to think extra hard about her answer. "I guess not. Come on in."

Finally, she moved out of the entry, heading straight for the couch.

Oh, this is going to be fun, I thought as I closed the door behind me.

She's testing you still. You hurt her best friend, Adira reminded me, as if I'd forgotten.

Sam's room was simple. A black couch and chair were in the middle, with a bed on the back wall and a sliding glass door leading to a small balcony next to a couple of white doors I assumed led to her closet and bathroom.

"Mind if I sit?" I asked, gesturing to the chair.

She kicked her feet up, lounging across the couch. "Go for it."

"Any news on Kyle?" I asked, even though I knew there wasn't, but I wanted to get the conversation going with something.

"Nope, but you already knew that." She grinned, purposely making me uncomfortable.

I shrugged. "I assumed the answer, but it never hurts to ask."

"Speaking of asking. Have you fucked my cousin?" she blurted out, and I nearly choked.

"Excuse me?"

"Not that I want any details," she shuddered, "but I am curious about your mate bond. It's not like others I've seen. You two seem to be capable of resisting each other beyond anything normal."

"Fucking isn't the only way to satisfy a mate bond," I replied dryly.

"But it is the only way to seal the deal and make things more permanent, but maybe that isn't why you're still here," she countered.

She was trying to rile me and succeeding, but I kept my emotions in check, choosing not to say anything else. If this was the only reason Sam asked for me to chat, then I was done with our conversation. I had no qualms about proving myself after the mistakes I'd made, but she was beginning to cross a line that I wasn't comfortable with.

"Nothing else to say?" Sam snarked with her brow raised.

"If you'd like to talk about something other than my personal life with Roman, then sure, I probably have lots to say. Otherwise, I think we're done here," I replied, frustration leaking through my words.

"Do you think you can dismiss me so easily? What if I'm not done?"

I stood up. "Listen, Sam. I respect that you're family to Roman and his best friend. I'm not here to change any of that. I also appreciate that you're upset on his behalf for my past choices, but I have already acknowledged I messed up, and Roman has forgiven me. Either accept that the rest of us have moved on, or just leave me alone. We have enough to deal with right now."

She got up from the couch, stepping within a foot of me. "And what if I don't want to leave you alone?"

"Then, I'll be forced to do something about it," I said, sure of my threat. Sam might be able to kick my ass, but I wouldn't back down from her.

She stared me down, trying to intimidate me, but I wasn't that easily swayed. I held her gaze and returned the challenge.

"You're not afraid of me," she stated.

"No, I'm not."

She took a small step back. "Why not?"

"Because I know I'm where I'm meant to be, and I won't let anyone try to bully me into thinking otherwise."

"I like you, Cait," she said, and I laughed so hard I had to hold my aching sides.

"Wow. I'd hate to be someone you disliked."

She shrugged and sat back down, so I did the same. Sam had crossed a line, but I wanted to move past the awkwardness she'd created.

"You're right. You have proven yourself, but I needed to push you a little further. You shouldn't ever let someone try to come between you and Roman. No matter who they are, or what they want. I wanted to know how far you were willing to fight for your position at his side. If you're willing to throwdown with a trained killer, I'd say that's enough for me."

"Well, I'm glad to have passed your test," I deadpanned, really hoping we could move beyond all of this.

"Roman is a good man. One of the best, and I hope you never forget that."

"I don't plan on it, but I'm sure if I ever waver, you'll be there to remind me."

"You can bet on that." She grinned and got up, reaching a hand toward me. "I'm not sorry I was so hard on you, but I am done now. I'm hoping we can be friends."

"Does Samantha McIntyre actually have friends?" I asked, accepting her offered hand.

She squeezed my fingers harder than necessary. "Not ones who call me Samantha."

"Except for Zeke, of course."

Sam let go, sighing as she went to her wet bar and poured herself a drink. "Zeke is an annoying bloodsucker."

"But you like him?" I asked, because he sure seemed fond of her.

She gagged. "Not like that. I only fuck shifters. Zeke is just convenient, and good at doing what needs to be done." She raised her glass. "Drink?"

I shook my head. "Do vampires offer help often?"

"No. Not ever. I only intrigued him because I shot him," Sam said, leaning against her bar with a smile.

"And why did you do that?"

"Because he's a vampire."

I raised a brow. "So, just because someone is turned into something evil, that automatically makes them worthy of death? No questions, just a bullet?" I didn't hide my condescending tone at all.

Sure, I was afraid of vampires, but I wasn't ready to kill them all just because they drank blood to survive. That didn't mean they were all murdering psychopaths.

"Okay, when you put it that way, you make me sound like an asshole," Sam sighed.

"Aren't you, though?"

She laughed. "You really aren't afraid of me. This is interesting."

"Dying a couple of times is a great way to get rid of fear. Though, I don't recommend it."

Sam finished off her drink. "No, I wouldn't imagine so. And no, I don't normally kill people just because. I'm not a monster, but Zeke had caught me on a bad day."

"Sounds like you've had a lot of those recently," I said.

"Working with the Supernatural Council used to be an outlet for the rage I'd built up as a kid after losing my parents, but then things changed. Someone started making rules that didn't make sense."

"Like what?" I asked.

"Well, I wasn't allowed at the council headquarters any longer unless I officially became one of their employees, which means I'd have to swear my allegiance to them instead of my pack. That was a hard no."

"Understandably so," I said.

"Then, mission details became more of information they relayed on a need-to-know basis only."

"Why did you keep taking jobs if things were changing?" I asked.

She smirked. "Because I *really* enjoy taking down the bad guy. Someone, or more than one someone, is pulling strings they have no business touching. I had intended on solving the mystery of who was doing what on my own, but then you showed up and made things more complicated."

"Am I supposed to apologize for having my wolf shifter genes activated and heaps of magic stuffed into my body without notice or explanation?"

Sam leisurely made her way back to the sitting area.

"I'd say yes, but I guess you don't have to take full blame."

Oh, she really was awful, but her attitude suited her, and I didn't let it get to me.

"Now that this has gotten bigger than I ever expected, I'll have to decide if I'm going to keep playing the council's games or see what happens when I quit and come after them."

"I'm assuming you already know what might happen if you choose the latter?"

"I do. They'll send hunters after me, and I'll kill every last one of them."

Sam was full of confidence every woman should have. She knew exactly who she was, what she was capable of, and she wasn't afraid or ashamed of any aspect of herself.

"You'll have to let me know what you decide," I said.

She winked at me. "I think you'll be well aware of my choice just as soon as I make it. We're in this together now. Whether any of us like it or not, a fight is brewing, and nobody will be off limits once shit hits the fan."

5

CAIT

The following day, I was back to my normal self. No more aches and pains from the previous day's obstacle course, and I had hopes of going on a day-date with Roman, which would hopefully lead into a night filled with all the things I'd been craving, but the unexpected return of Embry and Vaughn changed all of our plans.

"We have information, but we can't discuss it here," Vaughn said to Roman as we met them at the property line.

"Why not?" Roman asked.

"Our source won't come on pack lands," Embry answered, clearly annoyed.

I looked both her and Vaughn over. Neither of them had a scratch on their body, but there were a few tears in their clothes, telling me things hadn't been boring while they'd been gone.

"And who is your source?" Roman asked.

Vaughn grimaced. "He only offered to come if we didn't tell you who he was beforehand."

Roman and Vaughn began to have their own silent conversation, and based on Roman's creasing face, he wasn't getting what he wanted from his beta.

Embry hugged me. "Tell me everything about your final test. I'm so sorry I missed it, but hopefully what we were doing was worth it."

"I have no doubt your efforts have been worthwhile," I said before relaying the hell I'd gone through getting to the top of the tower.

Before I could finish, Roman and Vaughn were done arguing inside their heads, and Vaughn was laughing hysterically.

"Care to fill us in?" I asked.

"No, he wouldn't," Roman snapped. "We're headed into town. I'll be back as soon as I can be."

Yeah, that wasn't going to work for me.

"Don't you mean that *we'll* be back? I'm going with you," I said.

"No, you're not. I have no idea who we're meeting," he grumbled.

My eyes widened and I covered my mouth, letting out a small gasp in feigned shock. "Exactly. You're not going alone."

He wasn't the only one who was allowed to worry about their mate.

Vaughn snickered. "Told you."

Roman shoved him. "You stay out of this."

"Cait won't be in any danger. I think she's fine to come," Embry added.

Roman snarled at Vaughn and Embry. "Did you both forget who your alpha is? If I say she's not coming, then that's final."

My head turned as if I'd been smacked. My initial reaction was to argue with Roman, but I took a moment to breathe and reached for him. "Walk with me for a minute."

He took my offered hand and followed me a few yards away from our friends. "What's really wrong?" I asked.

"I'm not comfortable with taking you somewhere I can't keep you safe," he said.

"I understand that, but there's something more."

He groaned so deeply that it sounded more like a growl.

"You're only making this harder on yourself. Tell me what's really bothering you and maybe I'll see reason," I said.

Roman grimaced. "I don't like not being in control."

I smiled. "Now that I can understand. Let me see if I can help."

We walked back to Embry and Vaughn. "I know you can't tell us who we're meeting, but you can answer some questions, I'm assuming. Has Roman met this person before?" I asked.

Vaughn and Embry shared a look before she answered. "Yes."

"Is this person a danger to us?" I asked.

Vaughn flexed his muscles. "Not that I would be worried about."

I laughed. "Why does this person wish to remain unknown until we arrive?"

Neither of them answered this time.

"See? A good person wouldn't play games like this. They'd come to the pack and give the information without causing more issues," Roman grumbled.

"Unless said person is a supernatural who isn't supposed to interact with those outside their species and coming to the pack could get them in trouble," I said.

Vaughn pointed at me. "That one is smart. We should keep her around."

"I plan to." Roman wrapped an arm around me. "If the four of us go, and there is even a sliver of trouble, you both will pay dearly. Do I make myself clear?"

Vaughn saluted him. "Sir, yes, sir."

Oh, that beta didn't know when to shut his mouth, but I enjoyed his smartass remarks all the same. Vaughn was the perfect balance to Roman's alpha attitude.

"Let's go." Roman pulled me toward the garage, and we all rode in one of the pack trucks. I'd yet to come into town when everything was open.

The pack had everything I could want on hand and made it easy to never leave. Once I stopped needing an escape, I understood how everyone was so comfortable on the lands. There was a sense of safety and tranquility about every inch of the property.

We passed by the mill. The place was as busy as ever, considering they were shorthanded from having part of the pack up north for a while. I'd asked to help out there, but my training had been more important.

Town came into view, and it wasn't as busy as I expected it to be. In fact, while I could see plenty of businesses open, only a few cars were on the road.

"Is it always so quiet around here?" I asked.

Roman glared out the window. "No."

The person we're meeting is capable of making humans want to steer clear of the area they're in. Roman is starting to piece together why we didn't tell him who. He wants to murder us, Embry said through our mental connection.

I bet you're extra glad I'm here to make sure that doesn't happen, I replied.

She grunted out loud and caught Roman's death glare in the mirror as he pulled into the parking lot of an abandoned structure. It was the last building at the end of the main street in town but wasn't in disarray. Someone must have recently vacated.

When we got out of the truck, Roman was at my side. "Do not move out of my sight."

"I wasn't planning on it." I smiled at him, hoping to ease some of his tension.

He grunted in return. Clearly, my words and actions hadn't held the desired effect.

We entered the building. The inside was dark, but I could still see plenty of shadows. As my eyes adjusted, I realized the place likely used to be an old clothing store based on the racks I could see pushed against the wall.

"I have to admit, I'm surprised you came," a familiar man's voice sounded from the furthest corner.

"What do you know about Kyle?" Roman asked gruffly.

Zeke's face became fully visible as he slowly moved

49

closer. "No pleasantries? Now, that's not very alpha of you." The vampire tsked.

"Helping shifters isn't very vampire of you, either," Roman responded.

Zeke smiled, white, sharp teeth standing out against his dark skin. "My clan doesn't like problems, and we also don't like attention where it doesn't belong. You can accept my assistance the way I'm able to give it, or I can leave."

"We brought Roman to you. Now, tell us what you know," Vaughn snarled, showing a side of him he didn't often let out.

"You shifters rely on your animal instincts too much. Patience does wonders when you have a problem to solve. Thankfully for you, I'm a patient guy. I heard from Samantha about your wolf issues and decided to help because it seemed important to her that this was sorted quickly and quietly."

I wondered briefly if Sam was going to get in trouble for telling Zeke about pack business, but the more the vampire spoke, the more relaxed Roman became. Hopefully, that was a good thing and not the calm before the storm I knew he was capable of.

Zeke continued. "The wolf you're looking for is hunkered down in an old industrial section outside of Albuquerque, New Mexico. There might be a dozen or so wolves still with him. Several of them went off on their own and the rest back to the pack. Seems to be a bit of confusion on who their alpha is now, from what I'm hearing."

"And how are you hearing all of this?" Roman asked.

"Vampires have the best hearing and the fastest speeds of all supernaturals. We hear a lot of things when we want to." Zeke winked like the cocky vampire I was beginning to realize he was.

"Right. So, because of Sam, you wanted to *hear* the information we needed, and now you're relaying it to us instead of her, why?" Vaughn asked.

Zeke's smirk disappeared. "Samantha doesn't need to be out right now. There are people looking for her that I'd rather not find her."

"Like who?" Roman demanded.

"The same ones looking for your mate. I'd be careful where you go with her as well."

Freaking hell. Just what I needed. Roman to have another reason to worry about me.

Zeke cleared his throat, adding, "Though, seems like you've got some time where the Lavender Wolf is concerned. Isn't that right?"

Embry moved closer to me, and Roman took a step forward. "Because Sam trusts you, I'm hesitating to kill you right now, but if you know something about my mate, don't think you can play games with me. There isn't a line I won't cross for her."

Zeke straightened, adjusting his collared shirt. "Point made, Alpha Wolf. I only know as much as you do. The council wants your mate, but they've given you time to bring her in willingly. Not much longer now, though."

"I'm well aware of the clock counting down, and

you two can stop talking about me like I'm not here. I'm plenty capable of speaking for myself," I said.

Men were sometimes annoyingly overbearing, and I could only stay quiet for so long.

"I have no doubt about that," Zeke replied with a smirk.

I wasn't trying to speak for you. I'd just rather you not get any closer to the vampire than necessary, Roman said through our connection.

I squeezed his hand in reply. I wasn't upset with him.

"You all have a lot to do and not a lot of time to do it in. I'll text Samantha the address and then my part is done here. I'll be gone before you even get back to your truck," Zeke said.

"That would be appreciated," Vaughn replied.

Roman steered me toward the exit as Embry led the way and Vaughn covered our backs. I glanced back before the shadows swallowed Zeke.

He was staring at us with his red eyes and blew me a kiss just before taking a step back.

Weird ass vampire.

6

CAIT

We returned to the pack within ten minutes and found Sam waiting for us at the garage. Her arms were crossed, and she was glaring daggers at Roman.

"What the fuck?" she snapped.

"There wasn't time to get you... like I said the ten times before on our way home," Roman droned.

Apparently, Sam had begun yelling at him as soon as Zeke sent her the address.

"Bullshit," she said.

Vaughn wrapped an arm around her. "How about we take this inside?" There was a grin on his face, but his tone was serious.

I glanced around us, and sure enough, we were gathering attention. The pack didn't need any added stress by watching the high-ranking wolves argue.

Sam huffed, but turned around and headed inside the main house. We followed her to Roman's office, and I chuckled as she sat on Roman's desk, facing the door.

Roman released his hold on my hand and went to Sam. "You're acting like a child who had their favorite toy taken away. I'm sure you'll see Zeke again soon enough. He seems quite fond of you."

Sam snarled at him. "In a professional manner, yes."

"Get off my desk, Sam," Roman said, returning her glare.

She finally broke their staring contest and moved to glower against the wall. "What did Zeke say?"

"That *you* told him about pack business, and he found Kyle for us. The four of us will be leaving within the hour to check out the location he gave us," Roman answered.

Sam laughed too loud to be normal. "Not without me, you're not."

"You have the council looking for you, and I need you here in case someone shows up that shouldn't."

"I'm also the one with the address," Sam replied defiantly.

Roman's eyes darkened, and his fist made a noticeable dent in the desk as he turned back to his cousin. "I don't have the patience for games, Sam. I love you. You're my family and my best friend. I need you to have my back right now. Do you understand?"

I watched as the fire fizzled out of Sam's eyes. They hadn't had any alone time together since I arrived, and I could see the stress was wearing on their relationship.

"I understand." She walked to his desk, grabbed a pen, and scribbled down the address. "I will wait here, and everything is going to be fine. Just kill that bastard for what he did to our pack."

Sam dialed back her attitude completely, and Roman's sigh of relief wasn't missed by any of us. "Thank you, Sammy."

She bumped him with her fist on his shoulder, and I could feel the rise of his emotions through our bond. It was something that didn't happen often given we weren't officially mated, but I enjoyed the random times I could feel closer to Roman.

"I'm going to go check on the Super Squad before we need to leave again," Vaughn said.

Embry nodded. "I have some things to follow up on as well after being gone a bit."

Roman had grabbed on to Sam, keeping her close, and I took the opportunity to give them the alone time I'd just been thinking about.

"Ramona probably needs lunch. I'll be back in a bit," I said.

Roman took a step toward me, but I held my hand up. *Spend some time with your cousin. You both need it.*

He nodded as his eyes softened. *You're amazing.*

The door clicked closed behind me, and I leaned against it. We'd found Kyle. All we had to do was hope he was still there when we arrived to serve him the justice he'd earned.

Only I hadn't been completely honest with Roman. I was going to bring Ramona lunch, but I was also inviting her to come with us on the condition she was respectful of Roman's needs.

It had been her mate who was killed by Kyle. She deserved to be part of whatever was coming next. Roman might not like it, but deep down he could understand. His mother deserved the chance to avenge her mate. Of that, I was absolutely certain.

After stopping by the kitchen for some sandwiches, I made my way to Ramona's room. I knocked, and she called for me to come in.

When I entered, Ramona was looking worse than I'd yet to see her. Her shoulders were hunched, and she sat on the couch with her arms wrapped around her legs.

I sat the sandwiches down and went to her. "What happened?"

She turned her head, tears filling her eyes. "He's really gone. My Jack isn't ever coming back."

"Oh, Ramona." I cried with her, wrapping my arms tightly around her and holding on as hard as I could, as if my strength could put all of her broken pieces back together.

When I glanced around to see if there was anything that triggered the emotional breakdown besides the obvious processing of grief, I saw pictures of her and Jack scattered on the kitchen table. Ramona had been taking a trip down memory lane that didn't quite go as planned.

"I have news that might make you feel better," I said once her cries quieted.

"Kyle's dead?" she asked.

I shook my head. "But he will be soon and you're coming with us."

She wiped away the remaining tears. "Did Roman have you come tell me?"

"No. He doesn't know I'm telling you, but *I* know it's the right thing and so does he. At least, he will soon, but you will have to listen to him for this to work. He needs you to be okay."

Ramona latched on to me, hugging me tightly. "Thank you, Cait."

"You were there for me. I'm just glad I can repay the favor and do what is right."

Once we parted for the second time, she shot up from the couch and headed for her room. "What are you doing?" I asked.

"Showering and changing. I won't let Kyle see me broken. He doesn't have the right to know how he hurt me." Ramona's head was held high, and her eyes were bright with not only unshed tears, but the conviction to finish what needed to be done.

Yes, I'd made the right move coming to Ramona. Hopefully Roman would see that when I brought her downstairs with me.

7

ROMAN

I t had been a long time since I'd fought with Sam. We'd always gotten along, and the tension between us was not helping the rest of the shit blowing up around me. Cait, being the perfect mate I already knew she was, gave me the opportunity to finally have some time alone with my cousin.

Sam still stood near my desk after everyone left, but she wasn't speaking to me. We were both stubborn, but in this instance, I chose to make the first move. I was the one that had been too busy worrying about everyone else and I took majority of the blame for the strain between us.

"Sammy, I'm sorry," I said as I inched closer to her. She was like a wild cat, and I needed to tread carefully.

She raised a brow. "Why are you sorry?"

"I wasn't available for you when you came home. I was occupied with Cait, and while my mate is at the top of my priority list, I should have done a better job checking in with you. If I had, you might not have ended up in that rock."

Sam laughed. "You wouldn't have been able to stop me."

"No, but maybe I could have gone with you, or done something to make sure you weren't alone," I said.

"I wasn't alone. Though, Zeke isn't the first company I would have chosen. Regardless, I don't want the pack involved in whatever is happening with the councils. There is even chatter about the wolf council being compromised."

There had been a reason I'd been hesitant to include anyone else in the problems involving Cait. Not only did power make idiots do stupid shit, but my gut had told me more was happening around us than anyone realized. I was equal parts glad and irritated that I had been right.

"What are we going to do about it? I know you know more than you've told us," I said.

Sam grinned. "It's more about what I've seen in the past. History likes to repeat itself. As soon as we can find Embry's parents, things will begin to make more sense."

"Why are they so important to what you think is happening?" I asked. Embry hadn't seemed worried about her parents, but Sam had brought them up on more than one occasion. Something I hadn't missed.

"Because I trust them. Their loyalty might lie with the supernatural council now, but their hearts are still here. The fact that they haven't surfaced in weeks isn't normal, even for them." Sam's bright blue eyes met mine. There was a sliver of fear in them, something she rarely expressed.

"Do you think they're dead?" I asked, hoping like hell not. Embry might not be close with her parents, but they were still family. Her only blood family.

"I think that someone is playing God when they have no right, and anyone who might get in their way is being silenced by any means necessary," Sam answered.

We won't let anyone get to Cait, my wolf snarled.

No, not ever, but we might have to play a few games in order to keep her safe, I replied.

Or we could just find their secret base and blow the whole thing up.

And possibly kill innocent people? I countered.

Better than our mate being taken away from us.

My wolf wasn't wrong. I'd burn cities down for Cait, but we weren't that desperate yet. Cait wouldn't accept that option, either. We had to find out what was going on.

"Nothing immediate happening this week that you've heard, though?" I asked Sam, hoping to move the conversation along.

"No, but that's not necessarily a good thing, either."

I reached a hand to her, cupping her elbow. "Listen, Sammy. I know you want to help. It's in your DNA to fight, but I need you here, keeping an eye out and reporting anything new. We can handle Kyle as long as I know the pack is safe and there isn't anyone on the hunt for Cait yet."

She sighed, losing some of her earlier wrath. "I don't like it."

"I know, but we don't have a lot of options."

Sam stepped closer to me, and I wrapped my arms around her. "I miss before when I came home and we had movie nights and long runs with our wolves," she murmured.

"Me, too, Sammy. Things don't have to change forever, though. We just need to get past whatever is happening right now. I promise to binge your favorite superhero movies just as soon as Cait isn't in danger."

She pulled back. "I like her. I didn't want to like her, but I do."

I laughed. "She's a good person. Stronger than I expected her to be."

"Cait isn't afraid of much, that's for sure. I did my best to intimidate her, and she didn't cower. I admit I was impressed."

I narrowed my eyes at my best friend. "I hope you're done with that now?"

"I am. And I'll stay here where you need me. Just make sure you kick Kyle in the balls for me before you kill him," Sam said.

"Deal, and thank you. Knowing you're here will make this trip easier."

She nodded and we pulled apart as I sensed my mother getting closer. "I think Mom finally came out of her room. She's probably coming to yell at me some more," I said solemnly. I hated keeping her trapped, but I needed to keep her safe more than I needed her to like me.

"You knew she wouldn't take your command well.

That's your bed of shit to lay in and nobody else's," Sam said with a wink.

"Let's go make sure she isn't breaking stuff."

Sam followed me, and we headed toward the kitchen where I sensed both Cait and my mom. I heard laughter and was confused. Something had happened, and I wasn't sure it was a good thing.

I tried reaching out to Cait, but she wasn't responding to my mental calls. She'd done something.

We entered the kitchen, and my mom was dressed in dark jeans, black boots, and a grey shirt. Her eyes were alive for the first time since we lost my dad. My gut twisted as I began putting things together. My mate was in deep shit.

"What's going on?" I asked casually.

"We're just getting ready," my mother answered as Cait met my pointed stare.

"Ramona is coming with us. She will get the opportunity to avenge her mate," Cait said confidently.

I crossed my arms. "Is that so?"

Cait closed the distance between us and lowered her voice, even though everyone in the room would still be able to hear her. "If it was me or you in her position, we'd want the same thing. The situation will be controlled. We have the upper hand, thanks to Zeke. Ramona needs this, and I need you to give her this opportunity."

Cait's green eyes held a fire within them that said I wasn't going to win this conversation. I wanted to argue all the reasons why it wasn't a good idea, but my mate was smart. We'd kept my mother locked up long enough. Though, it didn't mean there wouldn't be stipulations.

"Okay," I said with a pause.

Cait's eyes widened. "Seriously?"

"But," I said, and she sighed, "there are rules."

My mom was eating a sandwich at the counter, grinning between bites. "And what would those be, Son?"

"You will not act without permission. If you take off on your own, I will drag you back to the pack by whatever means necessary, and you won't ever get another opportunity to find Kyle again. The location of where we're headed will only be known by me, and we will all travel in the same vehicle."

"Is that all?" my mom asked, and I didn't like the light tone of her voice. She wasn't taking this seriously.

I pushed away from the wall and strode toward her, turning her so that she faced me. "I will not lose both of my parents. This isn't a suicide mission. We will capture Kyle, and I will give you the opportunity to exact your revenge. Nothing more, nothing less. Do you understand?"

My voice was filled with alpha power that broke through the façade she'd been showing just moments before. The sorrow within her eyes was back, but there was a fury more powerful than any other emotion simmering beneath. "I do."

"Good. We will leave within the hour." I turned toward Cait, and she shrugged. I'd be bending her over my knee just as soon as I could.

Sam stepped between us. "You've already got the

address. I'll go meet with Vaughn and the Super Squad to make sure they know to report to me while the rest of you are gone."

I reached for her. "Thank you, Sammy."

"Two movie nights and an all-night run," she said before heading toward the back door.

Cait smiled. "Payment for making her stay back?"

I nodded. "It's also overdue."

"Embry won't complain about me having the free time so don't postpone because of me. We still need to do the things we did before, or we'll drive each other crazy. I'm not a fan of that thought," she said.

"Neither am I." I pulled her into my arms. "Everything is going to be fine."

"It's going to be better than fine," Cait vowed, and I did my damnedest to believe her.

8

CAIT

W e were halfway through our thirteen-hour drive. I sat up front with Roman while Embry and Ramona took up the middle with Vaughn yelling at everyone from the third row as if he was yards away from us instead of mere feet.

Night had fallen, and if we were able to keep pace by switching drivers instead of stopping to sleep, then we'd be to Albuquerque just after two in the morning. Our hope was to catch the wolves while they were sleeping, but that was probably wishful thinking. Kyle seemed smart enough to at least have a guard keeping watch. Then again, it wouldn't surprise me if he wasn't.

"Let's switch before we hit Interstate Forty," Roman said, glancing in the rearview mirror.

Vaughn leaned forward. "You got it, Boss. I made sure to get my beauty sleep. I'm ready for action."

Embry rolled her eyes. "First, no amount of beauty sleep could ever help your ugly mug. Second, there will be no action on this trip until we arrive at that warehouse."

"I second what Embry said. Well, I second her second point. I want nothing to do with the first," I said. Vaughn was attractive in his own way—the rugged biker way—but not my type.

Roman pulled into a rest stop. There was only one other vehicle and two more that followed us in. I saw vending machines and bathrooms.

"Who's hungry?" I asked, unbuckling before I reached for the cash I saw Roman toss into the center console.

"Me," Embry and Vaughn echoed.

Roman was already at my door when I went to open it. "I'll go with you."

"Overprotective alpha," I muttered not so quietly.

He smacked my ass as I got out of the vehicle. "And proud of it." He glanced back at his mother. "Stay in here. If you have to piss, get out now so you can come with us."

She narrowed her eyes at him. "I have no reason to get out of this vehicle until Kyle is within killing distance."

Roman hesitated. I was certain he didn't believe her, but Embry and Vaughn were hanging back, so I didn't stress too much on it.

Once I yanked him away from the SUV, I reached out and slid my fingers into his. He squeezed twice as I glanced up at the stars. We were away from city lights we'd been passing through, but the sky still had nothing on the nights we experienced in the pack.

East Texas had already become home, and I already missed being there after a short time.

"I'm going to the bathroom first," I said as we approached the rest-stop building.

He looked around, hesitant to let me go alone.

"I'll be sixty seconds, tops. I give you full permission to come storming in if I'm a moment beyond that," I added.

"Hurry up," he grunted as he released me.

Given what Zeke had said before, I had no problem complying with Roman's demand. I'd already been taken once; there was no need to allow it to happen a second time.

I took care of business in record time and was drying my hands under the loud air vent when I heard the door open. "I still have fourteen seconds," I called out.

"Technically, you still have just over two weeks left, but nobody will be the wiser if I keep you hidden until time runs out and I can collect my reward," a woman's voice said from behind me.

I had nothing to say back. There was no way in hell this chick was hiding me anywhere.

I can find the perfect place to bury her, Adira said as I channeled our energy. I had no doubts my wolf was right.

The woman blurred out of my sight, then reappeared, making me think she was a vampire. "Now, be a good little bitch and stay quiet so your guard dog doesn't hear us."

She wrapped a hand around my mouth, but I wasn't

complying. No, it was time to show her why the council wanted me.

I extended my canines and bit down on her palm until she released me, then swung my arm around, slamming my fist into her jaw. She stumbled, falling back into the grimy tile wall.

She hissed, showing off fangs, and was on me again before I could blink. Damn it, I hated how fast these suckers were.

Adira created the barrier around me that we'd been working on perfecting in my downtime. As the vamp reached for me again, her skin burned from the friction of my magic.

"What did you do to me?" she screeched.

Before I could even consider an answer, Roman stormed into the bathroom and wrapped his fist around her neck. I'd asked all sorts of things about vampires, but somehow, I'd missed the most important one of all: how they were killed.

Roman snarled in her face, keeping his hold tight until I heard bones snap in the vampire's neck. He dropped her to the ground, then glanced back at me, fury radiating from his shaking form. "Are you okay?" he asked.

I called my magic back inside of me and nodded. "Is it really that easy to kill them?"

"No. She'd heal and resurface within the hour if we left her as is, but she'll be dead before that can happen. Vaughn and Embry are dealing with the other two that arrived with this one. I didn't have time to grab the proper items to kill her after I sensed your energy flair.

Come on." He reached for me, and we exited the bathroom to find Vaughn with his phone in his hand and Embry standing over two bodies, smiling and waving at an older couple headed back to their car.

"What did you tell them?" Roman asked when we walked up.

Vaughn grinned and held his phone up. "That we're film students and making our first horror movie. I asked if they wanted to play dead along with our friends here, but they were already behind schedule due to a flat tire a few miles back."

The humans drove toward the on ramp, and the wife waved some more at Vaughn. "Bye, Susy!" he called.

"Her name was not seriously the same as your precious motorcycle," I said.

Vaughn shrugged. "Susanne, but close enough."

I shook my head and glanced at Roman as he spoke. "We need to kill these three and get out of here before anyone else shows up."

Embry moved toward the SUV. "I'll get the stakes."

"Seriously? We just have to stab them with wood?" I asked, shocked it was as simple as some of the movies made it sound.

"No. We have to stab them with wooden stakes soaked in holy water that have metal tips to pierce their hearts with," Vaughn answered just as Embry tossed him one.

The beta peeked left, then right, and no other humans were around. He grinned up at me. "Watch and learn, Witchy Wolf."

Roman sighed at Vaughn's theatrics, but I loved them. My eyes never moved as I watched the wooden stake slide with expert precision into the first male vampire's chest. Vaughn pressed down until six inches of the weapon disappeared, then leaned back.

"This is the only cool thing these bastards do," Embry said as the vampire's skin began to crack and shrivel like it was already decomposing. A strong smell of death hit me, making me cough and back up as the body started crumbling before my eyes. Before I could fully stand, I was hit by a shimmering cloud of ash.

I swiped at my face. "What the hell is that?"

"Vampires explode into a plume of sparkly dust when they die. Weird as it is, I appreciate not having to bury bodies," Embry answered, wiping vamp crap off herself as well.

"Now that you've had your fun, kill the second bloodsucker while we go take care of the third in the bathroom." Roman grabbed my hand and we walked together.

"I should have asked more questions before," I droned, feeling dirty even though there was nothing gory on me.

Roman wrapped an arm around me. "I think Embry purposely left that part out because it's been entertaining for her to watch you learn all of this, but don't stress. There isn't a spec of vampire left on you. The dust disintegrates quickly, and it doesn't actually sparkle. Natural lights like the moon can reflect off the ash almost making it seem that way, though."

I glanced down and, sure enough, where I expected

to find a glitter party happening all over my clothes, there was nothing. Everything else appeared just as normal as before. Still, I was in desperate need of a shower as soon as we found one.

"Is that the only way to kill them? A dagger to the chest?" I asked.

"It's the cleanest way. You can also cut their heads off, but you run the risk of having some of the human blood running through their veins spray back at you. Even though the bloodsuckers are undead, they still need blood coursing through their veins to survive. Just not their own."

A shiver ran down my spine as we turned the corner to enter the bathroom and Ramona came out, smiling and twirling a stake just like Roman was holding.

"Shit," Roman muttered.

"Forgot about me, huh? Well, good thing I'm not one for doing what I'm told when I'm not forced to. The vamp you left behind in here was coming to when I came to check things out," Ramona said. Even though she was grinning from the kill, Ramona's eyes were still dull and there was a heaviness around her she couldn't hide. Not from us.

"Thank you, Mom," Roman said, surprising her and me when he didn't reprimand his mother for leaving the SUV when specifically told not to.

Ramona nodded and walked past us to head back to the vehicle. By the time we made it to the parking lot, Vaughn and Embry were already in the front seats and Ramona was getting into the very back. I slid into the middle with Roman and was glad to be on the road again.

While the interaction with vampires had gone over smoothly, it could have been much worse. There could have been more of them, and I wasn't fond of the thought that there were people out there willing to keep me hidden until my deadline with the Supernatural Council expired, so they could turn me in themselves for a reward.

I'd asked for this, though. I wasn't going to hide. I'd be whatever I needed to be in order to keep myself from dying, either by psychopaths like those vamps or from the council.

Hopefully, the other supernaturals would get the memo. Even if they managed to get past my defenses, they'd never get through Roman's. Together, we were a force to be reckoned with.

Other supernaturals would soon learn. They couldn't come for me and survive.

9

ROMAN

Z eke was a fucking idiot. He'd warned Sam would be in danger if she came with us, but somehow, the parasite had no clue the time Cait had been given didn't much matter to the psychos out in our world.

I should have known better as well. There was a reason I'd been high strung since receiving word from the council. I knew how our world worked, but I'd let Cait's needs come before my desire to keep her safe.

While that might have been the right choice for my mate, it didn't make me feel any better.

The rest of the drive went smoothly, and we didn't make any other stops. We arrived at the address Zeke had given us at almost three in the morning and found a vantage point at the top of a hill behind some trees not far from where Kyle was supposed to be. There was one light on in front of the rusted metal building and no windows to tell if anyone was moving around inside.

"What's the plan, Boss?" Vaughn said as we all stared at where I hoped Kyle still was.

"We break down the door and kill every shifter we find. Just remember Kyle is mine," my mother spat before I could answer.

"No, that's not how we do things when we don't know if we can trust the information we were given," I said, already knowing exactly how things would play out.

"Zeke wouldn't be dumb enough to set you up," Embry said.

I grunted. "You'd think not, but power and money make people do stupid shit all the time. We don't know him, and just because Sam trusts him doesn't mean I do."

Vaughn slapped his hand down on my shoulder. "Good call. So, what now?"

Cait, who had been unusually quiet since we exited the car, leaned forward, and took charge. "We need two people to creep around the back, check the sides, and figure out where all of the exits are. Then, the remaining three will enter the building one at a time with the third giving the all-clear for the final two to enter behind us. Unless it's more beneficial for someone to watch potential exits depending on what's found."

I grinned at my mate. She knew my plan without me ever sharing it with her. It was exactly what I was going to say except for one part.

"What about the—"

She cut me off. "The roof? Wolves don't climb and unless there is a helicopter waiting for them up there that we magically can't see, I don't think it's anything to waste our time with."

"Okay, Alpha Female. Who is going where?" I asked, having no problem with Cait taking the lead. Clearly, she'd been more in tune with the situation than I realized, and she'd be in no less danger if I was the one calling the shots.

"Vaughn and Embry, you'll check the perimeter and the three of us will follow a minute behind and enter through the main door," Cait said, and nobody questioned her.

There was something off with her. The more she spoke, the more tension radiated from my mate. I tried reaching out through our bond, but she was closed off. A part of me wanted to ask her to stay back, but whatever was bothering Cait, she seemed in control of it, so I let the worry go.

"Leave your thoughts open, so we can communicate our every move. We can't let anything be missed," I added.

Cait's form shimmered purple, and her body shook from head-to-toe until the glow went away.

"What was that?" Embry asked before I could.

Cait shrugged. "Not sure. Just something my wolf wanted to try. She's rather stubborn with new information until she knows it's worth sharing."

I hoped that whatever tension I'd been sensing was the buildup of energy from her wolf and nothing more.

At the mention of Cait's wolf, mine rose to the surface. *We need to claim her soon.*

I know. We will, I replied.

My wolf's shock filtered through me. *Are you done making sure Cait is truly ready?*

77

I glanced down at our mate. I'd known she was ready since the week after she woke up. She'd been very clear with her wants, a trait I admired about her, but something had held me back. Something that had nothing to do with Cait.

I'd needed to know for myself that *I* was ready, and after my realizations during her final training test, I knew more than ever what was in my heart. I loved Cait beyond anything imaginable. She was the light that kept me moving forward, and there would be nothing in this world that could stop me from keeping her safe.

Cait nudged me. "Are you ready?"

My thoughts had taken more of my awareness than I realized. Embry and Vaughn were already disappearing into the shadows of the warehouse, and my mother was slowly trying to sneak past us.

"Let's go," I said.

Moving into the lead, I pushed my emotions down and called on my wolf senses. We had plenty of time once we all left here to worry about everything else.

There is nothing to worry about, only things to celebrate. Kyle will be dead, and we will make Cait ours. Officially. My wolf's eagerness to be done with Kyle was profound now that he knew what was coming next. I didn't fault him for his excitement. We'd waited long enough.

We approached the front door, and I couldn't hear anything inside. I held my hand up for Cait and my mother to wait, but neither of them listened as an all-clear came in from Embry.

One exit back here and a balcony on the second floor, Vaughn added.

Cait entered the building first, making me nervous, but I also trusted she was capable of taking care of herself. Though, letting go of my fear wasn't simple.

Vaughn and Embry, you're clear to come in through the back. Split up again as you come inside to cover more ground on your way in, I said.

They did as I requested, and I followed behind the two most important women in my life—important for two very different reasons. Regardless, I'd be crushed if anything happened to either of them.

We were ten feet into the building, and my mom was beginning to venture off on her own until she stepped on a trip wire, causing a flood light to shine down on us. I covered my eyes, trying to see through the brightness, but lights snapped on, one after another, in every direction I turned.

"Did you think I wouldn't be prepared for your arrival, dear cousin?" Kyle called from somewhere above us.

"Not at all. In fact, I hoped for the opposite. Given that you are, why don't you come down here and face me like a man?" I replied as I pulled my wolf's strength forward.

Kyle laughed and said nothing as he jumped from the second level. He landed on his feet, and I could hear the rumble of my mother's wolf when he came into view, but she stayed where she was, waiting on me. At least she wasn't acting irrationally like I thought she might.

"Came to die just like your father?" Kyle taunted me.

It was Cait who acted first, and I couldn't blame her. She launched herself forward, shifting into her wolf as she did so. My mate's teeth sank into Kyle's calf, and he bellowed in pain. Other shifters jumped down from the second floor, and the fight began.

Vaughn and Embry entered the room, blood already splattered on themselves, but neither appeared to be injured as they fought against the others.

I lost track of my mother, but I didn't worry about that for long—she wasn't going anywhere with Kyle inside the building. Cait was slashing her claws at Kyle's chest as he tried to get loose from her hold long enough to shift.

Unfortunately for Kyle, he didn't have a witch around to make Cait weak like before, and there was no way Kyle could overpower her. Kyle didn't have enough wolves coming to his aid to win this fight. It was almost too easy, which was just as concerning.

I grabbed him by his neck, squeezing tight. "You had a choice and chose wrong."

Kyle spit blood in my face. "I was stuck in that pack. I never had a choice."

"There are always options. You were just too weak to seek them out." Other wolves appeared in my peripherals, but they weren't coming to attack and assist their pack beta. Their heads were bowed, and it appeared Vaughn and Embry were already done with the fighting. It was only Kyle who needed to be dealt with.

His russet eyes bore into me. There wasn't an ounce of regret in them for the things he'd done, for the lives he'd taken and ruined. Kyle was my blood, but he wasn't my family. My father had been everything to our pack, and he hadn't deserved to be killed. Kyle did.

My mother's wolf snarled from behind me as I held on to Kyle's neck and Cait remained latched to his leg. I glanced back at my mom and the thirst for death was clear.

Kyle had nowhere to go, and nobody left to fight for him. I released my hold and nodded at Cait to do the same.

"I hope your wolf has a better life in the next go around," I said right before I shoved Kyle to the floor, offering him up to my mother.

He attempted to stand, but Cait had done a number on his leg and there was no hesitation on my mother's part.

Her wolf howled the most sorrowful sound I'd ever heard and then made her move. Kyle managed to shift to his wolf form before my mother sprung toward him. I inched to move in and help, but Cait's wolf stepped in front of me.

My mate was right. My mother needed this moment, but damn if it wasn't hard to remain protective of her. I couldn't let anything happen to her. Not so soon after losing my father.

Kyle put up a fight I didn't think he had left in him. His wolf snarled and snapped at my mom, but she was quicker than him and he'd barely made a scratch on her. She darted around him in circles until Kyle began to trip over his own feet. The damage Cait had already done prevented Kyle from any grand moves. It seemed the only thing he was capable of was biting, but that wasn't going to happen.

My mother barreled into Kyle, causing him to land on his side before she made her killing blow. Without hesitation, my mom's wolf ripped through the fur of Kyle's, snarling in victory and sorrow. Her light tan coat was quickly covered in crimson as her sharp teeth tore into the wolf's neck until they hit their mark. Kyle tried to fight back, but every slash of his claws was futile.

My mother was relentless in her actions, clamping down until the snapping of bones sounded and Kyle's body went limp. When she released his lifeless and shredded body, I thought she'd back away, but instead, she bowed her head and moaned over his body.

Kyle had been her nephew, yet he'd taken away the most precious person in the world to her. I'd known all along that killing him wouldn't heal her, but I hoped it would at least take away most of her anger.

I need time, Son. Her words were filled with grief as they echoed through my mind when she finally backed up.

I'd held her hostage at the pack for fear she'd get herself into trouble she couldn't get out of, possibly on purpose. Seeing her so raw after avenging her mate, I knew I needed to let her go.

Will you come home? I asked.

Just as soon as I'm ready.

I nodded and moved closer to her wolf, stroking the thick fur at her back. *I love you, Mom.*

I love you with all my heart.

Her wolf eyes shimmered with emotion as she took

several steps away from me and turned to exit the warehouse.

"Where is she going?" Vaughn asked.

"I don't know, but she'll come back to us when she's ready," I replied as Cait joined my side, grabbing on to my hand. I checked her over with a quick glance and there didn't seem to be a mark on her, but she was still closed off to me.

A throat cleared behind us, reminding me there were still other shifters to deal with. "You have lived within a pack that was led by an undeserving alpha for far too long. What do you want to do now?"

A man from the middle of the seven standing before us limped to the front. "We'd like to head back to our home and see what has been decided. Kyle did not automatically become alpha. In fact, he was growing weaker the longer we were away from our home."

Kyle wasn't meant to be alpha, but losing a leader shouldn't have made him weaker. It must have been his own subconscious doing him in. "I have my own issues to deal with, but don't hesitate to reach out if the West Texas pack needs help. Remember how our ancestors did things and listen to your wolves. Your home has the chance to start over. Don't take that for granted."

One by one, the other shifters filtered out of the building. Besides Kyle's, there were only four other bodies we had to do something with before we could leave. Four wolves who had died for nothing and before their time. All because one man could never be happy with what he had.

"Should we call in a crew to take care of this, or

burn the building?" Vaughn asked, seeming just as eager as I was to get home.

"There are no proper places around here to bury the wolves, and no other occupied buildings near enough. Burn it." That was better than risking someone digging them up later.

As I turned for the door with Cait still at my side, her grip on my hand was bordering on painful. Something had happened to my mate, and I'd done a piss poor job of figuring it out.

"What's wrong? Are you hurt?" I asked just as soon as we were alone.

"I'd wanted to kill him," she said solemnly.

"We all did, but you were right to bring my mother. Even though it won't make her feel better, she needed this closure."

Cait shook her head. "No, I wanted to *kill* him. I wanted to tear him apart limb-by-limb, making him suffer as he slowly bled out. I envisioned his pain, craved it."

I wrapped my arms around Cait. "What he did to you wasn't right, either. It's not surprising your wolf was pushing to finish him."

Her next words were filled with fear. "It wasn't my wolf's thoughts. They were all mine. Adira was the only reason I stayed in control."

I pulled back far enough to meet her eyes and cup her cheeks. "There is nothing wrong with thinking that way. I know you've learned a lot already about our way of life, but the most important thing to remember is that shifters are still beasts at heart. When someone threatens their pack, it doesn't usually go over well."

"But this wasn't my wolf's thoughts," she repeated, desperation lacing through her words.

"Kitten, you are your wolf."

10

CAIT

K*itten, you are your wolf.*
Roman's words repeated several times over through my mind as we made our way back to the pack. I'd been fine when we left East Texas. Even facing the vampire at the rest stop hadn't bothered me. I'd had a handle on my emotions, but as we got closer to Kyle's location, the thirst for his blood grew with every passing mile.

Adira had tried to talk me down. Her words had allowed me to keep control of the growing darkness, but it had been a fragile hold. Her suggestion of having me take lead in the mission seemed like a good plan, but there wasn't true relief until I expelled my energy and shifted.

The euphoria that ran through me as I tasted Kyle's blood in my mouth scared the hell out of me and awoke parts of me I didn't know existed.

Everything you did and felt was normal, Adira said for the hundredth time.

Why doesn't it feel normal, then? I asked.

Because you weren't raised this way. You might finally accept that this is your life, but there will still be struggles you have to conquer as you let go of your human past.

Her words held a truth to them I knew I should believe, and I did my best to do just that, even when it was hard as shit.

We'd been home for one full day, and I hadn't seen Roman much. He'd been busy making calls and finalizing plans for the other pack alphas and their families to come meet me. We only had fifteen days left before the time to turn myself over to the council was up, and we'd spent much of the previously given time concerning ourselves with finding Kyle.

It was worth it, but now we had to double down and figure out how to stop whoever was pulling the strings over there. Something wasn't right, and we were going to get to the bottom of things or die trying. Allowing anyone to use me in some sick attempt to steal power wasn't an option.

I felt Roman's presence getting nearer to where I'd been hiding out. The river that ran through the property was quiet and calming and just what I needed when he was busy. Embry had tried to get me to open up to her, but there were some things I needed to work through on my own.

"How is my mate today?" Roman asked before kissing the back of my neck.

"She's communing with nature," I joked, but in a way, that was exactly what I was doing.

He turned me toward him, a smile on his face. "I'd like to have dinner with you tonight."

"We have dinner together every night."

"Alone. Without an audience. The other alphas will begin arriving tomorrow, and I need time with you before they're here."

His words made my skin tingle. "Alone, alone?"

Roman's grin grew as the silver flecks in his blue eyes brightened. "Yes, Mate. Alone, alone. We'll spend the evening at the cabin."

I wasn't questioning him again. Sure, his room offered enough privacy when we needed it, but I was allowing my hope to grow that time spent in the cabin meant big things for us. Like the kind I'd been asking for rather bluntly lately.

I was ready to complete our bond and hopeful this meant he was, too. Maybe in doing so I'd find the peace I'd been searching for the past couple of days.

///

I SPENT THE REST OF THE LATE AFTERNOON LOSING MY MIND. It wasn't that I was nervous about having sex with Roman. We'd basically done everything else together, and I trusted him explicitly. I more so just hoped nothing went wrong.

Would someone unexpected show up at the pack? Would I have a magically charged episode during the bonding moment that wasn't normal? Would Roman even make it to the cabin? Or would someone need him more than we needed each other tonight?

Embry stormed into my room as my favorite green dress fell into place over my freshly shaven legs. "What are you doing tonight?"

"Having dinner with Roman," I replied casually. I'd tell her we bonded after the fact. I didn't need her making me more nervous with her version of twisted humor.

She shook her finger at me. "Liar, liar, pants on fire. Roman said he was staying at the cabin tonight and not to be disturbed unless there was a life-or-death threat against the pack. You're totally getting laid tonight, aren't you?"

I was a terrible liar. Instead, I said nothing.

"Okay, fine. Be that way. I guess I can wait to pry the details from you later when there is actual dirt to be given. I just hope Roman knows what he's doing and things don't get cockward."

I choked on air. "What the hell is cockward?"

She shrugged. "You know? Like, what if he has problems down there?"

"Oh, I assure you there are no problems down there. Now, leave me alone."

Are you ready? Roman's voice rang through my mind, and I silently thanked the gods I could walk away from Embry and all her cockward business.

I'll meet you outside, I replied and gave Embry my attention again. "I'm leaving. Please don't say another word involving cock."

She grinned and pretended to zip her lips before opening her arms to me. I went to my best friend and gave her a hug, even though she'd put more worries in my head. We left mine and Roman's room together, saying goodbye once we got to the bottom of the stairs.

"I love you, Asstie!" she called as I headed out the door.

"Love you, too," I yelled back and walked faster down the porch in case Roman was close. I didn't need her saying anything to him, too.

When I finally saw Roman standing on the gravel driveway, my heart sped up. His bright eyes only saw me as we stared at each other. He tossed his hair back as his smile grew, and I took in his white button-up collared shirt and khaki shorts.

He was sexier than sin and I couldn't wait to get him naked. All previous nerves were gone as he closed the distance between us and lifted me up into a hug. "I missed you."

"It's only been a couple hours," I joked.

"Seconds apart is long enough for me to miss you." Roman kissed me, and I melted in his arms. Damn, how did I get so lucky?

He loosened his hold until my feet touched the ground again, and he held my hand as we walked toward the cabin. "I already brought dinner over. Are you hungry?"

I eyed him openly. "Extremely."

He laughed, then picked me up. "In that case, we should hurry."

With Roman's enhanced speed, we were at the cabin in no time and my cheeks were sore from grinning. I had no clue why I'd been freaking out earlier. Roman was perfect for me, and I was his. Nothing, and nobody, would change that.

Once we were inside, Roman closed and locked the door and I took in the setup. Candles were the only light within the single room, soft music played from a small speaker on a shelf, and covered serving trays sat on the table. Even though the aroma of food was enticing, it was the bed that held most of my attention.

A new comforter and pillows adorned the mattress along with flower petals, not from roses. No, that would be too generic, and my mate was more creative than that. These were chocolates wrapped in red and pink foil. Something we could feed each other later after we'd satisfied other needs.

"Is everything okay?" Roman asked, gesturing toward the room.

I turned back to him and wrapped my arms around his neck. "Everything is perfect. Just like you."

His lips pressed down on mine, and I opened for him as his tongue begged for entrance to my mouth. I pushed up onto my toes, doing whatever it took to get closer to him.

Roman kissed down my neck, sucking behind my ear as I curved into his touch. "We should eat first."

My fingers made their way down his chest and traced the lines of his muscled stomach. "Is that what you want?"

I met his eyes, and they burned with a fire only for me. "Not at all, but we didn't really talk about what tonight—"

I cut him off. "We didn't need to. We both know what we want and how we feel."

He pushed me toward the bed until my ass met the comforter. "I'm going to love you for the rest of eternity."

I grabbed onto his shirt and pulled him closer. I'd never said the words out loud, but I'd shown Roman in many ways how I felt. It was time to make sure he really knew.

"I love you, Roman Chase."

His thumb rubbed over my lower lip. "I love you, too. More than life itself."

What I expected to be frenzied and somewhat rushed after all the time we'd waited, turned into something slow and passionate and sensual.

His fingers tugged at the straps of my dress and drew them down my shoulders one at a time, leaving kisses in his wake.

I worked at his pants, even as my mind was on overload and not functioning properly. Every sense was heightened. Every emotion wanting to burst from my chest. Every aspect of the moment perfect.

Roman had my dress around my waist, and I pushed his arms to the side so I could slide his shirt over his head, taking my time to pay respect to the sculpted lines of his body. I stood to finish the task and my dress fell to my feet, leaving me in the lace bra and underwear I'd been saving for this moment.

"Beautiful," Roman whispered against my lips.

His kiss silenced my response as he nudged me back onto the bed, then rid himself of his pants. His six-foot-three frame stood before me, bare and open, and all mine.

"Come here," I demanded softly.

Roman crawled over me as my chest constricted. This was it. We were going to finally bond, and I could feel the magic inside me fighting to escape. I focused on keeping a tight hold on the power, afraid it would ruin the moment, but my wolf eased any current worries.

Roman must accept you for all that you are. You can't hide this part of you now, Adira said before retreating.

Without hesitation, I let go of my hold and the room filled with a soft purple glow. I expected Roman to freak out, but he smiled down at me instead, pressing his hand to my chest.

"Your energy has called to me since the day I first saw you on that beach. I promise to cherish every part of you for the rest of my life," he whispered above me.

"In return, I promise to always stand by your side. No matter what we face, we do it together."

Our shared words were a vow I hadn't expected to make, but I meant every word spoken. Roman was my life now, and there was nothing in this world I'd let come between us.

Together, we had everything.

His rough palms trailed over my sensitive skin, relieving me of my bra and underwear before doing the same to his deliciously tight boxer briefs.

Purple fog still swirled around us, and Roman's body widened and grew before my eyes as his alpha power rose to the surface. The moment was overpowering and monumental. I took in every movement he made, not wanting to forget a single thing.

Roman leaned over me, his eyes smoldering and his touch burning me in the most sensual of ways. "Are you ready?" he asked.

"I've never been more ready for anything in my life," I replied with absolute truth.

His fingers blazed a trail from my chest, across my stomach, and over my core. I bucked beneath his touch that I craved, needing more. He tested my readiness, but it was futile. I was primed the moment I saw him in the driveway.

Roman's cock twitched above me, and I tugged him closer, ready for forever with my mate. He took my cues and aligned himself with me. I had no idea what to expect after he tortuously and slowly pushed into me. Instead, I opened my mind to any possibility and let all of me free.

Nothing could have readied me for the emotional overload as Roman fully entered me and I clung to him with every bit of strength that I had. My heart swelled with love, and my skin tingled with magic to the point where I wondered if I was going to pass out.

Roman seemed to be just as affected as he moved above me with measured movements. His elbows kept him propped up, while our hips did most of the work and I was able to stare into his endless eyes.

I love you so damn much, I said through our connection, unsure at what point our bond would be complete.

He leaned on one hand, using the other to brush my

hair back. *I love you more than anyone has ever loved another.*

With every thrust, the bond with Roman tightened around my heart. Our eyes locked as we continued to move together, solidifying our relationship into something that was forever.

My chest rose as I could feel an orgasm drawing near. I dug my nails into his biceps, hoping he was close as well. With the energy still surrounding us, I wasn't sure I could handle two epic releases that close together.

Roman's forehead lowered to mine as his hand slipped between us, rubbing over my center at the perfect moment. My hips jerked up, taking him deeper than before, and I cried out. My vision faltered, but I held on to consciousness, refusing to miss any part of our bonding.

Roman's jaw tensed as he pounded into me harder and faster, drawing out my orgasm, so we could finish together. As soon as he groaned, light from the candles flickered around us and wind whipped through the room.

Roman held on to me, and I focused only on him as our wolf magic worked its way through both of us. When the air calmed in the room, unknown power filled me and the presence of too many others filled my mind, momentarily taking away the high I'd just been riding.

"Take a deep breath and build a mental wall. You have complete control," Roman murmured against my ear.

I did as he said while enjoying the fact that he was

still inside me. Our bond pulsed through my blood like a lifeline I'd never release.

"What was that?" I asked once the sensations disappeared.

"The pack. You're connected to them through me. Now, how do I stop feeling like I want to explode with power?" he asked in return, which had me smiling wide.

"There's no stopping it. You just have to let go," I replied.

His face turned serious. "I'll never let go."

I gripped his ass. "Good, because I'd hate to have to kill you for doing so just to find you in another lifetime."

"We'll always find our way back to each other. From this moment forward."

"Forever and always."

11

CAIT

Any negative thoughts that had been lingering before were extinguished after a night of being loved by my mate. Once our bonding was done, Roman turned from the caring, sensual partner I knew him to be and into the fierce, insatiable lover I'd suspected was inside him.

I'd experienced the best of both sides for hours on end until the sun came up and we finally fell asleep, tangled in a mess of sweat, arms, legs, and love. The emotions that flowed within me were raw and powerful and nothing like I imagined, but everything I expected.

The fear I had held on to before had been because deep down I'd known that what I could have with Roman was enough to ruin me if I lost him. I'd been right, but the thought of losing him wasn't as terrifying as living a life without knowing his kind of love.

"Good morning, Kitten," Roman murmured as I stretched out next to him.

My muscles were sore from being twisted into

positions I hadn't known existed, but between a few hours of sleep and my wolf healing, the aches were merely a reminder of the ecstasy from our late-night escapades.

"Good morning, Mate," I replied as I tossed my leg over his hips, learning quickly that last night had not been enough for either of us.

He palmed my ass and moved me until I straddled him. "Shall we make it a *great* morning?" he suggested.

I moved onto my knees, answering him with my movements instead of words.

"Are you sore?" he asked.

"Not enough to stop me from wanting you all over again," I replied as I slowly positioned myself over his hardened cock.

He grinned, gripping my hips and guiding me down until he was fully seated within me. I ground against him, rubbing myself shamelessly as I let my head tilt back.

His rough hands moved up my sides, squeezing my breasts until I moaned from the pressure. I began to look down, but Roman was in charge this morning and I had no problem releasing control to him.

He grabbed a fistful of my hair, forcing my back to stay arched, and pounded into me as I rode him like there was no tomorrow. His other hand slipped between us, calling my orgasm too soon.

"Let go, Kitten. We're not leaving this cabin until I've made you scream many more times," he growled.

I did as he asked, and my nails dug into his ribs while I pushed harder to get him as deep as possible inside me. Everything about Roman made me want more. I couldn't imagine that the craving I currently had swirling inside me would ever die down.

When I came down from my high, Roman flipped me over and positioned me onto my hands and knees as he kneeled behind me. His hand smacked my ass so hard, I nearly came again from the pleasure-pain his touch offered.

He pounded into me with abandon, and I thanked the Moon Goddess for expedited healing, because having my mate own me like he did would be a damn shame to miss.

One of his hands held my hips where he wanted while the other pinched my nipples hard enough to make me moan in more of that pleasure-pain-filled way. He'd been more gentle than rough the night before which I'd loved the hell out of, but I couldn't deny the way he was dominating turned me on twice as much.

I was ready for my second release, and Roman was right there with me. His speed picked up, and the pressure of his hands intensified until we came together, falling onto the mattress.

Roman rolled us to our sides so he didn't squish me, but I had no cares left to give. He'd killed me with his dick, and I wasn't even mad about it.

"We need to start every day like this," Roman murmured against my shoulder.

"I'll never get anything done if we do that." I laughed.

His fingers trailed over my sensitive skin, then stopped suddenly. "What's wrong?" I asked.

"The alpha from Tennessee and his daughter have arrived early. He's demanding to see me," Roman answered, effectively bursting our love bubble.

I sat up, ready to face whatever was going to happen. "Then, let's go meet him, but first, we shower and change. Make him stew a little longer if he wants to be demanding."

Roman kissed me. "That is exactly what we should and will do. I might have invited them here, asking for their help, but another alpha doesn't get to tell me what to do on my own land. It's not my problem that they arrived four hours early."

After our bonding, I was more than ready to face the arriving alphas. It was time to figure out who was going to have our back and who we needed to keep an eye on.

///

THIRTY MINUTES LATER, ROMAN AND I MET THE IMPATIENT alpha and his daughter in the conference room downstairs. Vaughn and Sam were there as well, but nobody was speaking.

"Trey, Cassie. It's good to see the two of you again. I apologize I wasn't available sooner. We weren't expecting you until after noon," Roman said, reaching his hand out to the alpha.

Trey stood. He was just over six feet tall with stormy colored eyes and cropped dirty-blond hair. He was dressed casually in jeans and a t-shirt, which fit in since that was also what Roman and I had opted for as we got ready.

"We have other matters to discuss, so I thought it best that we arrive early." Trey nodded toward his daughter. "Cassie is here with me to officially challenge Cait for the position as your mate. You deserve a true wolf at—"

Roman's growing snarl cut the other alpha off. "Cait is not my chosen mate. She is the mate fated to me by the Moon Goddess herself. You are a fool to doubt our creator's choice, and an even bigger idiot for thinking Cait isn't a true wolf. She will kill your daughter."

"If my Cassie isn't strong enough to survive the challenge she has issued, then I will accept that is her fate," Trey stated with zero concern for his own blood.

I'd ignored Cassie until that point. She looked nothing like her father with black wavy hair and dull copper eyes. She refused to meet my stare, instead focusing on the table beside us.

"It doesn't seem to me that Cassie has issued the challenge," I said with bite, meeting the eyes of the alpha.

He sneered at me. "Will you allow your mate to speak to me that way?"

"Her words are much kinder than what I have to say, so yes, I will. Cait and I have completed our bonding. You have no challenge here to issue, even if Cassie decided to speak the words herself," Roman said.

An excited "yes" slipped from Vaughn before he tried to cover it up with a cough.

"A bond can be broken if the mate it's attached to

isn't strong enough to keep it," Trey replied with an air of confidence.

"No. I don't accept your challenge, and you're not welcome in my pack. The two of you can leave on your own, or I'd be happy to show you out. It's up to you how this ends," Roman said.

Trey shoved Cassie toward me. "Challenge her as I've told you."

The girl couldn't be much older than eighteen, and she was shaking with fear. She glanced back. "Father, they've already—"

Trey backhanded her. "Do as we've discussed!"

Roman was on Trey, slamming him against the back wall as I pulled Cassie to me. I thought she'd struggle, but she went willingly into my arms.

Roman's hand pressed against the other alpha's chest, keeping him pinned down. "A worthy alpha never harms his pack, let alone his own blood. If I didn't have more important issues to handle, I'd take you straight to the council to be dealt with. For now, I'll settle for dragging you off my land."

Vaughn and Sam were right behind him, so I focused on Cassie. "Are you okay?"

She held on to my forearm and muttered. "Morior Invictus."

My chest constricted, and I stumbled back as power swirled painfully within me.

"Fuck," Sam said before she pushed Cassie away from me.

What just happened? I asked Adira.

We've been challenged to the death.

And to think, I'd felt bad for this girl. Gone was the meek wolf who'd been cowering moments before. In her place was a wolf prepared to die for something that didn't belong to her.

Roman's fist slammed into Trey's face. "You have no idea what you've just done."

Trey spit blood onto the ground. "Oh, I know exactly what I've done. Tonight at sunset, we'll see the truth."

Trey shoved past Roman and grabbed on to Cassie as they strode out of the room.

"You're just going to let them go?" I asked.

Roman growled. "Not by choice. Morior Invictus is ancient wolf magic. I have no choice but to let him stay on our land until the challenge is honored. If you don't fight, you will lose your wolf. It's the same fight I had to complete because of Cohen."

"We'll prepare everything. Don't worry, Cait can handle her," Sam said.

Vaughn nodded. "Yeah, especially now that you guys finally got your freak on, Cassie stands no chance."

I sighed. I had no desire to be thankful for my bonding to Roman just so I could survive this challenge.

Embry stormed into the room. "Where is that dirty whore?"

I glanced at Roman, wondering if he'd called for her, but it was Sam who stepped forward. "I thought you might need a friend as well as your mate right now."

"Thank you," I said to Sam as Embry threw her arms around me.

"You're going to kick this wolf's ass, and her challenge will be nothing but a bad memory soon enough," my best friend said.

As much as I hoped Embry was right, after seeing what killing that other wolf had done to Roman, I wasn't sure I'd forget this day easily.

Regardless, Roman was mine. I'd do whatever it took and accept the consequences of my choices in order to keep him. It wasn't my life that mattered to me once I understood what was happening.

It was his.

12

ROMAN

I couldn't believe what was happening. Not again. Even if it wasn't me who had been challenged, it was *my* mate. The reason I existed and why my heart continued to beat. The thought of anything happening to her because she was mine nearly gutted me.

Still, those were emotions I had to keep to myself. Cait needed me to be strong for her, not fucking raging like I wanted to be.

Wolves had certain protocols we followed. Challenges weren't to be taken lightly and they were never ignored. I couldn't take Cait and run like I wanted. She'd lose her wolf and we'd be shunned by our kind, leaving us with no pack. That kind of life was worse than death.

"What now?" Vaughn asked me as the girls huddled together.

I took a moment to admire how close their relationships were getting. Sam had fought letting Cait in, but once my mate proved she couldn't be intimidated, Sam relented, something that would not only make life easier, but would also be helpful as Cait prepared for the challenge.

"It's nearly ten now. We'll each take turns fighting Cait, pushing her as far as we can without letting her get hurt. Then, she'll need rest and food before the challenge. We have nine hours to be ready," I said, keeping my tone even to hide my true feelings.

Vaughn nodded. "She's going to be okay. Cait is stronger than any of us. Just don't tell her I said that."

My lip curled. I knew my beta spoke the truth, but I hated that Cait had to prove it. Cassie was young, but I knew nothing about her and her wolf. I didn't know what they might be capable of, and that wasn't good.

"Do we know anyone from their pack we can trust?" I asked.

"No, but I might know someone near enough that could tell us something. I'll see what I can do," Vaughn replied.

I met his stare. "Offer whatever it takes. No price is too high for information that could help us."

"You got it. I'll make some calls and meet you guys at the training field?"

My head shook. "No, we can't be out in the open. Trey will have only heard rumors of Cait's abilities. When I called the alphas here, I gave minimal information, letting them know they'd be better off seeing her instead. I won't let Trey see what his daughter is up against until the fight has begun. We'll leave the pack and head out behind the mill. We have some room there where we shouldn't have any issues being seen."

"Good call. I'll head out the opposite way and go the long way through town in case he has anyone following us. What about the other alphas arriving today?"

Shit. I'd forgotten about them already. I needed more people I could trust. I'd already lost my father, my mother was God-knew-where, and Cait needed the rest of us for various reasons.

"What about us other alphas?" a deep voice boomed from the opening doorway.

A slow smile spread on my face. "Perry. How the hell are you?"

Cait's attention was on the oversized alpha as well when he entered the room alone. Perry was nearing seven feet tall with salt-and-pepper hair he kept short with a military cut. His light-brown eyes danced with mischief, and I couldn't be happier that he had arrived.

Perry's smile fell. "I'm sorry I couldn't be here to say a proper goodbye to Jack. He was one hell of a man. I'm going to miss our fishing expeditions."

Perry and my father had been long time friends. I wasn't sure how they'd met, but Perry had always been there for our pack when we needed it. I was glad to see that hadn't changed.

"We at least found the wolf responsible," I said with a grunt.

Perry's brow arched. "Did you kill him?"

"No. My mother took that honor."

He let out a low whistle. "She's always been a feisty

one. I should have known." Perry nodded toward Cait. "And from what I hear, you've found yourself a mate that just might rival Ramona's alpha female strength."

I reached for Cait, bringing her to my side. "Perry, this is Cait. My bonded mate that has just been challenged by Trey's daughter."

A rumble built within Perry's chest. "Are you shitting me? He's an even bigger idiot than I thought. What can I do?"

Cait smiled, but it didn't quite reach her eyes, making my wolf fill with fury.

"We need to prepare Cait, but the other alphas will be arriving throughout the day. Can you stay here and welcome them?" I asked.

"Am I allowed to tell them what a piece of shit Trey is and why you're not around at the moment?" Perry asked with a snarl.

"You certainly are. Vaughn will give you his number. Call him if there are any problems," I said.

"Does killing Trey myself count as a problem? Because I'm seriously tempted. We all know Cait is your true mate. For him to do this after agreeing to help you... it makes me want to break things."

I appreciated Perry's ire, and I couldn't control him, but I also knew leaving Trey in one piece was best for the time being.

"Try to keep your fists to yourself until after tonight. We've got to go, but I look forward to catching up after this situation is handled," I said, hating that I had no idea what the immediate future held.

Perry gave Cait his attention, offering her a big grin.

WOLF MATED

"Shame on me. I didn't even greet you properly. I'm Perry, Alpha to the South Carolina pack. I have a daughter about your age named Kelly. The two of you would get along well. I'll bring her with me next time I visit unless I can convince the two of you to head east for a vacation first."

"It's great to meet someone new we can trust. It's been a minute since that happened, and a vacation sounds great, but not exactly a possibility," Cait replied with a forced smile.

"Consider my family an extended part of yours. We will have your back with Trey *and* the Supernatural Council. Everything is going to be just fine," Perry said confidently, giving her a gentle pat on the shoulder.

Perry was the positivity we needed. He was always the first to provide solutions instead of problems. That was always something I admired about my father's best friend.

"We should get going," Sam said as she and Embry joined our small group.

"Where are you headed?" Perry asked.

I explained our plan and the reasons why.

Perry clasped my shoulder. "You're a smart alpha, Roman. Now, get out of here. I can handle things while you're gone. My beta Traci is also here. She'll keep an eye on things outside while I wait here."

"Thank you," I said sincerely, grabbing his hand with both of mine.

"No thanks needed." He glanced at Cait. "Don't let fear make you question who you are. Trey and Cassie sprung this on you purposely. Don't let them see you

113

shaken. I sense a powerful wolf within you. Let her shine and trust that no matter what happens, you are not at fault."

Cait tilted her chin up, and her eyes brightened. I had no doubt that she'd be worried about having to kill Cassie. The death part of our world wasn't something that was easy to swallow and normally didn't happen often, but Cait had been thrown right into the thick of things, having to fight for her life every step of the way.

None of it was fair, but she was strong enough to handle whatever came next. I was more certain of that than anything else.

"Thank you, Perry. I will do my best to remember that," Cait replied.

We all said our goodbyes and I went with the women to the garage while Vaughn headed in the opposite direction. Nobody said anything as we loaded up into one of the Jeeps, but Cait sat next to me, gripping my hand tightly.

She was nervous and rightly so. There was nothing wrong with that, but Perry had been right. Mistakes happened most when we let fear rule our decisions. I would do whatever it took to make sure all the fear inside my mate was gone before we left the mill.

///

THREE HOURS LATER, I HAD MORE BRUISES ON ME THAN Cait. Sam, Embry, Vaughn, and I took turns using various tactics against Cait. At first, I'd been worried.

She lost every single round against us, but on the second go around, I realized what she'd been doing.

Cait and her wolf were not the charge-in-and-hope-for-the-best kind of fighter. No, they were smarter than that and I should have known better. Cait observed us and made well-thought-out choices that had each of us on our asses for various reasons, and allowed her to conserve her strength.

"You're a damn savage," Sam groaned as she dusted herself off.

Cait shrugged. "You told me not to take it easy on you."

Sam snarled and stalked off, but when her back was to Cait, I could see the grin Sam tried to hide. We were all feeling the blows Cait dealt out, but we enjoyed them, because each of them meant Cait was just as capable as I knew her to be. I had been more worried about her not believing it.

All that was left was to know if Cassie had any hidden tricks that we weren't aware of. Vaughn had made some calls, but they'd led nowhere. Last anyone else had heard, Cassie was a gangly teen. That clearly wasn't the case any longer.

It was my turn again and then we were done. Cait hadn't needed the training to really learn anything, but she'd needed the reminder of how capable she was. None of us had taken it easy on her, and my mate had performed just as she needed.

With plenty of grace and vigor.

"Are you ready?" I asked as I approached Cait.

She grinned and nodded before shifting to wolf

form. I took a moment to appreciate the beauty that followed. Cait's wolf appeared within the blink of an eye, glowing lavender fur that was several inches long and the proudest eyes I'd ever seen on a wolf.

In the beginning, I'd worried that the wolf's pride would prove to be a weakness for my mate, but as she shook her tail out and stalked toward me, I knew there wasn't anything weak about either of them.

I shifted, and my wolf surged forward. *Finally*, he said.

Don't go easy on her, I reminded him.

She's about to see a whole new side of us.

I wasn't sure how I should feel about his statement, but I let things go as the two wolves circled each other.

Cait lunged, but she held back, testing our wolf. They could communicate now that Cait and I were bonded. The only downside was that their conversations were private. I had no idea what they might have been saying to each other and as my wolf launched at her with teeth bared, I worried it wasn't anything good.

Adira, as Cait called hers, rolled to the left, avoiding the brunt of my wolf's impact, then twisted around, biting us right on the ass. My wolf snarled and snapped back, but Adira was already on the move.

She's fast, but not fast enough, my wolf seethed while I was entertained.

Our wolves went back and forth, snapping and swiping at each other repeatedly until the fight became pointless. They were evenly matched, and we were only wasting Cait's energy.

I think it's time we concede, I suggested.

She is not the alpha wolf, mine replied instantly.

For as old as you are, you're not very smart. The moment we accepted them into our lives, they became alpha, I said, knowing that every choice I made would include putting Cait first. She owned me, and I wasn't ashamed of that fact. Not when it meant I was able to love her for the rest of my life.

My wolf paused for the briefest of seconds as he heard my thoughts, and it was enough for Adira to jump on top of us and bite into our neck. She growled, but it wasn't filled with rage.

"Uh, don't forget we're still here," Embry called out.

We don't really care that they're here, my wolf said.

No, we might not care, but Cait would.

Adira backed off, sitting on her haunches as mine got up. We circled her, then kneeled before our mate, conceding to the fight. She let out a howl before shifting back and a fully clothed Cait reappeared.

I did the same and pulled Cait into a tight hug just as soon as we were both on two feet. "You're just as incredible as I knew you'd be."

"This was just what I needed," she replied as we pulled apart, but she didn't go far, staying close to my side.

"What next?" Cait asked.

Vaughn glanced at his phone. "Perry says all of the other alphas have arrived. Trey and Cassie have set up camp outside the pack house and seemed to have stayed put all day."

I grabbed Cait's hand. "Let's head back then and we

can formally greet the others before resting. Cait and I both need sleep before tonight."

I might not be physically fighting, but as Cait's alpha and mate, I'd need to be prepared to help heal her after the fight.

Cait would win this challenge, and we'd move on to the next one until there were no more obstacles in the way. There wasn't a single person who could stop us from having the life I could clearly see for the two of us now that we'd found each other.

13

CAIT

There was nothing better than having a small group of people at your back that you could trust. When I first arrived in Texas, I'd had my issues. Embry was the only person in the world I thought I'd ever truly let in. After training today, I was more grateful than ever for the people I'd recently met.

None of them babied me. They all reminded me of what I was truly capable of, and seeing Roman's faith in me made me worry less about the coming fight.

I'd come out on top during this challenge, not only for myself, but for Roman and the future we deserved to have together.

After getting back to the pack house, there were ten new alphas waiting for us. Four females and six males —seven if we included Perry. I had expected there to be a lot of pissing contests going on, but everyone wore smiles when I was introduced to them and seemed to be equally disgusted by Trey and Cassie's actions.

It wasn't common for challenges to be thrown out

nowadays when it was easier to simply move on, and it was even rarer for a mateship to be challenged when there was a true mate bond in effect.

According to Orion from the Alabama pack, Trey would be considered an outcast after this. Nobody understood why he'd made the choice to act by old law instead of the new wolf ways. The unfortunate part was that even though laws had been made to override the way things used to be, if the right wording was used, there was no way for it to be undone.

Morior Invictus held magic within its words that couldn't be ignored.

Roman tugged on my hand. "Let's get you upstairs."

I nodded, knowing my body needed to rest just as much as my mind did. I needed a clear head for what came next. I was going to have to kill another shifter and while it wouldn't be the first time, all the other instances had been unexpected. It had been an in-the-moment decision to take another life.

Now, I was preemptively figuring out how I could kill Cassie before she took me out. That was a tough pill to swallow.

Your humanity is what will make you a great alpha female, but you need to know when to turn off those emotions, Adira said as I made my way up the stairs with Roman.

Easier said than done.

Just remember that if you lose, Cassie will have every right to touch Roman. To kiss him and share his be—

I snarled loudly, cutting her words off. Maybe I

wasn't going to have *that* hard of a time, as long as I remembered to focus on what it meant for Roman.

"What's wrong?" Roman hissed.

"Sorry. Adira kindly reminded me why I had to be okay with being a murderer."

Roman's lips thinned, but he didn't question me further. Probably for the best.

We entered our room and I headed to the bathroom. The night before and that morning had been nothing short of perfection. I'd been sure I was going to ride the high of bonding to Roman for days, possibly even weeks. All it took was one asshole to ruin everything.

I eyed the tub, but I dismissed the thought. Relaxing wasn't going to be something I could do until after I won the challenge and knew Roman was still all mine.

My chest rumbled as I rinsed my face at the sink, trying to settle my thoughts. Warm hands moved up my ribs while my eyes were still closed, and I sighed.

All mine.

Roman pushed my hair to the side and kissed the back of my neck, sending goosebumps down my arms. "Everything is going to be okay."

"It has to be," I replied, reaching for the towel to dry my face.

He turned me toward him, taking the towel from me. Roman was always finding ways to take care of me, and damn if I didn't love him even more for how in tune he was to my needs and wants.

"We need rest." Roman took my hand after drying my face, then led me to the bed. He sat me down on the bed with a bit of force, telling me there was no arguing allowed as he continued to dote on me.

My sandals came off first, followed by my shorts, but he didn't touch my underwear. As Roman's fingers trailed up my sensitive skin, his lips paid homage to every bend in my body, doing exactly what I assumed he intended—distracting me.

I leaned back onto my arms and let my head relax back. My hair fell in waves around me while Roman kissed my belly button. His hands found their way under my shirt and unhooked my bra. Before I could move to assist him, he was pulling me flush against his chest and sliding the bra out from under my tee. His ability to remove that death trap so gracefully was pure talent.

My legs wrapped around Roman's waist, and he kept me close, walking us to the side of the bed. "We need rest," he said, repeating his previous words.

"Rest can come in various forms," I murmured, biting at his neck and ear.

"Mate," he growled. "You need sleep."

I nipped harder. "Then, you shouldn't have put your hands and lips all over my body."

"I was trying to calm your mind." He dropped me onto the bed. "Do I need to leave so you can sleep?"

Lines formed around his eyes, telling me just how hard it was for him to offer that and showing me how important it was to him that I did in fact sleep.

"Absolutely not. Get your ass in this bed and spoon me, Mate." I reached for him, and he grinned before taking his jeans and shirt off. It was hard not to stare at his growing arousal, but Roman always did so much for me. I wasn't going to push him beyond his limits, even if I was pretty sure we'd both be satisfied in the end.

His strong arms enveloped me, and I sighed heavily. I couldn't imagine a day that didn't end with me in Roman's arms.

"I love you, Kitten," he whispered against my shoulder.

"I love you, too." My words were barely audible as I tried to hide the emotions that wanted to break free.

I had to kill Cassie. I had to kill her to keep my mate.

What a damned nightmare.

※

SEVERAL HOURS LATER, I'D MANAGED TO GET A SOLID HOUR of sleep. The moment I opened my eyes, nerves jackhammered throughout my gut.

The clock on the nightstand said it was just after six, which meant we had less than an hour until it was time for the challenge.

You're ready for this. You have nothing to fear. Just focus on what you're fighting for, and everything will be fine, Adira said.

Having her support and faith that we could do this together helped to keep my confidence up. A month ago, I wouldn't have thought we'd get along so well, but once we began to understand each other better, things clicked into place for the both of us.

"I can hear you thinking," Roman murmured, tightening his hold around me.

"And?" I countered.

He rolled me over, cupping my cheek. "And nothing. Though, we should go check in with the others. See if they've learned anything helpful."

I nodded and moved to slip out of bed, but Roman held me tighter. Our eyes met, and there weren't any words needed as our souls connected with just one stare. Our bond awoke and flared within me, filling me with strength, love, and pride.

I was Roman's true mate. I was the female alpha to this pack. This was my home now. Nobody was going to take that away from me. Not ever.

"Thank you," I whispered.

"No thanks needed, Mate."

We got out of bed together, and I headed to the closet while Roman went for the bathroom. I had no idea what I was supposed to wear for a challenge, so I reached out to Embry through our wolf connection.

Hey, Asstie. Any special garment requirements I should be aware of for tonight?

Want me to come up and help? she asked instead of answering.

It will be quicker if you just tell me, but I appreciate the offer, I replied with a chuckle.

Nope. Just make sure you're comfortable. That's most important. I'd suggest something similar to what we normally train in and that you won't mind getting ruined with that dumb bitch's blood. Embry's snarl echoed through my mind.

Got it. So black workout pants and tank top. Thanks. We'll be down in a minute, I said, then cut off the connection before she could put any more images in my head. I knew what needed to be done, but that didn't mean I wanted to visualize the mayhem beforehand.

I chose black, because Embry's mention of blood made me think the darker color would also hide my blood if things didn't go my way. I hated to think that, but I needed to be prepared in case Cassie was more capable than the others thought. I would not underestimate her, not for a single second.

There had been a confidence and darkness in her eyes when she'd uttered the challenge to me. I hadn't seen it for what it was then, but as I thought longer about how things went down in the conference, I realized she'd sought out my compassion and had a feeling she'd attempt to use my humanity against me.

Roman joined me in our walk-in closet as I was sliding the tank top over my head. He appraised me and nodded. "Good choice."

"Thanks." I pushed up onto my tippy toes and kissed him. "I'm going to brush and braid my hair, then I'll be ready."

"No rush." There was a hint of frustration in his voice that told me Roman had already reached out to Vaughn and learned nothing new.

I purposely hadn't asked Embry, because I didn't want to be disappointed, but at the same time, I also expected there to be no new information. Something told me Trey had been waiting for an opportunity to do something big and when Roman had shown the smallest of vulnerabilities, Trey set things into motion.

Though, how the plan had to come to fruition didn't

much matter anymore. We could only do our best to control the outcome of the tornado that had been dropped on our doorstep.

I brushed the knots from my hair, focusing on the purple flecks within my green eyes. A reminder that I wasn't weak. I had true, original power within me. All I had to do was harness the energy and focus on what needed to be done.

And kill that shifter before she can think twice about touching our mate, Adira added.

Yes, I couldn't forget that motivation.

My fingers moved deftly through my brunette strands until all the pieces were braided. Then I twisted my hair into a tight bun at the back of my head. I wasn't sure if the fight would be done in my wolf form or human one, so I needed to be ready for both scenarios.

Once I was done, I gave myself a once over. My skin glowed from the pulsing power within me. My eyes narrowed with determination. Clothes clung to my body, showing off new muscles I'd been working hard to build the last couple of weeks.

I was as ready as I was ever going to be.

As I left the bathroom, Roman was waiting for me by the door as if he'd known I needed that moment to myself.

"Ready, Mate?"

I nodded. "Let's do this."

He grabbed on to my hand and opened the bedroom door. I tilted my head up and removed any emotion from my face. I wouldn't give anyone a clue as to how I was feeling. Mostly because, if I was being honest, I wanted to tuck tail and run. Fighting to death sounded archaic and dumb as shit, but I wouldn't lose Roman or Adira. I had to keep myself in check long enough to make sure of that.

Vaughn, Embry, and Sam greeted us when we got to the bottom of the stairs. The girls grabbed each of my arms and guided me away from Roman. I glanced back at him, and he merely shrugged as Vaughn began to talk to him.

"What are you ladies doing?" I asked calmly.

They shoved me into a room and slammed the door closed. As soon as we were alone, Embry threw her arms around me. "I love you so damn much. You're a badass. A true alpha female. And you're going to bury this bitch in the ground."

I accepted her hug and laughed. "I love you, too, and thanks for the pep talk."

Embry backed off and Sam approached me. She straightened the strap of my tank top and brushed a strand of hair back that had already gotten loose. "Embry is right. You've never been afraid of me, so there's no reason to be scared now. I've been watching this chick since we got back. She's got nothing on you."

"Did Samantha McIntyre just give me a compliment?" I feigned shock.

She jabbed her elbow into my ribs. "No, I was merely speaking the truth, but I can take it back if you'd rather."

Even though I knew she was normally only soft with Roman, I pulled Sam into a hug. "Thank you for your support, Sam. It means a lot."

She hugged me back, taking me by surprise. "You're family, Cait."

Embry joined us, and we all stood there for a moment, just soaking in the support being thrown around. I had been so afraid of the world I'd been tossed into, but being here with these people was exactly what I'd been missing in my life before.

"Alright. Now, we're going to exit this room with our heads held high and as a united pack. We're going to make Cassie regret stepping foot in our pack before she even gets to throw a punch," Embry said, and I couldn't agree more.

With the support of the pack, there wasn't anything I couldn't do.

14

CAIT

I hadn't taken a moment to think about where we would be fighting or what it would look like. All I'd known was that the fight would begin after the sun set. When we exited the main house, the entire pack was present. Even many of those who had previously left had come back after news spread.

My chest swelled as I sensed each of the pack members and I slowly lowered the wall that had kept them from overwhelming me before. Pride, love, faith, and strength hit me the hardest as the wolves began to notice our arrival.

These people hardly knew me, but they believed in me. That nearly brought me to my knees. Pack love was unconditional and unlike anything else in this world. I hadn't truly understood how true those words were until that moment.

The other alphas were gathered together, including Trey, but there was a visible distance between him and the others. My eyes briefly scanned the area for Cassie, but I didn't spot her before I focused on where the fight would take place.

Torches were placed in a circle. Ten in total, spread about five feet apart each. Between them were rocks and I could see shimmers of magic flowing between the flames and stones.

Roman's grip tightened on me as we approached the alphas, but greeting them before our pack didn't sit right with me. I pulled my hand from Roman and diverted with Embry and Sam at my heels. There were rows and rows of shifters. I'd never be able to thank them for their presence individually, but I could acknowledge them as a whole and hope my message traveled to those further back.

I bowed my head to the first row of wolves, then met each of their gazes while placing my hand over my chest. "Thank you for being here and supporting me. I can feel each of you, and I vow to make you all proud tonight."

Two men parted, and someone I hadn't seen in much too long stepped through. "No matter what happens, you are our alpha female. I told Beatrix I had to come home as soon as I felt you had accepted your place within the pack."

"We missed you around here, Serene," I said with a small smile.

"Of course you did, but my time away wasn't wasted. We'll discuss that more after. Now, go greet the alphas you just shunned for us lower wolves," she said, pushing me away.

I dug my feet into the ground. "None of you are lower. Our pack needs every member."

She winked at me. "Good girl. Now, go on."

Crazy old woman.

Embry and Sam stayed just a pace behind, still flanking me and keeping our united front intact. I hadn't expected their support to lift me up so much, but as I strode confidently back toward my mate and the other alphas, the worry I'd been trying to push down began to dissipate.

Sure, I was still well aware that I could lose this challenge and die, but if that happened, it wouldn't be because of any doubt on my part.

Power flowed freely within and around me as I headed toward the alphas. So much so that I even heard Embry let out a slight grunt when she stepped too close.

Roman nodded at me with a gleam in his eyes, and two of the five alphas surrounding him glowered.

"Orion, Brandie, Max, Robert, Anthony." I nodded at each of them as I said their names, surprising myself when I remembered them without assistance from Roman or Embry.

"How are your pack members?" Robert said with a tip of his head.

I smiled and pushed my energy out until I was certain he could feel the pulsing. "Very well. Thank you for asking and thank you for being here today. I'm sorry Roman and I weren't around much, but tomorrow is another day."

He nodded, sweat beading on his forehead. "Yes, it is."

"Well, it is for some of us," Trey piped in from his corner, but I ignored him. He wouldn't get under my skin.

"Where is Cassie?" Roman asked, just as eager as me to get this challenge done with.

Trey smirked. "Missing her already and she isn't even your mate yet."

Roman snarled and stepped forward, but Perry appeared at just the right time. "Don't give him the satisfaction."

Roman shrugged Perry off and grabbed hold of me. I turned to him, wrapping my arms around his neck until I felt him relax from my closeness. "Everything is going to be fine," I reminded him.

"As long as I have you, it will be."

He kissed me long and hard, then tensed as Vaughn's voice sounded in both of our minds.

She's here. Not sure what she was doing in their tent for so long, though.

I moved to Roman's side while Embry and Sam stood next to me again. Having them so close was definitely something I could get used to. My own girl gang. We could do some serious damage together.

Cassie finally appeared at the side of the pack house. She was wearing tiny black shorts and a white sports bra that left nothing to the imagination, showing off a muscled stomach and legs along with boobs I was certain would fall out at any moment. Her previously black wavy hair was slicked back into a ponytail, and she wore charcoal paint over her eyes, creating an intricate mask.

I took a step forward as her gaze met mine, and there was nothing dull about her eyes any longer. The copper color was streaked with gold as I sensed her wolf challenge me in an alpha stare. I smirked and pushed back with my own power until Trey stepped between us, either by pure coincidence or because he knew I was about to shame her before the fight even got started.

Embry and Sam placed a hand on either of my shoulders and I brought my attention back to Roman and the other alphas.

Roman nodded at me, tapping into our mental connection. *You're doing tremendously well. Not that I thought anything less, but just making sure you knew.*

Thank you, Mate, I replied.

"It's time," Embry said as Vaughn joined us. The only person missing that I would have preferred to be around was Ramona, but I knew she was here in spirit and that was all that mattered.

"Ten of the present alphas will take position at each of the torches. Their power will hold the magic that keeps the two of you locked into the challenge until there is a winner. Trey and I are not allowed to interfere. You will not be able to hear us, either. Not even mentally. You will be on your own," Roman said, and I shook my head.

"Just because I can't hear you or the pack doesn't mean I'm alone."

He smiled, but it didn't reach his eyes. Time for pretending everything would be fine was over. Even winning... there would still be consequences, but I was prepared to pay for them in order to keep my pack, my family.

Trey and Cassie were huddled together with their foreheads touching. She was doing a lot of nodding and he was muttering words too low for me to hear.

Embry got my attention back by pulling me into a hug. "Throat punch that bitch for me."

I nodded against her shoulder. "I'll see what I can do."

Vaughn was next. "You got this, Witchy Wolf. I've already planned your after party. You wouldn't want to disappoint me by not showing up, right?"

"Of course not," I laughed.

Sam gave me a solid pat on the back, offering a single nod of support. Apparently, she only hugged me in private, which was fine by me. She had a reputation to uphold after all.

Roman was last, and while every part of me wanted to hold onto him the longest, I gave him a single kiss and quick hug. "I'll see you soon."

His eyes showed the concern we were both feeling, but his voice and presence remained solid. "Yes, you will."

Without postponing, I took a step toward the torch circle. Perry was waiting at the nearest one. "When you cross this line, you are officially locked into the challenge."

"I understand," I said.

"May the Moon Goddess be with you." Perry bowed his head, and I took that final step without turning back.

My skin tightened and heartbeat sped up. I flexed my fingers as a heaviness settled over me.

Adira? I called.

I'm here. Just give our energy a moment to absorb the challenge.

She was right. As the seconds ticked by, the tension along my body eased and my own magic took precedence. Silence surrounded us, and I finally turned around. Roman was as close as he could get, his jaw tight and eyes filled with the fury he'd been withholding.

Cassie entering the circle pulled my attention from Roman. She snarled as she went through the same process that I had but held my stare, even as I could tell she was in pain. Girl was brave, I couldn't deny that.

Perry's voice echoed around us. "On the count of three, the fight will start. We all know how this ends, and there are no rules. Ready?" He paused as each of us nodded. "One... two... three!"

Remember to let her make the first move. It might hurt, but whatever she chooses to do will tell us a lot, Adira said.

With the pack watching, I wanted the fight to be done and over with quickly, so I took my wolf's advice. Cassie and I circled each other with no words exchanged. She was staying quiet, which I didn't expect, but I guess there wasn't much to say.

Claws extended from Cassie's hands, and she snarled, revealing sharp incisors before making her first move. I bounced back and forth on my feet, acting as if I was going to attempt to move out of the way, but I took Adira's request seriously. Cassie's right fist connected with my jaw, and her left hand raked down my thigh, tearing my pants and breaking skin.

The cuts aren't deep. They'll heal within minutes, Adira said as Cassie came at me again.

I moved out of the way this time, sidestepping the shifter and coming around behind her. She swung around quicker than I expected, but I could tell she was weaker on the right side and a small wolf. She should have cut me to the bone and knocked me on my ass with her first two hits.

Now, it's time for us to do the same, Adira said.

Damn right.

I called my energy forward, creating a barrier around me until I glowed purple. Power pulsed around us as magic bounced around the enclosed area. Cassie's left shoulder lowered, and I went to her right, sending my claws into her chest.

She howled in pain and hobbled back, but I wasn't relenting. I punched her ribs three times over, then backed up to assess the situation once more. Cassie heaved and fell to the floor. I stalked closer, and she lifted her head.

"You're going to die." Her smile faded as her wolf came into view. A small ebony colored being that nearly disappeared before my eyes. Shit, she was fast.

As I turned around, the wolf was already on me, teeth sinking into my bicep even as my magic burned the hell out of her.

Fast with a high pain tolerance. Great.

I shifted as well, forcing the wolf to let go of me. We snarled at each other, and I knew Cassie had also been testing me before. While we'd both learned a little about the other, even I could admit she'd played me well.

That didn't mean I thought she had a chance of winning, though. Her wolf might be quick on her feet, but mine was one-of-a-kind. I still had full belief that we would be the ones walking away from this fight.

Cassie attacked swiftly, but Adira was ready for her. We gathered our energy, dodging the wolf as well as we could until we were ready for our next big move.

The ebony wolf darted out of reach, then began running in circles until her claws kicked up grass, dirt, and rock around making it hard to see. I had no idea what she was attempting to do, but it was annoying the hell out of me. Maybe that was the point.

Adira launched for Cassie's wolf, catching her backside, and the two wolves tumbled together until we slammed into the barrier. *Mother freaking ouch!*

Neither wolf stayed fazed as the real fighting began. No more testing each other. It was time for all claws, teeth, and power. Cassie was quick, but she wasn't as strong. We just had to use our strength at the right time, and we could finish this fight on top.

We swiped at Cassie's wolf as she tried to get past us. Adira made her trip, and jumped onto the wolf's back, biting into her front flank. An ear-piercing howl echoed around us, and Cassie managed to roll over, putting us on the ground, but that didn't stop our movements.

Adira's claws were long and sharp, made for gutting a bitch when the occasion required, and that was exactly what she did. My wolf sank her paw into the stomach of our attacker and jerked down hard and fast. Blood spilled from Cassie, and Adira moved to bite the wolf's neck, but she was out of our grasp before we could deliver another blow.

How is she so damn fast? I asked Adira.

Magic. Similar to your Luna Mark, but nowhere near as powerful. Likely something she inherited from her mother, given I didn't sense anything remarkable about her father.

I'd have to ask later what other accelerated abilities some wolves had. It felt like something I should be prepared for given I kept finding myself battling for my life against them.

Blood dripped profusely from Cassie as she charged back for us, and nothing seemed to deter her. The wolf launched for us, taking me by surprise considering her injury, and slammed her head into our ribs. Adira stumbled, but only briefly. We gathered our energy and pushed with everything we had as we whipped back around.

We weren't fighting to win. We were fighting to the death. A part of me had been trying to block that part out, subconsciously drawing the battle out even though I also wanted it over. Cassie was growing more agitated with every move we made, and we were both done with this.

As much as I don't want to, we need to end her, I said.

All I was waiting for was your acceptance, Adira replied. Cocky freaking wolf.

Adira and I worked together, drawing on my Luna Marked energy as we stalked forward. Cassie wasn't bleeding any longer, and there was a determination in her eyes I hadn't seen before. She wasn't going to go down easily, but that didn't matter. Whatever it took for us to be the one walking out of this circle is what would be done.

Our wolves went head-to-head once again. More snapping of jaws and swiping of claws until there was no way to tell whose blood was whose. Cassie was finally slowing, and I had to admit I was impressed with her ability to keep fighting despite the injuries she'd received.

It's time, Adira said.

Finish this, I agreed.

With one last swell of energy, Adira slammed into Cassie's wolf, pinning her to the ground. We let out a sorrowful howl as Cassie struggled beneath us. She was a young wolf. She didn't deserve to die, but she'd also had a choice. Just like Kyle had.

Adira bit into Cassie's neck, tearing chunks out as the ebony wolf tried desperately to get free. Unfortunately, no matter how quick she was on her feet, Cassie's endurance had run out before ours. She would not win her challenge. She would never lay a hand on my Roman.

With one last bite, Adira snapped her jaws closed and jerked her head around until Cassie fell limp against the ground. There was nothing satisfying about what we'd done. Another wolf died a pointless death.

Cheering roars sounded all around us as our mate's presence finally came back and I shifted back to my human form. Besides knowing Roman belonged to no one other than me, there would be no celebrating for me. I just wanted my mate and to be alone. At least for now.

Roman's voice bellowed over the crowd. "Back. Off." The noises quieted, and I considered shifting back to my wolf form to avoid having to speak to anyone, but Roman picked me up before I could. "I have you, Mate."

And I knew he always would.

15

ROMAN

N ever before had I been so out of control. My
bond to Cait had been cut off. I couldn't feel her
or hear her, and nothing anybody did calmed me. The
only saving grace was that Cait couldn't sense how
furious I was.

Vaughn, Sam, and several others had held me back.
Even when I fought against them, they stayed by my
side, knowing I needed their support. My wolf was the
biggest reason I didn't kill anyone, though. Sure, he
wasn't happy about watching Cait get punched and
bitten and bleeding, either, but my wolf was old. He
knew no amount of rage would change our situation.
Wise fucker.

*Getting yourself killed by trying to interfere wouldn't
have been helpful, either. I was keeping us alive,* my wolf
muttered.

Again, I knew he was right, and once I had Cait in
my arms, it was easier to accept that there had been
nothing I could do while I watched Cassie move with

lightning speed, shocking the hell out of everyone except her father.

As I walked with Cait through the gathering crowd, Trey was scowling at his daughter's body. "You are a disgrace to your pack and your family," I spat at him, still holding Cait tight.

"You have no idea what you're talking about. If you didn't hide out here, keeping *that* power hidden, maybe things would have been different," Trey countered, nodding at Cait.

"What my mate is capable of should have made no difference in your actions. Your greed killed your daughter. Be thankful I'm a better alpha than you. You have twenty minutes to be off my pack lands. My wolves will assist you out."

I turned away from Trey as Cait began to stir in my arms. Vaughn nodded at me, confirming he heard my demand and would make sure Trey left quickly and peacefully. We didn't need any other issues.

"I can walk," Cait said, sounding stronger than I expected her to be after the fight.

"Probably, but you're not going to. I need you close to me right now," I said truthfully. I needed Cait more than she needed me. I always would.

She held on tighter to me, and our bond ignited within my chest. Given we'd only made things official the night before, the connection was still growing and solidifying its place between us. My father had told me his version of the bond before, but the process was different for every wolf.

This slow build of intensity was exactly what I

expected with Cait. There was nothing fast and wild about the two of us. Every decision was made with thought—sometimes too much—and I wouldn't have it any other way.

The pack wolves created a pathway for us to the house, all of them bowing their heads as we passed by. Cait tried to sit up further, but I knew adrenaline had blocked out the worst of her pain. I kept my hold on her secure until I could lay her on our bed.

We still had so much to deal with. The other alphas would need my attention, and I needed their agreement to stand by our pack if things went as far as I believed they would with the Supernatural Council.

Yet, none of that made me rush with Cait. She needed my closeness to heal quicker, and I knew she'd want to be part of the conversation with the others. So, the sooner I got her alone, the sooner everything could move forward.

We made it to our room, and I took her straight to the bathroom, adjusting my hold to start the shower while still keeping Cait in my grasp.

Cait's lip quivered, and I sensed her grief before she spoke. "I didn't want to kill her."

"I know you didn't, Kitten, but you had no choice. It was you or her, and I'm selfish enough to be fucking thankful it was her," I said.

She nodded and I sat her on the counter so I could do one of my favorite things—get her undressed.

Cait had been in wolf form most of the fight, but that didn't mean her human body wouldn't have taken a beating. Cassie had been fast, and her hits were hard.

Cait had bruises along her stomach and ribs, as well as a cut on her cheek. Those injuries weren't what I worried about, though.

My hand rested over her chest. "Everything hurts right now, but you did exactly what you had to and, as shitty as the situation is, you did nothing wrong. I know my words are only that, and time to process what happened is what you need most, but I'm here for you. Don't forget that you're not alone anymore, Cait."

I feared that with all the choices she'd been forced to make as of late that a part of Cait would begin to retreat from me again. Even if we were bonded, it didn't mean we would always get along. I had to make sure she knew she could talk to me instead of feeling as if she was suffering alone.

"I know. You are nothing short of perfect, Roman. I just need a minute to… I don't know, but nothing has changed. I accepted the life I was meant for already. There is nothing that will change that. I'm exactly where I belong. Right here with you."

I cupped her cheeks, kissing her slowly as not to further hurt my mate. The press of her lips to mine had my emotions going wild. There had been a chance I'd never feel this again. Never feel her pulse spike because of my touch. Never see the fire in her eyes that told me just how damn strong she was.

I'd blocked a lot of my fears out because I'd had to believe Cait would win the challenge, but now that she was okay, the realization of how close I'd come to losing her again rocked me to the core.

Cait wrapped her arms around me. "It's okay, Ro.

I'm right here and I'm not going anywhere. Not for as long as I can help it."

Her love for me filled my chest as we held on to each other. Here, I was supposed to be making her feel better and she was taking care of me instead.

"How about that shower?" I suggested, needing to focus on her for my own sanity.

"Only if you join me."

I already had every intention of doing so. Cait's energy was already on the rise, and I knew my closeness would only keep helping. She needed time to process the challenge, but I trusted her to decide when that would be. I wouldn't force her to do anything she wasn't ready for.

After getting undressed, I carried Cait into the steaming shower, gently setting her on her feet and keeping my hold around her waist. She hissed as the water washed over her cut, then moaned as she leaned her head forward and the spray covered her aching muscles.

Carefully, I rinsed her off, hoping with every touch that the bruises would fade.

Cait's eyes closed as she rested her forehead against my chest. Once she was cleaned up, I held her as tight as I felt she could handle. As the silence took over, there was nothing awkward about it. In fact, I had never been closer to my mate than in that moment while the bond between us grew, holding the two of us together.

The longer we stayed connected, skin-on-skin, the more charged I became. My own strength, which had seemed normal before, was bursting at the seams. It needed some sort of escape, which I attributed to the power I'd taken on from Cait.

My wolf had done a good job at helping me disperse the excess magic, but the longer I stayed connected to Cait, the more I realized we had no clue just how powerful she truly was.

"Is it always going to be like this?" Cait asked with a contented sigh.

I squeezed tighter. "If we want, yes. As long as our souls continue to search each other out, the bond will never fade."

She looked up at me with her bright green eyes and smiled. "Good."

I leaned down and gripped her chin before kissing her like it would be the last time. Her toes curled over mine and energy swirled around us, making the steam swirl within the shower.

Meeting her eyes, I grinned. "Might be time to get out if you're ready."

"As long as I have you, I am."

"Always," I replied.

We'd only been gone from the chaos outside for maybe thirty minutes. That was past the time I'd given Trey to be gone. A small part of me hoped he was still around just so I could teach him a lesson he wouldn't soon forget, but regardless of whatever drove him to make his daughter challenge my mate, I believed he would pay for his choices long after today.

There was a reason Trey was invited to my pack. At one point, he'd been a friend to my father. While nothing could justify his choices, I had to assume something happened to force his hand. Though, his problems weren't mine, especially when he decided to handle them on his own.

I had a mate to keep safe and that was all I could concern myself with for the time being. Well, that and my pack.

We got dressed and headed downstairs in hopes of finding everyone back to where they'd normally be.

Vaughn met us in the hallway, a smile on his face. "Good evening, Alpha. Alpha Female. I didn't get to properly congratulate you before."

I narrowed my eyes. "Not necessary."

"Are you sure, because I prepared a speech and even picked flowers?"

"Absolutely sure," Cait and I said at the same time.

Vaughn grimaced. "You two are boring."

Oh, there was so much I could say to that, but Vaughn wasn't going to know more than he needed to. At least not about my bonding to Cait.

"Where are the other alphas?" I asked.

"Around the fire pit. I was just about to join them. First, I made sure that Trey made it off pack lands. He seemed to be pretty torn up about what happened here, but he didn't say a word as he gathered his daughter."

I eyed Cait when I felt her tense next to me. "What happened here today is nobody's fault but Trey's. If he was in some sort of trouble, he should have known where to turn, just like I knew when to ask for help."

Vaughn nodded, but my words didn't make Cait feel any better. I knew they wouldn't, but I'd keep saying them anyway.

The three of us headed out to the side yard where the fire pit was, only to be stopped by Embry and Sam. Both of them zeroed in on Cait, checking her over for injuries before focusing on her face.

Embry threw her arms around Cait just as I stepped to the side. "We just wanted to make sure you were as okay as could be expected," Embry said.

Sam stepped forward, surprising even me when she reached for Cait. "You are quite the force to be reckoned with."

My cousin was a private person and sharper around the edges than most people I knew. When she said she had finally accepted Cait, a part of me had worried that only meant Sam would quit giving my mate a hard time. I wasn't sure it was a good thing for me that the two of them were getting so close, but it would be good for Cait.

"Do you want to stay with them while I see the alphas?" I asked Cait.

She glanced from Sam and Embry to me, clearly torn.

"Sam and I have some work to do. Let us know when you're back inside the pack house and, if you're up for visitors, we'll come over to your room," Embry said, saving Cait from having to choose.

Cait smiled. "I will definitely do that."

After they said goodbye, we continued to the fire. I could have invited Embry and Sam, but a meeting with alphas wasn't an open invitation, no matter how involved the other pack members were. Not even Vaughn would be staying for the meeting.

When the three of us arrived, Perry was standing up and making gorilla noises that likely had something to do with a story and at someone else's expense.

I glanced down at Cait. "Are you ready for this?"

She grinned up at me. "Absolutely."

16

CAIT

W hen Roman had carried me back to the pack house after the fight, I'd been certain the need to drown in guilt would take precedence over everything else. Except I hadn't known how the bond with Roman would change everything for me.

The fears I'd previously held on to, the guilt, the sadness... all of it was diminished to manageable levels when he held me and our energies collided. It was as if I'd been reborn again and there was nothing in this world that could stop me.

Sure, I still held on to the former emotions, but they weren't overpowering when I allowed Roman to be there for me. He balanced me in ways I never knew possible.

Which was good, because I didn't have time for being stuck in the darkness. I needed to figure out how we kept the Supernatural Council from getting their hands on me. Ramona also needed to come home. I was equally as worried about her the longer she was gone, even though I knew she was capable of taking care of herself.

What I didn't trust was everyone else. Someone could grab Ramona and use her as leverage to get to us. That wasn't a situation I wanted to find ourselves in.

As we arrived at the fire pit I'd never seen in use before, Roman pulled me closer to him and shook his head at Perry's antics. I had no idea what the alpha was going on about, but it had the others around him nearly falling to the ground with laughter.

Well, all except one person.

"Oh, come on, Bruce. You know I'm just messing with you," Perry said when he was done dancing around like a gorilla.

Bruce snarled at the other alpha. "That's not a moment in my life I like to relive."

"But the rest of us sure do," Orion called out.

I couldn't remember where all of the others were from, but I was getting better at remembering names and I took that as a win.

Vaughn nodded at Roman before taking his departure. It hadn't been necessary for the beta to walk us down to the others, but even though he'd already been throwing jokes, I knew the challenge had rocked all of us. A little extra eye on things never hurt anyone.

Roman and I stood as the group sobered when they realized we were present. Perry stepped forward and shook Roman's hand. "We weren't sure we'd see you tonight."

"You all have your own packs to get home to. I didn't want to keep you waiting," Roman answered.

Perry moved toward me and pulled me into an unsuspecting hug. "You will never find me on your shit list. Whatever you need, you make sure to count my pack in."

I hugged him back awkwardly. "Thanks."

Perry smiled at me before taking a seat with the others.

Roman took a step forward. "We appreciate that you all have traveled the hours to get here and meet Cait. I had intended on having my mate share her story with you all, but I believe what you've seen tonight is enough to know that the Supernatural Council can't get their hands on her."

Murmurs of agreement sounded from the group.

"If we didn't already know there were things amiss within the ranks of the council, we'd have no problem offering our assistance to them on a case-by-case basis. Unfortunately for them, we have, or well, had someone on the inside that confirmed not all is as it has been in the past. We're not sure if it is one person pulling the strings or multiple people. Either way, supernaturals have been forced to the council stronghold and haven't been seen since," Roman said.

Brandie stood, brushing her shoulder-length brunette hair back and focusing her hazel eyes on me. "I've heard mumblings as well. Your power has caused quite the disruption in our world."

I smiled. "Glad I could shake things up for you."

She grinned back. "That's one way to see things.

Our pack is up near Canada in rural Montana. Some have said the Supernatural Council's lair is also along the Canadian border. There is a shift in power up there that makes me believe these rumors have merit. We've had two wolves disappear, and I know several witches who have gone missing as well."

"What about the other pack down here? Will they join you now that their alpha is dead?" Robert asked. I couldn't remember where he was from, but his accent made me think East Coast somewhere.

Brandie sat back down, and Roman spoke next. "The plan is for them to have their own alpha still. If that isn't something they can work out, I will help them figure out another solution, but I have no intentions of showing up and taking over. The wolves there deserve better than what they've had and a chance to prove they're capable of more."

"So, what is it that you need from us exactly? We all understand the importance of keeping Cait away from greedy hands. How far are you willing to take this?" Perry asked.

Roman's eyes met mine, and I knew his answer, but I wasn't sure how the other alphas would perceive it. Though, there was no point in trying to hide anything from those willing to assist us.

"We aren't exactly sure what we need. That all depends on the true intentions of the Supernatural Council. As of now, they've merely sent a formal notice for Cait to appear before them within thirty days—more than half of which have already passed. My gut tells me that if we show up there, we're not leaving on our own. At least not without help."

"So, what if you don't go?" Max asked.

I stepped forward this time. "When we went out just a few days ago, I was ambushed in a bathroom by a vampire. Whoever wants me at the Supernatural Council has made it known. The vampire made that clear when she mentioned the reward she could collect by bringing me in, which tells me there is nothing good about going to the council, but I'd rather not live a life on the run. I don't imagine any of you want the council coming for you next, either?"

That last part hopefully gave everyone something to think about. This wasn't just about protecting me. It was about making sure none of the other supernaturals had their freewill taken away. The council was overstepping, and we needed to stand up for what was right.

Heads nodded in agreement and Perry spoke again. "Are you only asking for the help of shifters?"

"No. I plan to call Beatrix next, and I've been in touch with a vampire who seems to have a conscience, unlike most of the ones we meet. From what I know, and as Brandie confirmed, we are not the only race having an issue with the Supernatural Council. My hope is that we can get to the core of the problem. The council has always been fair and just until recently. Something has happened to change that.

"If we can figure out what, then maybe we can avoid a fight, but I will not back down until my family is safe. I don't expect you to put your packs at risk for my mate, but I will advise you to protect your own. However you believe that is to be done is your choice. If the thought of fighting against the council and their guards is too much for you, then I understand your need to stay out of this." Roman's eyes scanned the group of alphas slowly as he finished speaking.

Each of them wore varying expressions of concern and wariness, neither of which was surprising. I didn't imagine it was often they had to worry about going against the one group of people who were created to protect their current way of life.

An alpha whose name I didn't remember stood. He'd been the quietest one in the bunch from what I'd seen, and he was the smallest at maybe six feet tall. His light-colored hair fell in front of his eyes before he brushed it back, revealing wrinkles on his previously shadowed face.

"You speak strong words for such a young alpha, Roman. As you are newly mated, it is my belief you are acting on emotion and not fact. Supernaturals go missing. That is not new. Alphas are challenged. That is also not new. Most importantly, your mate, as we've all seen, is unusual even under magical expectations. I can see why the council is curious."

I reached for Roman's hand when I saw his body flinch. We didn't need a fight with any of these wolves. We needed to remain calm, even if they didn't agree with us.

Max stood next. "You're correct, Nathaniel. About all of the things you've spoken, but do you not feel the changes in the air? Does your wolf not warn you of trouble? Roman might be young and willing to die for his mate over something we are not, but that does not mean he is wrong."

Thank you, Max.

"No, Roman is not wrong," Perry said, unsurprisingly. "We are shifters created by magic. We don't require proof of something to believe things are amiss. There have been enough instances to make me believe we need to stand up and do more to protect our packs. Cait might be unique, but she has caused no problems within our communities. She is not a threat so long as she's not provoked, as we've seen. What happens if the wrong person gets a hold of Cait and turns her into something the rest of us cannot fight against?"

Nathaniel nodded. "You've given me a lot to think about, old friend."

"What is it that you hoped to get out of this meeting of alphas, Roman?" Orion asked.

Roman glanced down at me and smiled. The tension in his jaw was faint, but I knew he was holding back as best he could. Without looking away from me, he spoke. "Exactly what has happened. I wanted you all to see who Cait was, so that you could understand why she is worth protecting. My words would not have done the convincing needed for something of this importance."

Roman looked away from me finally and back at the others. "I hope to have you and your packs at our side when we find the council's stronghold. You have enough information to make your choice. There are two weeks left until the council's deadline for my mate. With the remaining time, my intention is to keep searching for answers as to why things haven't been as they should. All I ask for now is that you keep your ears open and consider what might be needed in order to protect our packs."

The air was tense, and I could sense several of the alphas were ready to tuck tail and get the hell out of our pack. They hadn't expected everything they learned here, that much was clear, and I wanted to say a thing or two myself.

"We truly are grateful to each of you for coming to meet me. I understand there is much unknown about the Luna Marked, but it's not as if I was created under suspicious circumstances. Your Moon Goddess chose me for a reason, and I won't stop until my purpose has been fulfilled. I could have run and left you all to figure this out on your own, but I didn't, and I hope you won't either."

"And what is it you think you're staying to fight for?" Brandie asked me.

"I haven't been part of this world for long, but I'm fighting for family and freedom. For the right to be with my pack and not somewhere I don't want to be. You all might believe you have that option now, but all it takes is one person to change everything."

As heads nodded and eyes widened ever so slightly, I knew I'd got their attention which was exactly what I wanted, but I still wasn't sure if our words would be enough.

If they're smart alphas, they'll listen to their wolf. If

they're worthy wolves, then we have nothing to worry about, Adira said, making a valid point. We'd done all we could for the time being.

"Would anyone object to some alpha meeting crashers?" Ramona's voice sounded from behind us.

I turned around to find her standing with a smile on her face and two others at her side.

"Mother," Roman said with irritation, and I went on guard. He didn't seem pleased at the arrival of the other two.

They're friendly. Roman is upset because of the lengths Ramona would have gone to find them, Adira said.

Are those Embry's parents?

I believe so.

"I'm not your child, so don't look at me with that tone, *Son.* I got done what needed to get done," Ramona said as the three of them sauntered closer.

Roman gave his mother a once over and nodded. Ramona had made her grand appearance at just the right time, and by the gleam in her eyes, she knew it as well.

"If you all needed proof that the council has been compromised, look no further than Kye and Lillias Daughtry," Ramona said, moving aside so Embry's parents could step forward.

A few murmurs sounded through the alphas, but I didn't understand why. I knew Embry's parents worked for the council, but I wouldn't have expected such shock by their arrival.

"I know most of you thought we were dead, but that was never closer to the truth until recently. If you have time to hear us out, we have some information to share," Kye said.

Roman guided me toward an empty spot next to Perry, who didn't seem as surprised as the others about the arrival of Kye and Lillias.

Apparently, Roman and I weren't the only ones making a statement tonight.

CAIT

Ramona sat next to me and squeezed my thigh. "I'm sorry we weren't here sooner. I heard about the challenge. Are you okay?"

I smiled at her, just glad to have her home. "I'll be fine. How about you?"

She grinned back. "We'll talk about me later. Listen to Kye and Lillias. It's important information for you to know."

Roman observed our conversation, but didn't join in. His thoughts were closed to me, but his emotions were all over the place. His mood was something he couldn't hide as easily from me as our bond grew stronger. I grabbed onto his hand and intertwined our fingers. He sighed, but the tension he was holding onto didn't release.

Kye stood near the fire pit with Lillias at his side before he spoke. His hair was a perfect silver color, falling just beyond his ears. Lillias had deep burgundy hair and, for the first time, I believed Embry. She's always said her rose-gold hair was natural, but I hadn't thought it was possible before seeing her parents stand side-by-side.

They wore near-matching black outfits that were threadbare and ripped in several places, and dirt smeared their faces. Wherever they'd been all this time wasn't anywhere I hoped to visit.

"As most of you know, my mate and I have worked for the Supernatural Council for quite some time now. A couple of years ago, we were sent to bring in a powerful witch. Things didn't go as planned, and a lot of people assumed we died," Kye said first, looking to Lillias to speak next.

"The council advised us that it was better this way for our future missions. At the time, we agreed. Our loyalty was to them, and while we have missed our family here dearly, we thought what we were doing with the council served a greater purpose. Until recently, that is."

Nathaniel, the alpha who was previously skeptical, cleared his throat. "If you're loyal to the council, then how are you here?"

I remembered learning that Sam had chosen to remain a contract worker with the council because she didn't want her loyalties to change from her pack. While I hated Nathaniel questioning us, he made a valid point this time.

"Magic works in ways we don't expect sometimes. We've all experienced that ourselves at some point, I'm sure," Lillias said, pausing for a moment. "When things began to change, and missions became more about killing rather than investigating, Kye and I started to ask more questions. The more curious we became, the less freedoms we were given."

Kye spoke again, picking up right after Lillias, as if it was still the same person speaking. "As time passed, the council broke their promise to us. They stopped being loyal to *us*. Their commitment shifted to someone else, and our freewill grew. By denying us their promised safety, they lost our allegiance without realizing it until too much had already happened."

Nathaniel narrowed his eyes, then sat back down with a nod. I wasn't sure we should keep having this conversation with him around, but none of the other alphas seemed to mind his lack of trust, so I kept my opinions to myself.

Nathaniel is the oldest out of all the alphas present. He has held his title for nearly a century. There is a reason for that, and those who question that normally don't win. I invited him here to do exactly what he's doing. He's asking the hard questions. As long as the answers given are truthful, then he will be a great asset to us, Roman said through our connection.

You know it's not fair that you're listening in on my thoughts, but I don't get to hear yours, I said in return. Clearly, the bond gave more perks than I was aware of yet.

We haven't really had the time to sort out all aspects of the bond. He squeezed my hand and we resumed listening to Kye and Lillias.

"Have any of you heard of a witch-wolf hybrid named Demi?" Kye asked.

Heads shook all around, but something triggered for me. Demi. The name didn't sound familiar, but I just knew I was supposed to know it for some reason.

Voices sounded around me as everyone tried to figure out who this person was, but I retreated inside my own head.

Any thoughts? I asked Adira.

You've never mentioned this person since my arrival in your mind, but I'm searching my memories as well. If this Demi has been around a while, it's possible I've met her before this life.

Demi. I thought the name over and over until finally I remembered why, but it wasn't Demi that had been used. It was D. Just a singular letter I had overheard before, but maybe it was short for whoever this woman was.

I replayed the memory of listening to the woman approach the guard while I'd been trying to sleep when captured by Cohen and Kyle.

A woman's voice sounded. "Everything staying quiet tonight, Felix?"

"Sure is, D. I think she's sleeping," a guy much closer replied.

"And nobody has been down there since the alpha gave orders?" she asked.

"I've been here the last four hours and haven't seen anyone."

"Good. You call me if you do."

I'd been so tired at the time that I hadn't questioned the interaction, but it had stuck with my subconscious. I pushed the memory to Roman, not sure if that was how our connection worked, but when he turned toward me and creases lined his face, I figured I did something right.

"When did this happen?" he asked me.

"The night before the full moon. I never heard her voice after that. Do you think it could be the same person?"

"I believe it's worth checking out," Roman replied.

"What's worth checking out?" Ramona asked, but Roman stood to share the information with everyone instead of just her.

"When Cait was being held captive at the West Texas pack, she overheard a short conversation between another wolf and a woman called D. There was also a witch working with Cohen, and I never understood why she would have done so when he had nothing to offer her in return. If this Demi person was present, that could have made all the difference."

Kye and Lillias shared an unreadable look. "How long ago was this?" she asked.

"Almost a month ago," I answered.

Another shared look, but this one held more concern between them. "It's very possible Cait heard the person we are referring to. From what we learned before we left, Demi was gone from the council stronghold for many days at a time. The last time she returned, about four weeks ago, is when everything changed within the council and prisoners were moved to underground bunkers outside of the normal areas."

Roman glared at his mother, knowing that must

have been where Ramona had ventured off to and likely could have gotten herself killed.

"I told the wolves who surrendered during our fight with Kyle that I would be checking in on them. Maybe it's time I did just that," Roman said, then turned to the other alphas. "As I said before, I won't beg you all to fight, but I urge you to consider the possibility that all of our packs are in danger. Cait's power isn't something you want to see in the wrong hands. Especially that of a wolf-witch hybrid capable of infiltrating the Supernatural Council."

One-by-one, the alphas got up and headed either to the guest rooms in the pack house, or to the tents they'd set up outside. Nobody would be traveling tonight, but I had a feeling they'd all be gone before we woke in the morning.

"Dad? Mom?" Embry's voice sounded and I felt like the worst best friend ever for not giving her a heads up that her parents had returned.

Lillias teared up and ran to her daughter, calling her by a name I assumed had everything to do with my best friend's hair. "Oh, Rosey."

Embry fell into her mother's arms and, not long after Kye joined them, enveloping them both. It was an emotional reunion that had me turning around to give them some privacy.

Vaughn joined me, Roman, Perry, and Ramona. "How did everything go?"

"Better than I expected," Roman answered. "How is the pack?"

Vaughn smirked at me. "Glad they don't have to kill their alpha for going rogue."

"Too soon, Beta," I said sharply.

"They're all very grateful you're alive and Roman still has his mate. Though, they are wondering what is happening next. The alphas being here have drawn attention," Vaughn added.

Sam joined us then and slammed her hip into mine. "Next, the pack is going to stay here where it's safest and the rest of us are going to take a little trip."

Roman stepped toward his cousin, a rejection on his tongue, but Sam stopped him. "If you want help from the vampires, you will not keep me prisoner. Of *course* I was listening to your little meeting. I'm the one who told Embry to join you. This is beyond me, and you'll need all the help you can get."

I hated to put Roman in a hard position, but I agreed with Sam and said as much.

"I knew this would happen," Roman grumbled. "Fine. You can come with us, but you will listen to me while we're out. If something is too dangerous, we all leave together."

Sam stuck her hand out. "Deal."

"It's late, and we've had a long day. Everyone should head to bed, and we'll get together again tomorrow about traveling to West Texas. We need to know what they know about this D woman in hopes of confirming she's Demi," Roman said, and there was a bit of hope in his voice.

I imagined learning his grandfather hadn't been acting on his own when he took me or attacked our pack would give Roman some much-needed closure. They might not have been close, but Cohen was still blood, and his and Kyle's betrayal had hurt worse than I suspected Roman, or Ramona, let on.

Perry grabbed Roman's forearm. "I'd like to stay here an extra day or two. Keep an eye on things while you head west. Maybe do some fishing with an old friend."

My eyes pricked with tears at the sorrow in Perry's voice. Jack's death was still so raw for everyone.

"You're welcome to stay as long as you'd like," Roman replied.

Perry held his hand out for Ramona. "Lovely night for a walk with an old friend."

She nodded, accepting his offered hand. "Agreed."

The two of them disappeared into the darkness, and I was ready for bed. I had no idea what time it was, but I was done with the day and eager to wake and start over on another.

Roman wrapped his arm around me before looking at Vaughn. "We're headed to bed unless you need anything first?"

Vaughn grinned. "No pack-related needs, but don't think the two of you have gotten away with bonding and not telling anyone. I had epic plans for a bachelor party that could still happen."

"Wolves don't have bachelor parties," Roman droned.

"They do when their best friend is me."

Sam punched Vaughn in the ribs. "That's my title. Good try."

"No, you're the cousin. I'm the best friend," Vaughn countered.

Roman leaned down and whispered, "Let's get away while we still can."

He'd find no objections from me. I smiled and nodded as he guided me back inside. Though, the closer we got to the house, the more sleep didn't sound as appealing as I'd previously thought.

18

CAIT

After getting back to our room, I undressed and showered, all with the help of Roman, of course. He'd remained by my side, allowing me to absorb what had transpired over the last—and longest—twenty-four hours of my life. The extreme high of bonding with him had nearly been overshadowed by the challenge issued from Cassie.

While I still felt sorrow for the life taken, I wasn't going to let it ruin me so thoroughly. I'd been through too much to get where I was, and there was still plenty of fight left to get through before there would be much peace.

Dwelling on the choices of others wasn't going to make anything better. My mate and pack needed me to be strong. I had to be the alpha female they needed. One who didn't wallow over killing another when it was the only option.

Those were the realizations I'd come to while I'd taken my time rinsing off for the second time that night.

Those thoughts would be what helped me move forward. Well, those and the support of Roman.

After I brushed and braided my hair for bed, I found him already laying under the sheet with his arms behind his head and eyes full of concern.

"I'm okay," I said as I crawled onto the oversized mattress.

A crease formed between his brows. "That's what worries me."

"It shouldn't. I know we're more alike than either of us realized in the beginning and you've been through the same challenge, but you didn't have me when you went through yours. Well, not me in particular, but a mate. Between my wolf, our newly formed bond, and my drive to be okay for the pack, I'm just stubborn enough to be able to push beyond the events of today. Maybe I won't be okay every day, but tonight I am."

By the time I was finished speaking, I'd crawled on top of him and positioned my legs around his hips with only the sheet separating our bodies.

His hands came down from behind his head and fingers splayed over my ribs. "Just remember that you don't always have to be okay. You are allowed to break and feel and anything else."

"I know and I will, but not now. Right now, we need to figure out who this Demi person is and what she is trying to do. I didn't even know hybrids existed. Does that make her more powerful or less?"

He grinned and shook his head but answered my question anyway. "Depends on the parents. It's different every time one is born. The council tried to outlaw relationships outside of individual races, but when true mate bonds appeared, there was nothing they could do."

I leaned forward until our faces were only inches apart. "I bet you're glad I didn't stay human."

Roman flipped me over without notice and tugged the sheet away from us as he came down on top of me. Neither of us had any clothes on, and our bond flared within my chest as we laid skin-to-skin.

"I would have loved you all the same no matter if you had a wolf or not. You are mine, Cait. Forever and always." His lips pressed softly against mine.

I reached up and held his face between my palms. "You are everything to me and always will be."

My legs wrapped around his waist, urging him closer. Everything inside me simmered with energy that could only be satisfied by having my mate as close as possible. I needed my connection to him. I needed Roman's love. With that, everything else was manageable. No matter how bad things got.

With slow and precise movements, Roman's hands travelled over my body until he turned me into a writhing mess beneath him. Only then did he give me exactly what I needed: all of him.

He made love to me in a way that had tears falling from my eyes. Our bonding had been special and perfect, but tonight was something else entirely. Tonight, Roman was healing me from the outside in.

With every touch and kiss and thrust, our bond grew to new heights I never wanted to come down from. I needed every inch of him and no amount of time with my mate would ever be enough.

Roman brushed loose strands of hair from my tear-streaked face. "Forever and always." He repeated his earlier words, and I did the same.

His movements sped up, and I lifted my hips in time with his as we held on tightly to each other until both of us were at the edge of release. Roman's fingers gripped my chin as he kissed me with his eyes open.

While tongues and lips clashed in sync with our bodies and our stares locked, we came together, never letting go of one another until the magic of our bond released us from the bubble of euphoria we'd been happily trapped in.

I watched my mate leave the bed, muscles in his ass flexing as he walked to the bathroom. I heard a cabinet door open and the water turn on. Just as I moved to go to clean up, Roman reappeared with a washcloth in hand.

I settled back into bed as he prowled toward me, the predator in his eyes clear as day, even in the darkened room. Except there was nothing about Roman that scared me.

The warm cloth pressed to my stomach as he slid it over my hips and down my center, all without breaking eye contact with me. With his free hand, he lifted my ass and cleaned every crevice until he seemed satisfied, and I was smirking at his thoroughness.

Roman tossed the dirty washcloth toward where our laundry basket was, then pulled me into his arms. "Sleep, Mate."

With his command, I did exactly that. Filled with love and safety and happiness. No matter how shitty the day had turned, I considered myself lucky to be exactly where I was.

///

THE FOLLOWING MORNING, I AWOKE IN A PANIC. I'D HAD A dream. The most perfect one I'd ever experienced, but it had also scared the hell out of me.

"How do wolves get pregnant?" I asked Roman as I sat straight up in bed.

He chuckled. "Well, when a man and a woman—"

I glared at him. "You know what I mean. We've been having sex and you haven't used a condom and my birth control shot is due for renewal and…"

"And what? Why are you freaking out now?" he asked calmly.

"I had a dream."

He raised a brow. "About?"

"You and me and… a baby. Could I be pregnant?" I asked, not really wanting to know the answer. I was absolutely on board with being Roman's mate, but I wasn't sure I was ready to be a mother yet.

Roman's hands pulled me toward him. "While nothing would make me happier to know you were carrying our pup, you're not pregnant. Wolves go through heats, and you haven't experienced one. You will know when you do, and you won't be leaving this room when it happens."

Warmth crept up my neck. "And why won't I be able to leave the room?"

"A female wolf in heat needs constant release. It only happens once a year and lasts for a day or two depending on the need to create life. I won't be able to leave your side, and my wolf won't allow another male near you until the heat is over. Our primal instincts come out in full force when our mates are fertile."

"And if we aren't ready to make babies, how the hell am I supposed to survive up to two days of... whatever is going to happen?" I asked, because nothing he'd just said made me feel any better.

Roman grinned and got out of bed. "We don't have to have sex to keep you comfortable, Mate."

My mind was instantly filled with dirty thoughts, and I was glad he'd already moved toward the bathroom. We still had things to do and a trip to make to West Texas. Spending every waking minute in bed wasn't going to keep anyone safe.

I heard the shower turn on and stayed in bed. If I joined him, I'd only end up attacking him.

If you don't get your naked ass in here, I'll throw you over my shoulder and make *you join me,* Roman's voice echoed through my mind.

On second thought, maybe a quickie in the spray of steaming water wouldn't be the worst way to start our day.

I scrambled out of bed and joined Roman in the shower as fast as I could. As I stepped under the water, Roman was already lifting me up and pressing me against the wall. "You can't think about sex and expect me not to smell your arousal, Kitten."

"Oops," was all I got out before Roman thrusted inside me and had me crying out in pleasure.

With my back pressed against the tile wall and the fog steaming around us, I merely held on and enjoyed the ride as Roman made my orgasms his bitch. My nails dug into his shoulders as magic shimmered around us, and I tightened around Roman.

"All mine," he grunted as we came together within minutes. While I slowly fell from the unexpected high, Roman's teeth scraped over my shoulder, nipping at my sensitive skin before letting me down.

"We really should hurry up," I said, even though I didn't want to.

"We don't know what tomorrow will bring. There's nothing wrong with taking these moments to ourselves. It only makes us stronger."

He wasn't wrong about that. The more we made love, the more I could sense the little emotions from him. Like right then, Roman was filled with happiness, but there was an underlying sense of responsibility and worry that I hadn't sensed before.

That alone was enough to make me take a step back and clean myself up. Roman did the same and we were out of the shower within minutes. We each moved about the room and we were ready for the day in record time.

"Where to first?" I asked as we stepped into the hallway.

Roman grabbed my hand. "I'd like to leave by ten

for the other pack. Vaughn should have already made preparations, so we find him first and figure out if he's learned anything else."

"Sam is going to want to come with us. She said so last night," I reminded him.

He sighed. "Yes. I won't fight her on that since we'll be staying within pack territories. Embry can come as well, but that's it. We shouldn't need anyone else."

"What if D is still there?"

"From what Kye and Lillias said, it's doubtful. We'll be on guard and if anything seems off, I have no problem leaving if that's what is best. We don't know enough about this Demi person to fight her on our own. It's too big of a risk, no matter how powerful you are," Roman said, and his words brought me comfort.

I was capable of a lot of things, but my gut told me that I wasn't prepared to fight a wolf-witch hybrid that could overtake an entire supernatural council. Even if she wasn't working on her own, we still needed to know more about her.

Where are you? I asked Embry through our pack connection.

With Sam in her room. You going to join us?

"I'm going to go see Embry and Sam while you find Vaughn, unless you need me to go with you," I said

He leaned down to kiss me. "I always need you, but go see them. You can let them know that they need to be ready within the hour.

"Of course," I replied as we parted ways, then let Embry know I was on my way toward them.

Embry was waiting with the door open, and I

walked in to find Sam lounging on her couch, dressed in black shorts and white crop top that made her platinum-blonde hair stand out. "It's about damn time you surfaced."

"Oh, did someone miss me?" I teased Sam.

She scoffed. "Hardly."

She was lying and we both knew it.

"Roman said we're leaving within the hour to head to West Texas," I said.

Embry took a seat. "Are we automatically invited now?"

"Sam invited herself last night. Plus, I think Roman has realized until this is all over, it's best not to try and keep any of us out of what's happening," I answered, and Sam nodded as I moved her feet so I could sit, too.

"Em, are you sure you want to come with us? What about your parents?" I asked, hoping she'd enjoyed her time with them the night before.

Embry's smile grew. "We stayed up through the middle of the night catching up. While I've missed them like crazy, making sure you're okay is also a priority. They understand this more than anyone else. I can be gone for the day and see them again tonight."

"So, they're sticking around?" I asked.

"At least for now. Just depends on how everything unfolds with the Council. Their job brings them happiness. Well, it did until the council was compromised, but that is likely only temporary and then they'll be back to work. While I wish I could see them more, I know what they do makes a difference in our world. I'd never ask them to stay and stop being who they are. They did while they raised me and gave me a good childhood. That was enough for me."

I'd never heard Embry so sure of something, and I was glad she didn't hold resentment toward her parents. That meant the moments they did have together could truly be cherished, and that was most important. Embry had a family here in the pack and I was glad she was happy with how things had worked out.

Sam kicked me in the thigh. "How are you doing?"

I shoved her foot off the couch again, adding a bit of power that sent a shock through her leg. Sam's chest rumbled, but she didn't say anything in return. Smart wolf.

"I'm doing better than expected," I finally answered. "The bond with Roman is helping me keep things in perspective. Or at least, that's how it feels."

"I take that to mean things didn't get cockward between the two of you?" Embry waggled her brows at me, reminding me of Vaughn in that moment. They either should have been brother and sister or mates, they were so much alike.

"Definitely nothing cockward," I answered, and Sam covered her ears.

"Don't you dare talk about screwing my cousin around me. While I'm glad the two of you sorted your shit out, I don't need details. Not now, not ever."

I laughed. "Good thing I don't plan on sharing them then. Though, I am curious how wolves survive the heat Roman was telling me about."

"Already thinking about babies, huh?" Embry asked.

"Not at all. It just came up." Neither of them needed to know about my dream. That would provide too much ammunition for them to taunt me with.

"This is why it's nice being able to go on missions. I can find another wolf to shack up with and come home with nobody the wiser," Sam answered.

"Or vampire like Zeke?" I asked with a wink.

She glowered. "I don't know what you guys think happened with me and the vampire, but there isn't anything sexual shared between us. Sure, he's hot, but the thought of fangs anywhere near me... that's a hard pass."

Embry nodded. "Bloodsuckers are the worst. Zeke is actually the nicest one I've met. I've only had two heats. The first one caught me by surprise, and I found myself alone with a visiting alpha much older than me. No, I won't tell you who he was and no I didn't have sex with him. He merely took care of me. The second time, I was prepared to handle things on my own. While not as enjoyable, it is safest."

Sam and I both leveled our gazes on Embry. I saw a drunk girl's night in our future where Embry was more likely to spill all the details if she was so inclined. Or at least enough of them.

"You'll talk sooner or later," Sam said with a smirk, and I had a feeling she was picturing more torture than alcohol to get the information out of Embry.

"Before things get really awkward, how about we head downstairs and find the guys, so we can get on the road?" I suggested when I sensed Embry's rising embarrassment about her admission. Not only was my bond growing with Roman, but my senses of the other wolves were as well.

Embry was up first. "Great idea. I need to run to my house first. I'll find you guys after I grab my things."

She darted out the door before either of us could respond.

"There are only so many alphas who have visited in the last couple of years. I'll figure it out," Sam said.

I faced her after I stood up. "Or you could let Embry have her secret just like you have yours. You know, that's what friends do. They support each other's choices."

Sam groaned. "Where's the fun in that?"

I shook my head at her. "You haven't done this *friend* thing very often, have you?"

"Nope." She didn't seem at all ashamed of that fact.

ROMAN

My energy buzzed with heightened senses. Every sound, smell, and movement was new. The more time I spent with Cait, the more I felt her power grow within me.

She's helping you become the alpha you were always meant to be, my wolf said.

How so?

A lot about Cait is unknown. We all know that the Luna Marked are powerful, but each one has been different in their own ways, and information about them has been lost over the years, but from what I'm sensing, the two of you will be equal in every way eventually.

Are you saying I'm going to be Luna Marked? I asked.

I don't know, but I'd bet this lifetime that you'll be something more than you are now.

I thought about my wolf's words during most of the drive to West Texas. Vaughn sat up front with me helping keep watch for anyone following us, and the girl's hung in the back, rambling about random things.

It was nice to see Sam have some normalcy. She'd only ever opened up to me after losing her parents. She was still rough around the edges, and I never wanted her to change who she was, but letting people in wasn't a bad idea, either.

As we arrived on the outskirts of the other pack, I thought about Cohen. I hadn't allowed thoughts of my grandfather to consume me since killing him. He tried to take my mate away and was close to killing my mother—his own daughter. In the end, the man had been filled with more darkness than any of us had ever known.

But I couldn't stop from wondering if Cohen had been acting of his own accord. If this Demi person had been targeting us from the very beginning, it's possible not. Witches were capable of knowing things before they happened. If Demi knew about Cait somehow, there was a chance my grandfather wasn't as vile as I thought.

Unfortunately, I'd never get the chance to know the real answer. Even if Demi revealed anything to us once we found her—given what we knew about her power— it would be hard to tell the truth from lies.

What was done couldn't be undone. Moving forward and finding safety for my mate was the only thing left. The first step to that was figuring out if the pack next door knew something we didn't.

I parked in front of the pack house, and we all went silent. Wolves were walking around, smiling and laughing. Something I'd never seen here.

"What's wrong?" Cait asked.

"Nothing, but that's the odd part," I answered as I opened my door.

A man I recognized approached us with a wide grin and open arms. "Roman. It's good to see you. It's been much too long."

Felix held his hand out to me, and I accepted with slight hesitation. "It sure has. I just came by to see how the alpha and beta selection was going. Congratulations are in order I see."

Felix was pulsing with beta energy. Something that was very new for him.

His brown eyes sparked with joy. "Yes, things were made official just yesterday. It's been rough losing the alpha and beta so close together, but the pack is stronger than ever."

I raised a brow. "Is that so?"

"Of course. We need to be. You never know when the next challenge will come. Our pack needs to feel safe," Felix answered, then eyed Cait as she came to my side. "Is this your mate? I heard you took one. It's lovely to meet you."

"You as well," Cait replied with uncertainty.

Felix was speaking as if their pack hadn't attacked ours just weeks before. I'd have thought it was an act, but his words were sincere, and I wasn't picking up anything negative from him.

"So, who is your new alpha?" Vaughn asked with Sam and Embry at his side.

Felix pressed a palm to his forehead. "Well, that would be important to know, wouldn't it? Follow me and you can meet her."

Each of us tensed when Felix said *her*. Was the D woman Cait had heard still around? Would we be able to confirm she was Demi sooner than we thought? Were we about to walk into a trap?

So many questions I didn't have answers to, but my wolf and gut were telling me to proceed. This pack was not a danger to us. Not any longer.

I intertwined my fingers with Cait's, wanting to keep her as close as possible until we confirmed who the new alpha was.

Felix led us into a pack house that seemed to be newly under construction. They'd wasted no time in making changes, and I couldn't decide if that was a good or bad thing.

We entered the foyer and Felix turned back to us. "She'll be out in just a moment."

"Does *she* have a name?" Sam asked.

An older woman strode into the room, head held high, blonde-greying hair that reminded me of my mother and similar eyes. "Why yes, *she* does. I'm Moira, new alpha to this pack. It's a pleasure to meet you all."

Does her voice sound familiar? I asked Cait through our bond.

No, not at all, but she sure looks familiar.

Yeah, I hadn't missed the family resemblance either.

"I'm Roman. This is my mate Cait, my beta Vaughn, and two of our wolves Sam and Embry," I said, pointing at everyone as I spoke, then asked, "Where are you from, Moira?"

She smiled, and I saw so much of my mother in her. "I'm from here, but I haven't been back in many decades. I saw the direction this pack was going as soon as my parents died. My brother changed the day they passed and not for the best. I tried to help him, but I had to do what was best for me at the time."

"Do you know how Cohen died?" I asked.

Her lips pinched. "You killed him."

"And do you know why?" Something still felt off about all of this. Felix was standing against the wall, whistling without a care, and Moira seemed uncertain when she said I killed her brother. Almost as if she didn't believe the words coming from her own mouth.

"I was told he challenged you for your pack. Am I mistaken?" she replied.

"No. Cohen did want control of both packs, and I wouldn't let that happen," I said.

She nodded. "You made the right choice. I obviously didn't know my brother any longer, but it seems as if he remained on the path that I wanted nothing to do with. I'm sorry you had to deal with that."

"Did you know Cohen had a daughter?" I asked, because she didn't appear to be making the family connection like I already had.

Moira gasped. "No. I was only told he had a son that died long ago—the father to the previous beta Kyle."

"He also had a daughter. She lives with my pack," I said, deciding at the last moment to keep the family relationship to myself. My mother could decide if she wanted Moira to know more. Clearly, none of us knew she existed.

"I'm glad she got out like I did. Please tell her to

visit if she would like. Things around here are going to be different now. As soon as I heard of Cohen's death, I came back to take my place as alpha."

"Why didn't you before?" Cait asked.

Moira's smile was filled with regret. "Women weren't as widely accepted as alphas back then. I could have taken my rightful place when our father died as I was born first with the alpha gene, but Cohen made too many threats and I had no one to back me. It seemed best for me to just walk away. I see now that might not have been the case."

Moira eyed each of us, suspicion still filling her emotions. "Is there something I should know? Why are you all here?"

Moira wasn't bad. I knew that, but something held me back from telling her the truth of recent events. The pack had been messed with, and I didn't want anyone to figure out we knew. For the time being, it seemed best to leave them out of our situation.

"As you know, Cohen wasn't the best alpha. I just wanted to make sure the pack was taken care of now," I said with a smile.

"And if they weren't, you were going to take over?" Moira asked.

My shoulder lifted. "I would have if it was necessary, but I can see that's not the case. We can visit another day, once you're more settled in. I'd like for our packs to get along better than they have in the past."

Moira wasn't dumb. I could see she sensed the omissions in my words, but she let things go. "I'd like that as well. You're welcome to stay for a while if you'd like."

I glanced at Vaughn. Given how Felix acted and knowing Moira wasn't a threat, I didn't see the point. He nodded in agreement with my thoughts.

"We actually need to be getting on the road. This was just one of the stops we were making. I'll be in touch, though." I reached a hand to her.

She accepted the simple gesture and squeezed my hand tighter as my energy buzzed. "I look forward to learning more about you, Roman."

We exited the way we came, once again taking in the changes of the pack. Groups of shifters were working together on various projects like a new garden, repairing fences, and water lines. Nobody seemed worried or out of sorts, and I had a feeling I knew why.

Moira and Felix stayed at the entry of the house as we got back into the vehicle. I waved before backing out of the driveway. It wasn't until we got to the end of their dirt road that anyone spoke.

"What the hell was that?" Embry asked.

"I felt like we were in a twilight zone," Vaughn added.

My fingers gripped the steering wheel as I considered what we did learn. Felix had no memory of Cait. Moira didn't know what led to Cohen's death, and the pack was too happy from what little we saw.

"I believe Cait was right to connect this D person to Demi. From what we just saw, I think Demi was here and guiding Cohen from behind the scenes. She likely posed as a wolf shifter and used her magic however she needed to get what she wanted. When she was done with the pack, she spelled them to remember a completely different story before moving on with her plans" I said.

"And what plans would that be?" Cait asked.

"I'm not sure, but I'm certain they have everything to do with you." It caused me physical pain to say those words. I wasn't fond of the thought that a powerful hybrid wanted my mate, but there was no denying Cait was tied to the bigger picture.

Nobody else said anything, because as the thoughts all came together, our wolves wouldn't let us deny that I was right. We still didn't know who Demi really was, but we knew what she wanted.

Someone she'd have to kill me to get.

20

CAIT

Three days had passed since we'd visited the West Texas pack. We were down to nine days left of my deadline from the Supernatural Council. Time was going by fast, but we weren't wasting a moment of it.

Our group spent hours plotting our trip that would begin with a stop to meet the vampires, and then the witches, before heading to the area where we assumed the council to be located, based off the knowledge that Kye and Lillias had retained.

Even though Embry's parents weren't controlled by the council members any longer, the magic that had kept them from sharing their secrets had messed with their memories, so while I'd hoped they'd be able to give us an exact location, it was still only an approximate area. Though, closer than we'd known before.

Brandie, one of the other alphas, had been correct that the location was near Canada, but it was actually in

Northern Washington somewhere, not Montana where her pack was.

When we weren't meeting to hash out details of what needed to be done before and after we left, I was spending time with Roman, growing our bond in every way we could think of.

That didn't only include sex, even though that part was my favorite. We also spent time working together on our shared abilities. My senses had grown in the last few days, and I was feeling a whole new level of confidence in what I was capable of.

Of course, you listen to a man instead of me, Adira droned.

She'd been telling me all along that I was powerful, and it wasn't that I hadn't trusted her; I was just having a hard time believing in myself.

My bond with Roman opened my mind even further, but it was my connection with you that made me see this pack was where I belonged, I said to my wolf. Without her, I might have still run away from the best things in my life, all because I was too afraid to lose them.

I guess that's acceptable, she muttered, and I just smiled. I really did adore my wolf.

How about we go for a run? Just the two of us. It's been a while since we've done that.

That might put me in a better mood.

Roman was with Vaughn and Perry finalizing our plans before Perry went back to his pack to ready them. They'd meet back up with us once we got to the coven location. Beatrix said that would be the best meeting place to come to an agreement about their needed support in standing against the Supernatural Council.

I'd also asked Roman about the fae, but he was hesitant. Last he heard, Lucinda wasn't even in Fae Islands any longer, and he didn't know who to trust there. Not that he trusted Lucinda, but she did tend to do the right thing in her own way from what I'd been told and had witnessed in Australia.

I was already downstairs, so I headed out the front door. Fall was near, and the heat was lessening, but it was nothing like the cool temperatures I grew up with in Eastern Oregon.

As soon as my feet hit the driveway, I called my wolf forward. Other pack members stopped what they were doing and watched. Even after the weeks that had passed, seeing my purple wolf still marveled the other shifters.

I have a confession to make, Adira said as we ran for the forest line on all fours.

What's that?

I don't have to be purple. Our true color is the ebony underneath the purple.

I only laughed. I saw no reason to be upset by her admission. Sure, I might not have drawn as much attention if my wolf was a normal color, but our fur was still longer than any other I'd seen, and our energy wasn't easy to hide.

We'd have never blended in, no matter what color our coat was, and I was more than okay with that.

Can you change the color to anything other than purple? I asked.

No, but I'll show you our true color when we get to the water, and you can see our reflection.

Adira ran with purpose after that. We dodged in and out of the trees, expelling excess energy and stretching our muscles. I needed to do it often, or I became fidgety and uneasy.

Before we made it to the edge of the forest, a light-grey wolf appeared in our path, causing us to halt.

Serene, I said.

Mind if I join you? she asked.

She has something to tell us, Adira added.

Given my wolf didn't seem to object and it had been a while since I had a full conversation with the eccentric pack historian, I nodded our wolf head. *Follow us.*

Serene did just that. When we got to the river by Roman's cabin, I slowed and shifted back to human form in hopes Serene would do the same. It was easier to gauge her tone when I could see her face and body language.

She followed my lead, and we both sat on the bench facing the water. "Is everything okay?" I asked.

"Is anything ever just okay?" she countered.

I chuckled. "I guess not."

"I do have something to share," she added.

"I suspected as much." Before Serene continued to speak, I opened my connection to Roman, something we'd been working on. By doing so, he'd be able to hear what Serene had to say without me having to relay the information, a bond perk I was happy to learn.

"When I was in LA with Beatrix, I kept in touch with Vaughn about the happenings in the pack. There isn't anything that has gone on that I didn't know about. Once Roman decided to gather the races, I shared what I knew was acceptable with Beatrix."

I nodded, not at all surprised.

"She made some calls after I left and agrees things are amiss. The witches have already decided that they will stand against the council with you, but under one condition."

"What would that be?" I asked, not surprised they would want something in return.

"Beatrix wants the power that will be released when the hybrid dies. Demi has no coven that anyone is aware of, and the energy has to go somewhere."

"What about the other covens that might stand with us? How is it fair to give Beatrix all of the power? How can we know that it won't corrupt her?" The one thing I knew about too much power was that in the wrong hands, it usually did irreparable damage.

Serene waved a hand as if my question was nothing but silly words. "Let Beatrix handle that."

"No, I don't think I will, Serene. She might be a powerful witch, but there are lives at stake. If she wants something in return for helping save all of us, then I need to be certain that we're not starting another fight by agreeing to her demands."

I could sense Roman's agreement. We needed more assurances from the witch. Otherwise, we were better off without their assistance.

"Fair enough. I will have Beatrix provide the needed proof that the power absorbed from the hybrid will be divided amongst the covens and there won't be a fear of too much going to any one person. Happy?" Serene's stare bored into me, almost demanding my agreement, but I wouldn't be rushed.

While I was okay with her offer, I didn't reply until Roman confirmed through our bond that he was good with it as well. Finally, I nodded. "That works for us. I appreciate you coming to me."

She winked. "People would rather talk to you than Roman now that you're officially the alpha female."

Oh, I hope he didn't hear that.

I heard it, he grumbled.

Sorry, Mate.

He grunted and I closed off the connection. He had more important things to worry about than Serene's crazy talk—even if what she said might have been true.

"How is the wolf pup you went to help with?" I asked, changing the topic on purpose.

Serene sneered. "Not much of a pup. Beatrix didn't give me all the information I needed. All is fine with the packs now. I wasn't even really needed. I think she just didn't want to deal with the local alpha herself once she stumbled upon the lone wolf."

"What happened to his pack?" I asked.

"Not sure. He wouldn't really say. The memories were too painful, and he wasn't causing trouble, so I let it go. I convinced the alpha to offer him refuge for the time being, and Foster, the stray wolf, promised not to cause any trouble. So far, everyone is keeping their end of the deal."

"Good to hear. Let us know if we can help in any way," I said.

Serene laughed. "Right, because the other packs would want you leading trouble to their territories."

I gave her a pointed stare, and she straightened.

"That was rude, wasn't it?" she asked.

"Yep."

Shocking the hell out of me, she bowed her head. "Sorry, Alpha Female. I know you didn't intentionally bring trouble. It's not your fault you were destined for this power."

My head shook. "It's fine, Serene."

The crazy old woman grinned at me. "Glad to hear it. I'm going home now." She took several steps back and shifted to her wolf.

Ready to head back as well? I asked Adira once Serene was gone.

She pushed her essence forward in answer and, once we were on all fours, trotted toward the water. I'd forgotten all about her showing me our black coat. With the sun beaming down on us and having only the river as reflection, our fur appeared to shine like diamonds in coal.

It's the energy we hold. Even when it's not purple, we can't ever keep it fully contained, Adira said in response to my thoughts.

Thank you for sharing with me, I replied as we turned to the side, taking one last look before heading home to Roman.

///

ROMAN FINISHED HIS MEETING WITH VAUGHN, AND OUR plans were officially approved by the other alphas involved and finalized within the pack by the time we arrived at the house.

There would be no more waiting. We already had the support of the packs that we needed and now the witches. All we had left to worry about was the vampire group that Zeke belonged to. Normally, vampires weren't to be trusted, but given Zeke had already been there for Sam several times, Roman decided it was worth the risk to involve them.

All races had agreed that we needed to meet up as soon as possible instead of waiting out the deadline the council had set. I hoped the timeline would work in our favor because, by now, nobody expected us to arrive at the location given on the letter requesting my presence.

Roman had even gone as far as to finally reach out to the wolf council, but he received no response in return. At least he'd tried, even if it was much later than they probably would have liked once they knew everything that was happening. They'd just have to figure it out after the fact.

We were set to leave within the hour, and our first destination was Glacier National Park in Northern Montana. It was almost two-thousand miles of driving to get there. If we switched drivers instead of stopping to rest when needed, we'd be there in just over twenty-eight hours with minimal interruptions. Being in a vehicle that long wasn't something I was looking forward to.

"Do you have everything you need?" Roman asked me as I zipped up my backpack.

"As long as I have you, I do." I winked at him.

He picked me up, holding me tight against his chest. "I don't like this."

"Neither do I, but we agreed not to run."

"Can I take that back?" Roman asked.

I knew he wasn't being serious, but I also understood why he'd ask. We had no idea how things would turn out over the next few days. We were headed into an unknown territory to likely start a battle with who knew how many people.

"Zeke confirmed the vampires were on board?" I asked, hoping to remind him of the things in our favor.

Roman nodded stiffly. "Mostly. His leader wants to meet us first before he officially commits. Should be more of a formality than anything else. Their nest isn't as big as I was hoping, but there should be enough of them to make the council guards take pause. Vampires are the most ruthless of our races, which is also why they're the least trusted."

"Beatrix provided proof that the power from Demi would be handled carefully once she's dead?"

"As soon as Serene delivered the message, I had a signed statement from four covens in my email," Roman said.

Beatrix had been prepared, it seemed. Almost as if she'd just been messing with us with her one condition. Pain in the ass witch.

"And we have ten packs headed in the same

direction to help, with plenty of wolves to stand by our side, right?" I confirmed.

He growled against my neck. "I see what you're doing, Mate. It didn't work. We could have every supernatural join us on the way to council and I still wouldn't feel right about having you so close to someone who wants your energy."

"I know, but I had to try."

"I love you for trying," he said before kissing his way up my neck.

I tilted my head back while wiggling within his tight grasp to get free. "The others are waiting for us."

"They can wait a little longer."

"But they shouldn't have to, and you know it."

A rumble grew in his chest. "I don't want to let you go."

"I won't leave your side."

"Promise?"

I nodded. "Forever and always."

"Okay. Let's go."

That was one promise I prayed I didn't break.

21

CAIT

We were twelve hours into our drive and in the middle of nowhere. The tension within the SUV kept building with every passing mile. The only person I didn't want to murder was Roman. Nothing Vaughn said was funny after the first two hours. Embry constantly whined about cramps in her legs. Sam just glowered at everyone, and her face made me want to punch her.

I had no idea what happened, but nobody was getting along. Well, except me and Roman, but I think that was only because we weren't talking to each other. I figured we were safer that way.

"I'm tired and we're almost halfway. Who is driving next?" Roman asked. He'd been behind the wheel since we left the pack. I was pretty sure he only lasted as long as he did because keeping his hands busy prevented him from punching Vaughn like I wanted to.

"Not me," Embry grumbled before burying her head beneath a blanket.

Vaughn's snores sounded from the third row, so he was out as well.

"Yeah, not a fucking chance. I offered to drive earlier, and you said no. My time has passed," Sam snapped.

I reached for Roman. "I can take over."

"You haven't slept, either, since you had to help with directions. I'm not letting you drive," Roman replied. His eyes were dark and stormy, something I wasn't used to and didn't particularly like.

"Then, what are we going to do?" I said with more bite in my tone than I intended.

Roman nodded to a billboard. "There's a motel up ahead. We'll stay there for a few hours to sleep. But my worthless beta stays in the car since he's not waking to drive."

Yeah, I wasn't going to argue with that. We all needed some separation before this trip blew up in our faces. Clearly, the stress of everything the pack had been going through as of late was finally getting to everyone. I should have known it was only a matter of time before the utopia of pack life faded away.

Nothing could be that amazing forever.

As Roman pulled off the highway, I stared out the window and wondered what my life would be like if I'd never seen him on that beach. If the mark had never appeared on my wrist. Or even if I'd only kept the mark to myself instead of immediately reaching out to Embry.

So many choices that could have been made differently and yet... here I was. In a car full of cranky wolf shifters because of some stupid Moon Goddess. Oh, what I wouldn't give to let her know how I felt about the shit situation she'd dropped me into.

Don't say things you don't mean. Putting words into the universe gives them the power to come true, Adira said.

Yeah, and what if I want them to come true? I retorted.

Then, by all means, keep blabbering like an idiot.

Her presence faded away. Stupid freaking wolf. I didn't need her. I didn't need any of these people.

Roman reached for me and shocked my arm with his fingertips. "We're here."

Some of the rage that had been building dissipated as I met his eyes. Eyes that were only for me. Shit, what was wrong with me? My emotions were unlike anything I'd ever experienced before. I grabbed hold of Roman, soaking up the bond between us, hoping it helped to calm me.

"Are we really leaving Vaughn in here?" I asked after a moment.

Roman glanced back with a snarl. "We can leave them all in here. They're the ones that didn't want to drive."

Embry was fast asleep as well, but Sam was still coherent. "I don't think so, asshole." She opened her door with a bag in hand, and the three of us got out.

Sam leaned against the rotted siding of the motel, just beneath a flickering pale-yellow light. Maybe it would have been better for all of us to sleep in the SUV.

Roman stomped into the office and the glass door cracked at the bottom as it slammed shut behind him.

I stared up at the sky, taking in the bright stars. We

were surrounded by trees and city lights were nowhere to be seen as the moon shined down on us. If it didn't smell like ass in the air, it would have almost been peaceful.

My wolf nose was picking up on trash that hadn't been taken away in weeks, or possibly months, making me want to gag. Before I could do so, Roman came back out with two keys, throwing one at Sam's face. "114."

She grunted in response and disappeared into the shadows.

"Where are we?" I asked, grabbing on to his arm to soak up the calm I knew I could find with him. My earlier thoughts were maddening. I wanted to kick myself for even thinking them. I just needed sleep and my mate. Everything would be back to normal after that. It had to be.

"Some shit motel along the border of Wyoming and Colorado." He nodded. "Our room is around the back." Roman gripped my hand tighter than normal as he dragged me along the cracked and uneven sidewalk.

There were only three cars in the parking lot beside ours, and it was nearly two in the morning. Everything was eerily quiet as we headed toward our room. My stomach twisted at the thought of staying here, but I also didn't think we had much of a choice. Not with the way everyone was acting.

Roman stuck the key into the doorknob for room 136. As soon as he opened the door, the stench of body odor, mildew, and bleach slammed into me, causing me to start coughing until I almost choked.

Roman rubbed my back. "Focus on me and not the

human smells. You can block them out if you concentrate hard enough."

I had to bite my tongue—literally—to prevent myself from snapping back at his comment of concentrating hard enough. The rising anger helped me to forget about the smells, and I finally straightened.

We entered the dingy room with peeling wallpaper, a queen-sized bed, and a TV from the eighties.

It's only a few hours, I thought to myself as I eyed the bed. There was no way I was getting under the covers. I had no idea what had been on the mattress before our arrival. Certainly nothing good or clean.

Roman eyed the bed just as suspiciously as I had, but his hesitation didn't last as long. He laid down on top of the comforter, the springs creaking as the weight of his body pressed onto the mattress. His arms opened to me, and I couldn't ignore the needs of my mate.

We needed each other. Badly.

I crawled onto the bed, trying to keep my cringing to a minimum. As soon as my head lay on Roman's chest, I sighed. This was definitely what I'd needed.

His arms tightened around me, and his fingers trailed up my spine.

"Don't even think about trying to get lucky in this place. We'd get some sort of disease, I'm sure of it," I grumbled.

"Shifters don't get diseases," he replied, making me grin and shake my head before he added, "Sleep, Mate."

I closed my eyes, doing just that.

///

THE SOUND OF A SQUEAKING DOOR WOKE ME. AT FIRST, I thought Roman was up, but the steady thrum of his heartbeat sounded underneath my ear. I tensed but kept my eyes closed as I listened for any other noises.

Nothing else made a peep, and I started to relax. Before I could go back to sleep, I rolled over to check the time to make sure we hadn't slept for too long. As I reached out for the clock I knew was somewhere behind me, my fingers felt jeans instead.

"Hello, Cait," a man's voice sounded.

Not fucking again.

We were never stopping on a road trip again. Not ever.

I zapped Roman with my energy to wake him as I moved into action. I had no idea who was in our room, but whoever he was, he was going to die. Really freaking quickly.

"Today is not the day, buddy," I grumbled while swinging a punch packed full of power.

The newcomer stumbled back, knocking the curtains around enough that his burnt-orange hair and freckled face came into view from the light of the moon outside.

"Today is not *your* day." The guy created a yellow orb between his hands and flung it my way. I ducked down, and the magic crashed into Roman who I hadn't realized was right behind me.

I glanced back long enough to see I was on my own. Whatever that dude had thrown made Roman's body seize up. He'd fallen back onto the bed.

As fun as it sounded to take some aggressions out on this guy, I needed to make sure Roman was okay, which meant the witch—or whatever he was—needed to die.

I need all we have, Adira.

Her growl echoed within my mind as we charged for the Weasley lookalike. Purple light emitted around the room as the witch's eyes widened.

He threw another orb, but the spell fizzled out against my power. Whoever had sent him to attack us made a poor choice. My hands wrapped around his throat, and he punched me in the side of the head, sending a shock of magic through my body even as the energy radiating from me burned his skin.

Okay, that stung a little, but not enough to make me let go of him. He drew his arm back again, but I wasn't going to get hit a second time. I used my hold on his neck to slam his head down onto the side table, enjoying the sound of splintering plywood while his face became my plaything.

Grabbing the back of his greasy red hair, I slammed him into the wall nose first while sending my energy down his spine until the bastard sparked with my purple magic.

I turned him around to finish the task I'd never asked for. His mouth opened and closed, but no words came out as my fingers turned into claws.

I considered dialing my rage back to ask him who'd sent him after us, but I had little faith that he'd tell us the truth anyway. Before I could think twice, I ripped the witch's throat out, flinging blood along the already-stained curtains.

He slumped to the floor, green lifeless eyes staring up at the ceiling.

I immediately went to Roman, who hadn't moved from the mattress. My hands traced over his body, soaking up the energy that didn't belong to him until my own demolished it. I didn't even know that was something I could do, but I was running on pure adrenaline and acting on instinct.

"Come on, Ro. Wake up," I demanded, tightening my hold around his biceps.

When his eyes started rolling around instead of focusing on me, I did the only thing I could think of: I pressed my hands to his chest and zapped him with my power.

He gasped, sitting straight up and almost knocking me off the bed. "What happened?" he roared.

"Someone tried to attack us in our sleep, but I got him first," I replied calmly.

Roman eyed the corpse leaning against the wall. "I see."

A knock sounded at the door, and we both tensed until we heard Sam's voice. "Let me in."

I got up to do just that. As I went to release the lock, I realized the door wasn't locked. The witch had gotten in, and nobody else would have locked it after.

Roman shouted, but it was too late. The door opened and another man stormed in with a glowing dagger in hand. "You killed my brother."

I moved to protect myself and knock the weapon

from his hand, but his movements were faster than mine. Too fast for me to process what had happened until there was a ten-inch blade buried into my stomach and magic moving through my veins from said blade.

Roman's snarls echoed through the room as I fell to the ground. I tried battling the foreign power invading my body, but everything burned, and I couldn't even move my arms to remove the object causing all of the damage.

The head of my attacker flew over my line of sight and across the room as I heard the thud of what I assumed was his body crash onto the floor. At least that asshole was dead. Unfortunately, I wasn't too far behind him.

Roman kneeled next to me, crimson coating his hands. "Cait?" He took the knife out of my stomach, but that only made the pain worse. "Cait!" he roared when I started fading away.

My heart slowed, and all I could think was, what if the third time wasn't the charm when it came to dying?

22

ROMAN

Unfiltered wrath stormed through every inch of my body as I shook Cait's bloodied form. Her skin was still warm, but her heart was no longer beating as her lifeless eyes stared at the ceiling.

One second, everything had been fine, and in the next, it was a fucking nightmare I couldn't wake up from.

Sam busted into the room. The real Sam this time. I'd known a second too late that my Sam would have never asked to be let in. She would have kicked down the door after hearing the commotion.

The warlock that had stabbed Cait was dead, and I wanted to kill him a thousand times over.

Sam was covered in blood splatter, and the rapid rise and fall of her chest told me our entire group had been ambushed. "A small coven found us. There were eight of them."

"Are any of them still alive?" I asked, my words were clipped while I stared at my mate.

Sam didn't answer my question as she kneeled next to me. I knew the moment she realized Cait was... gone. She gasped, grabbing on to my shoulder, but I shook her off.

"I said, are they still alive?" the volume of my voice growing louder by the second.

"No, but I think more are coming."

Good. Let them come. I'd kill every fucking person who appeared in my path.

"Roman, your skin is on fire," Sam said with caution.

My head snapped up, and I met her eyes. "My soul is burning to ash. Seems fitting the rest of me would be, too."

"She's come back before. Maybe—"

I snarled, pushing past Sam. I'd already thought the same thing, but something about this felt different. I wasn't around the first time Cait had died, and when Kyle attacked her after killing my father, Cait's heart stopped, but I'd still felt a part of her soul present. I'd still sensed her deep inside my own.

This time, there was nothing but darkness. An inky blackness that needed to be coated with crimson before I could find my way back to Cait.

Stepping outside, I ripped the motel room door from the hinges before turning to see Embry and Vaughn cleaning up the bodies from their own fight. I moved in the opposite direction of them, heading for the trees and where I sensed incoming power. Witches and warlocks liked to show off, which normally annoyed me, but not now. Not when I wanted to find every member of this coven and rip their heads from their necks, one-by-one.

Sam had been right. My skin was like fire. With every step I took, I channeled the rage flowing through me, unable to get the image of Cait's bloodied body lying in that piece-of-shit motel room out of my head.

"FUCK!" I roared. Why had we stopped? Why hadn't I just pushed through and kept driving?

My fists slammed into the trees around me as many times as needed until they'd each fallen to the ground from the force of my hits.

My wolf rumbled alongside me. He was quiet, but his ire was not. We fueled each other, soaking in the grief and the thought of spilled blood.

Purple flickers sparked from my heated skin where my knuckles were cut from the rough bark of the trees that I'd taken out only a sliver of my fury on.

I held my fist to my chest and closed my eyes. Purple swirls filled my mind as I thought of Cait and the joy of watching her grow into the beautiful wolf she was.

My mind filled with love as memories of her energy flowed through me so intensely that I could feel her affection for me, her pride and respect for the life we were trying to have together. She hadn't been part of our world long, and she might have been scared of it to begin with, but my Cait was an all-in kind of person. When she'd finally moved beyond fear, there was nothing that could keep us apart.

Nothing except death.

The crunching of leaves on the forest floor snapped

me back to my current situation. I still had witches and warlocks to kill.

I could sense Sam, Embry, and Vaughn moving closer behind me, but I paid them no attention. These kills were mine to have. Even if the approaching supernaturals hadn't killed Cait, they'd still had a hand in the taking of my mate.

Each of them would pay with their lives.

Whistles sounded before the group of witches and warlocks appeared in my path. I drew on my wolf power, and it flooded through me like never before. My height grew, my muscles strained against my clothes, and flashes of purple sparked around me.

I knew I'd taken on some of Cait's power when we bonded, but anytime I'd tried to utilize the magic like she did, the results were always lackluster. Now, when I needed her most, I clung to the familiarness of the energy within me.

I clenched my fists and snarled at the approaching group. Some of them hesitated, but others continued forward. My fingers turned to claws, canines extended within my mouth, and fur sprouted up along my arms and likely other parts of my body. Partial shifts weren't usually this complex, but I wasn't questioning anything as long as increased strength continued to pulse through my veins.

I lunged for the nearest witch, not even seeing her face before my claws made contact and snapped her neck. There was a fizzle of magic that landed on my shoulder, but nothing like what I'd been hit with earlier.

This second witch was weaker than the first, disappointing me there wouldn't be a drawn-out fight.

No, the witch isn't weaker. We're stronger. We're taking on Cait's power, my wolf said as another wave of power hit us, this time making me take a step back.

The thought of taking Cait's power was like rubbing salt in my bloodied wound. I didn't want my mate's power. I wanted her. All of her. Not this essence that was currently filling my body without satisfying any part of me.

As my ire doubled in strength, the need to expel the energy filling me was unstoppable. Acting on instinct, I lifted my hands up, palms facing down, and roared into the night sky. The ground beneath my feet shook and trees snapped around us as I moved toward the remaining warlocks standing.

Several of them disappeared, but two couldn't get free from the energy I'd let loose. I drew them closer to me with mere thought, then wrapped a hand around each of their throats.

"Who sent you?" I sneered.

Their dark eyes bulged from their faces. I lightened my grip just enough for one of them to answer. "We don't know. There was a message left, and we were promised—"

I squeezed tighter. I didn't care what they were promised. If they didn't know who sent them, they were of no use to me. I'd keep killing every witch and warlock I found until I figured out which coven leader led them to us.

The purple energy around me turned dark, almost

black with flashes of light that got dimmer as I sucked more life from the two in front of me. At the sound of bones snapping, I tossed both bodies onto the ground with disgust before turning back to the motel to get my mate. After I avenged her death, I had every intention of finding a way to be with her again. This lifetime was over for me without Cait by my side.

I'd left her body, assuming Sam would stay with her. Except, my cousin appeared with Embry and Vaughn in my path through the trees, which only served to further fuel my rage.

"You left her." My voice didn't sound like my own. Without Cait, nothing would ever be the same again. Not a single part of me.

"I wanted to check on you," Sam replied as Embry sniffled beside her.

I couldn't handle looking at them. I needed space. I needed to do something with the power flowing through me that would get me closer to being back with Cait.

"Roman, you're..." Vaughn started, then paused.

"I'm what?" I shouted in his face.

"You're on fire."

Embry wiped at her cheeks. "It's not fire. It's friction energy. The same as Cait."

Hearing my mate's name on another's lips caused me no comfort. I wanted to rip Embry's tongue out, so I'd never have to hear her speak it again.

With that thought, I knew I had to get away. I had to get back to Cait and not just her body. I would never be whole again without her. I no longer had a reason to live. I could kill every magic user in this world, and it would never be enough to fill the void I now had within my soul.

My mate was gone, but I'd soon find a way to be with her again. There were no other options left for me.

23

CAIT

This was not good. Not fucking good at all.

I looked down on my body, and I was all alone. My stomach was covered in blood and a pool of crimson was growing underneath me. The door to our room had been ripped from its hinges and I tried to force whatever form I'd become outside where I sensed others.

I needed to find Roman. I needed to make sure he was okay. My soul ached for him and the pain I knew he'd be feeling.

Every part of me wanted to comfort him, but then again, I was pretty sure I was nothing more than a ghost or spirit or something.

As I tried to move from where I floated in the motel room, another force was pulling me in the opposite direction I wanted to go. I fought against pressure until something thumped the back of my head, making me lose whatever hold I had to Earth.

Darkness descended around me while I was

hurtling through… well, I didn't know what, but the further I got from my body, the less okay I was.

Adira? I called, but I couldn't even sense her.

I couldn't really be dead. It wasn't possible. I'd only just found Roman. I wasn't ready for our time to be over. Sure, I could find him in another lifetime, but how many years would that take? I didn't know and I didn't want to find out. I just wanted him.

My body landed onto soft grass, my head narrowly missing a jagged rock. I blinked my eyes, trying to figure out where I was. The trees seemed familiar, the night sky was peaceful, and the moon was bright, but none of it seemed real. More like a figment of my imagination.

"It's more like *my* imagination, actually," a singsong voice sounded as a shadow fell over me.

I scrambled back, jumping to my feet with my hands out.

"You have no reason to fear me, child."

Luna, the Moon Goddess, stood before me in a billowy pink gown. Her silver eyes twinkled with magic and her ebony hair was twisted in braids atop her head.

There was an unearthly beauty about her that I didn't remember from our last meeting. Her essence had me wanting to bow before her and soak in the pureness of energy I could sense within her.

"I'm sorry to have brought you here under such circumstances, but time is running out, and I'm being blocked from Earth right now. Demi has acquired more dark magic than any of us expected," Luna said, and a growl built in my chest.

"What did you just say?" I said slowly.

"Oh, Cait. You're focusing on the wrong things," Luna chided.

I threw my hands in the air. "You killed me!"

She shrugged. "It wouldn't be the first time."

"You've got to be kidding me," I grumbled and began to pace.

"I was pretty sure you knew I made sure you died after the first fight with Callista. I didn't think you'd be so shocked." Luna's eyes scrunched together, and her lips thinned.

"Shocked? No, I'm not shocked. I'm fucking furious. You took me away from my mate!" I was seething now. It was one thing for her to get inside my head and show me I was being a fool for being fearful of a life with Roman, but killing me just so we could have a little chat was crossing a line.

"I can send you back, Cait."

My head snapped up. "Excuse me?"

"This life isn't over for you yet. There is still much to do. I just needed a few minutes with you."

"So, you killed me without warning?" I didn't understand this woman... goddess.

She sighed heavily as if *I* was the one inconveniencing her. "Listen, Cait. We don't have a lot of time." She glanced up at the moon before continuing. "I needed Roman to see his full potential, and I needed to pass along some information. This was the best way. I'm sorry about killing you, but I couldn't warn you.

Will you also tell the others I'm sorry for making you fight enough that the idea of staying at the motel didn't sound as horrible as it actually was?"

"*You're* why everyone was fighting?" I couldn't believe her.

"I had to get you to a place where you could be vulnerable to attack. You and Roman both have things to accomplish."

"Is Roman okay?" Regardless of how things had happened, my mate was still my biggest concern. I hadn't seen him when I regained consciousness in my spirit form or whatever I'd been.

"He is figuring out what he is truly capable of. Now, it's time for you to do the same," Luna answered.

"What does that mean? I've been utilizing my Luna Marked power for weeks, and I'm stronger than I've ever been."

She smiled down at me from her nearly six-foot height. "And you've made me incredibly proud with your progress, but there is more. Once you and Roman bonded, I expected him to lose control. When he didn't, that prevented you from unlocking your full power. Both of you are far more stubborn than I thought possible."

I smirked. That was what she got for messing with people's lives so drastically.

"The two of you needed to be on equal levels of strength before facing Demi. Now that Roman has fully tapped into the energy you shared with him during bonding, you will be able to act as one. Your mark didn't just make you a shifter, Cait. The Luna Marked are all different in creation, and your abilities differ from other wolves."

"Yeah, I've noticed. They don't glow like I do," I said with annoyance.

She held an arm out for me to join her. "Let's walk and talk. You need to be directly under my moon in order to go back, and the window to do so is closing."

Well, I wasn't going to argue with that. I hurried to join her, and we began following a shallow stream of water toward an open field of wildflowers.

"As I was saying, you're unique. None of the books telling of those who came before you would have ever given you the answers you needed to become your true self. Your wolf gives you strength and the courage needed to protect your pack. She also guides you onto the right path. The power you received from Roman through the mate bond solidified who you are as a wolf and the alpha female you were born to be."

She grabbed my wrist, pressing her thumb over my crescent mark until my skin burned. When she pulled away, the previously dark mark was now lined with a deep purple.

"Your Luna mark is now unlocked. You weren't strong enough to wield its full power before, but you are now," Luna said.

"I thought I was dead. How can I be stronger?" I asked, mostly being a smartass, but also curious.

"Your spirit form isn't benefiting from the mark being unlocked, your physical body is. When you awaken, everything will be different. The bond between you and Roman will have finalized, and your true form will be revealed. Listen to Adira. Her memories will guide your next steps, but also trust your instincts. The two of you have bonded closer than I expected, which will only benefit you in the coming days."

"What about Demi and my Luna Marked power?" I asked, a bit panicked because the meadow was only mere feet away. I was more than eager to get back to Roman, but I wasn't stupid enough to ignore the chance at getting answers that could help us.

"You are my child. You hold an amount of my power within you unlike any other shifter currently walking the Earth. You are capable of anything that you believe is possible. All you have to do is have faith in yourself and those who stand at your side."

"And Demi?" I pressed, because from the sounds of it, this hybrid wasn't going to be easy to fight if she'd left Luna no other option besides killing me just so we could have this conversation. Well, amongst other things I'd be finding out soon enough from Roman.

Luna's hands gripped both of my shoulders as she turned me until my back was to the meadow. "She is the exact opposite of you. She lives her life with hate and darkness. She was shunned by both wolves and witches, then again by the Supernatural Council. Each of their actions turned her into a monster you must now defeat, but what you need to remember most is that you can't do this alone."

Before I could ask anything else, she shoved me backward with a force so intense that I lost the ability to breathe. Bright light shined over my face, and I squeezed my eyes shut as the ground disappeared beneath me.

Hold on to what you know to be true, Cait. Don't lose your faith, Luna's voice whispered through my mind as I was sent plunging south, hopefully back to my body.

I tried to call back to the Moon Goddess, but her presence was already gone. Her parting words didn't make me feel any better.

Neither did the process of being sucked into my body. At least, that's what it had felt like when I sensed I was back on Earth. My head throbbed like a jackhammer had a party inside it. My stomach muscles were stitching themselves back together and freaking me out, because I could feel every thread knitting my insides closed until they were back where it belonged.

My heart raced when I heard Roman's howl cut through the night sky. I wanted to run to him, hold on to him and never let go, but my body wasn't done coming back to life yet.

Adira, are you there?

She moaned. *I want to kill our creator.*

Yeah, get in line. What did she do to you? I asked.

Gave me back memories that were suppressed. There was a slight pause. *She took so much from me.* A sorrowful sound weighed heavy in Adira's voice that made me want to die again just to show Luna how I felt about hurting my wolf, but then I heard Roman shouting.

Adira and I both forgot about our own pains as he came closer. Every inch that lessened between us and our mate filled us with the strength we needed to finish healing.

He needs us, Adira said.

We need him just as much.

"Vaughn, you fucking come near me again, I will end your life," Roman raged.

"That's a risk I'm willing to take. I'm not going to let you do something that will get you killed."

There was an unnerving pause before Roman spoke again. "I'm already dead."

Only one set of footsteps came closer. Slow at first, then faster. A light entered the room, so bright that even through my closed eyes, I wanted to turn my head away from it, but no matter how hard I tried, the light followed my movements.

"Cait!" Roman half-yelled and half-cried my name, then he hissed in pain while I tried to figure out how to get away from the brightness surrounding me.

Roman's continued shouts were drowned out by a ringing in my ears. Finally, my hands were able to move and cover my ears, but nothing helped quiet the rising sound.

I curled into a ball, remembering that Luna said I would become my true self when I woke. She certainly had a way of unveiling power within her children. Nothing about this was enjoyable as I rocked back and forth, holding on to my legs, and hoping I wasn't about to die again.

Sweat built up along my skin as my temperature increased. My clothes turned to ash while my hair floated around me. My previously brunette strands were turning into a midnight color: a perfect mix of the ebony color Adira had shown me our wolf form could be and a shimmer of the purple I was used to.

Stinging seared where I knew my mark to be and then moved up my forearm before stopping. I once again tried to open my eyes, but there was still a glow around me preventing that from happening.

My arms and legs stretched out once again and I lay on my back, staring into a nothingness. Agony tore through my body, and my spine arched until I felt like I was floating just inches above the floor. Screams bounced around inside my head as the rest of my body went limp.

Finally, arms grabbed a hold of me, dragging me against a hard body. "Cait, baby, I need you to wake up and tell me what's happening. *Please.*"

The ache in Roman's voice gave me the final push I needed to break through whatever had been holding me hostage. My arms obeyed my wants and wrapped around Roman's neck as he squeezed me tighter.

"I thought you were..." The anguish in his voice nearly killed me all over again.

"I was, but I'm okay. We're okay. I'm right here with you where I belong." My hands stroked the back of his head and between his shoulders, trying to calm the beast within him.

I might have died again, but Roman had suffered far more than me.

Gasps sounded behind us, and Roman turned me away from the door with a snarl that had whoever was there backing up before I could see them. "I just need you to myself right now," he whispered.

"I'm not going anywhere," I murmured against his ear. The tighter I held him, the more he relaxed and the better I felt. We were healing each other as the minutes ticked by, and I was in no hurry to let go of him. That was until he stroked my hair and spoke again. "This color suits you."

I'd forgotten about the changes while I was coming back to life. Roman must have sensed my curiosity, because he let me stand as we both inspected my body.

The first thing I noticed was that I was completely naked. The warmth shared between me and Roman hadn't made me realize that earlier. The next was that not only was my hair the color of the night sky, but it was also at least six inches longer and quite a bit thicker.

When I ran my fingers through it, shimmers of purple could be seen, but nothing bright or obnoxious in color.

Roman's fingers gently grabbed hold of my wrist and turned it over so we both could see. My mark still had the new purple outline around it from the Moon Goddess, but there were new additions as well.

Roman traced his pointer finger along the intricate silver lines that surrounded the crescent shape before swirling up toward my forearm, crossing over each other so many times that there was no way to find where the tattoo began or ended. I twisted my arm under the moonlight and the ink reflected before darkening a few shades, just like my Luna Mark had done when I first got it.

"It's beautiful," Roman whispered, moving his gaze

to mine. Our stares locked for the first time since I'd woken, and I didn't miss the specks of lavender in his eyes that hadn't been there before.

"You've changed, but you're still you," he said reverently.

"So have you." I smiled and held his face to pull him closer.

The mood shifted once we realized both of us were okay. His lips crashed against mine until our tongues danced together, soaking each other in and drowning in our bond. His love for me nearly made me weep as I dug my nails into his shoulders, holding on with every strength I had in me.

"I love you so damn much," I said between kisses.

"I love you more than my own life." Roman kissed my cheek before burying his face into my hair. His body began to shake, and I felt tears drop onto my shoulders. "I would have died just to find you again."

"The world would have been a worse place without you," I replied, finally allowing my sadness to shed while we continued to hold each other.

"The world wouldn't have survived my wrath if I'd stayed."

There was so much truth to his words that they had me crying harder than I had in years. The love I shared with Roman. The bond we'd created. There was nothing more powerful than that. Our love would destroy worlds if we let it. That I knew without a doubt in my mind.

Once we both regained our composure, Roman pulled back just enough to take in my naked body. "I want to get your bag from the car so you can get dressed, but I don't want you to leave my sight."

"As long as you didn't kill the others like I heard you threaten, then don't worry about it." I mentally reached out to Embry, asking her to bring me my stuff.

Don't you ever fucking die again, was her only response. I didn't bother to reply. Embry had every reason to be pissed off, but at least we had more answers now. Though I still wasn't certain what the changes about myself meant, I had no doubt we'd figure them out soon enough.

Embry tossed my bag into the room without entering. "Come out just as soon as you're decent. We need to get out of here before the cops show up. We've only had this much time because we're in the middle of BFE."

I snorted at her choice in words while Roman grabbed my pack from the bloodied ground before it could get ruined. I hadn't paid much attention to the bodies around us, and that wasn't going to change. I just wanted to be dressed and back on the road before anything else could go wrong.

Another minute later, I walked out the door and Embry pounced on me, sending both of us crashing back into Roman, who surprisingly didn't growl at my best friend.

Your bond to her is important, too. Roman's words sounded inside my head and nearly put me on my ass. He really was perfect.

Sam stalked toward me next, her hands clenched, and I worried she was going to punch me. Instead, she hugged me while pounding her fists against my spine. "Welcome back."

I coughed as she let go. "Thanks."

Vaughn had a black eye, blood all over his clothes, and a sneer on his face as he pointed at me. "I don't like you."

He stalked away before I could reply, and I considered chasing after him, but Roman held me back. "He's only upset because of what losing you meant for all of us. I wasn't the only one hurting, but he'll be okay. I'll talk to him once we get to Montana and he's had some time to process tonight."

Damn, I hoped so. Facing Demi with any tension in our core group wasn't good for anyone but her, and I refused to give that power-hungry psycho any sort of advantage against us.

24

CAIT

Due to the events at the motel, we were several hours behind schedule. Vaughn drove this time with Sam in the passenger seat, me and Roman in the middle, and Embry in the back. Roman held on to me while Embry played with my hair every five minutes to make sure I was really alive again.

I told them everything that had happened with the Moon Goddess, and nobody really had anything to say, which worried me even more. The longer I spoke, the more restrictive Roman's hands became around my waist.

"I mean, at least she apologized, right?" I said when there wasn't anything left to share.

"Apologized? She said I'm sorry for nearly getting us all killed, but did she really mean it? What do we truly know about our Moon Goddess other than she plays God with all of us? She decides when we meet our bonded. She decides who that mate is. She decides when we die and when we're reborn to go through the same shit all over again. What good is she really to us?" Vaughn spat, angrier than I'd ever seen him.

"Easy, Brother. I know tonight wasn't—" Roman tried saying, but he didn't get to finish before Vaughn jerked his head back, glaring at both of us.

"No, the two of you don't know anything. I would have died for the both of you tonight. I'm glad you're okay, but for a while, neither of you were. Don't forget how that makes the rest of us feel."

Shit, that cut deeper than I expected. I adored Vaughn. He was a dear friend and often the glue that kept our sanity together with his humor. Because of that, it was easy to forget that he had deeper feelings. Ones that mattered above all else.

I leaned forward and placed my hand over his forearm. "I'm sorry, Vaughn. I truly am for what you've gone through since my arrival, and most of all, I appreciate everything you have done for us. I never thought I would have a family again. Then, I met all of you, and I don't know what I would do without each of you."

Vaughn sniffled and shrugged. "It's fine. I was just overreacting."

"No, you weren't. You're allowed to be something other than happy all the time," I said.

He glanced back, offering me a small smile before wiping at his cheek.

Sam punched his thigh. "Are you crying?"

"No, it's your stench that's making my eyes water. Worse than an onion," Vaughn said, plugging his nose for full effect, then winked at me. "Thank you, Cait."

I gave his arm one more squeeze before leaning back into the bench seat. "No thanks needed."

The drive was much more enjoyable after that, and conversations flowed easier. Nothing like before when we'd all been pissy due to whatever Luna had done to us.

I'd avoided one particular topic, because it had felt too soon and I didn't want to upset Roman, but we were running out of time to chat before we arrived at our destination and met our first group of supernaturals.

I nudged him and spoke through our bond, so he didn't feel pressured to talk about it. *Luna said that you needed a push to become your true self which would also help me. Do you feel up for telling me what happened after… she took me?*

His chest rumbled and eyes focused on me. I placed my hand over his black t-shirt, trying to calm his racing heart.

"She didn't take you, she killed you, and I won't soon forget that," Roman said outside our bond, but none of the others seemed surprised by the random comment.

When he didn't elaborate, I took that to mean he wasn't ready to tell me what happened to him. While I was mildly disappointed, I understood. Our group was finally calm again and having to talk about me dying just hours after it happened wasn't going to help anyone stay in control.

Sparks of energy flickered off Roman as his ire rose.

Our bond strengthened, pulling us closer together as he tried to gain control of his emotions.

"I'm okay. I'm right here with you," I whispered to him.

"But you weren't. You were dead. Your heart had stopped beating and mine didn't, but I wanted it to."

I forced him to look at me. "I'm glad it didn't. Our story isn't over yet."

His forehead pressed against mine while he took a couple of deep breaths before speaking again. "I was furious beyond measure. I wanted to kill everything in my path and then I wanted to die. Everything I'd felt was amplified by your energy flowing through me, taunting me and begging to be set free. I half-shifted into my wolf, but not like normal. I was stronger than ever before and capable of more than I thought possible."

He paused, glancing out the window. Everyone else stayed quiet as we waited for him to continue. They might have seen Roman lose control, but hearing how he felt was completely different.

"The energy inside me… I don't know how you live with it. I couldn't control it when I saw the witches and warlocks. I unleashed something dangerous and when that should have scared me, it empowered me." His darkened eyes cast down at me. "I took the energy from their bodies. I squeezed their necks until they couldn't breathe and watched as the life left their bodies."

Well, that was something new.

Sam turned toward us, face solemn. "He also had the heat thing happening that you do when you run too hot with power. Plus, his height took on an extra foot or so of mass. Between the growth spurt and the power radiating from Roman, he was the freakiest and scariest dude I've ever seen, and that's saying something."

Sam's words had Roman fighting a smile. That little smirk told me everything would be okay. Eventually. We just had to find a way to keep putting one foot in front of the other.

"So, you turned into a super wolf on steroids and tried to get yourself killed. Big freaking deal. How about the guy that did everything to make sure he didn't lose his best friend and alpha?" Vaughn added. I could tell he was trying to keep his tone sharp, but there was still an underlying resentment in his words. Roman was still going to need to chat with him once we got out of the vehicle.

He really cares about you, I said to Roman through our bond.

Vaughn's the best beta I could have ever found.

Roman was right about that. We had to find a way to make Vaughn move past the evening's events. They were bringing him down more than the rest of us, and we had to figure out why just as soon as we could.

"So, when we get to Montana, we're meeting up with Zeke and then headed to the coven where Beatrix is?" I asked, trying to lessen the tension in the vehicle with a different topic.

Sam nodded. "I heard from Zeke. He's there already with his group. The guy who leads them is rich as hell. Old family money that his ancestors probably stole from humans and then got passed down to him.

Apparently, the cabin we're headed to is one of many houses the vampire owns."

Great. Hopefully the guy we needed to work with wasn't some rich prick who only cared about doing things that benefited himself. We couldn't handle anymore psychos.

///

WITHIN ANOTHER HOUR, IT WAS EARLY EVENING AND WE arrived in the middle-of-nowhere Montana at a structure I'd have never called a cabin. The home was two stories and made mostly of logs with stone accents along the first floor. There were huge windows that came out to a point in the front, and a porch that was big enough to hold the hot tub that was currently steaming under the awning.

"I want to live here," Embry sighed.

"Seriously. We need some upgrades to our cabins, Roman," Vaughn added, finally reminding me of his regular self.

Before Roman could respond, a man appeared at the bottom of the porch. He eyed each of us with cold, reddish-brown eyes. His skin appeared hard like stone with a light-tan color to it. His jaw was squared and hair dark with long strands that landed about halfway down his ears.

He wore black slacks and a charcoal long-sleeve dress shirt, but no tie. Though, the accessory wasn't needed to tell me this was Zeke's leader, the rich guy Sam was talking about before.

Roman stepped forward and I followed, staying at his side. "I'm Roman. It's good to officially meet you, Maciah."

The vampire leader nodded at Roman, reaching his hand out. "I'm not sure I'd say there is anything good about this meeting. I was intrigued enough to allow it to happen."

Oh, he wasn't going to play friendly. Interesting. He was definitely the alpha type with the way he kept all emotion from his face and looked down on the rest of us even though he and Roman were the same height.

Zeke joined us then. "Sorry I wasn't here to do introductions. I got held up." Zeke glared at Maciah, and something told me the leader had wanted to meet us on his own, but I had no idea why.

Roman accepted Maciah's offered handshake, then introduced the rest of us. "This is Cait, my mate. Behind us is Vaughn, my beta, and two of our best wolves, Sam and Embry."

Maciah stepped around Roman and grabbed Sam's hand. "You're the wolf who has had Zeke running around the world."

"I never asked for his help," she retorted.

Maciah chuckled, softening for the first time. "No, I don't imagine you did."

"How about we all head inside?" Zeke suggested.

The vampire leader turned away from Sam and led the way to the cabin. I shared a glance with Roman. This guy was weird. I wasn't liking it. If we were going to rely on someone for help, I didn't want the mystery that Maciah was throwing off.

Sam trusts Zeke, and I'm trying to do the same. Let's just see how this plays out, Roman said through our bond.

Fine, but if I see fangs, I can't be held responsible for my actions.

Roman's chuckle echoed through my mind. *Deal.*

We entered the log home. The second story was more of an open loft from what I could see. There was a large antler chandelier taking up the open space above us and enough furniture for a dozen people. There was a large sectional facing a wall that was made up of a massive stone fireplace. Opposite to that, there were individual chairs facing toward the windows.

Rugs lined the hardwood floors, directing the best path through the room, but Maciah ignored them and cut through to a dining room area. There was a stone-top table with wooden benches on each side. Our group gathered to one side and only sat once Zeke did. Maciah and Roman settled at the same time which had me smirking. Yep, these two were a lot alike.

Maciah nodded toward me. "So, you're the Lavender Wolf?"

"No, I'm Cait," I replied with a grin, then added, "but people who don't know me sometimes call me that."

He nodded. "I see. I know what Zeke has said, but I'd like to hear from you what it is that you all know about the Supernatural Council that the rest of us don't."

"There is a wolf-witch hybrid that has corrupted our leaders. She has convinced them to hunt down my mate if she doesn't turn herself in to them. There is no good reason for the council to require Cait's presence, so I can only assume this is an attempt to take her power. I'm not letting that happen," Roman said.

"How does this affect the rest of us?" Maciah asked.

Once again, Roman explained what could happen if my Luna Marked energy ended up in the wrong hands. The two alpha males went back and forth, and I appreciated that Maciah was asking so many questions, even if I didn't want to relive this conversation every time we encountered someone new.

Others moved through the cabin. I could see three vampires in the loft—two females and a male—and I caught shadows moving outside as I watched for anything that might mean trouble for us while Roman explained our story.

"I appreciate your candor with me, and I believe you're right about the council. The vampires have had new nests popping up where they don't belong and causing trouble for those of us who like living among the humans. I didn't think the issue laid outside of our race, but maybe it does," Maciah said.

"How many vampires do you have in your nest?" Vaughn asked.

Maciah smirked. "That's not shared information. Just know that there will be enough of us to assist you. When do you plan to approach the council?"

"Possibly tonight, or tomorrow at the latest. The witches are working on pinpointing the location in Washington, and other packs are gathering teams to meet us," Roman answered.

"I have something I want to show you if you're up for a run," Maciah said to Roman.

"Can my pack come?"

Maciah glanced at the rest of us. "It's better if just the two of us go. Too many might draw unwanted attention. They'll be safe here. Zeke will make sure of it."

"I'm not worried about their safety," Roman replied. "You're okay if I go for a bit?"

I was already pushing him to stand, even though I knew he was hoping I'd object. "We're good here, I promise."

His internal struggle at leaving my side so soon after I'd died again was clear as day through our bond. I opened my mind to him, so he could hear all of my thoughts. "You'll know the second something is wrong should anything happen."

Roman grunted, then kissed me. "I'll be back soon."

The two men left the cabin and Zeke grinned at us. "So, how's things?"

Sam huffed and stalked off, which surprised me. Vaughn moved to stare out the window as if he was expecting someone. Or maybe it was more because the beta wasn't okay with Roman going off on his own. Probably the latter.

Zeke slid down the bench until he was seated across from me and Embry. "Why is everyone so tense? I mean, besides the fact you're surrounded by vampires that I know none of you really care for."

"Things didn't go as smoothly as we'd hoped on the

drive up," I said, deciding to keep the details from the motel to ourselves.

Zeke glanced over his shoulder, staring at Sam who stood in front of the fireplace.

"You like her," I said.

The vampire's attention fell back to me just as Embry elbowed me in the ribs. "Vampires don't like wolves," she said.

I ignored her and waited for Zeke's response. He was the complete opposite of his leader. Zeke's dark-skinned face was welcoming. Well, besides his red eyes. His bright smile was what made me want to trust him most. At least when it wasn't covered in witch blood like the first time that I met him on the Australian beach.

"Sam reminds me of someone that was the center of my life until she died. I wasn't always a vampire, you know. I had a family before this life. A baby sister and parents who loved me. The fire inside Sam is a lot like what I'd seen in my little Mia. The way Sam talks about your pack made me miss my own family. Don't get me wrong. Maciah is a great leader, but there is something different about packs. You hold family above all else, and it reminds me of a time in my life I'll never get back."

Zeke's obsession with Sam wasn't just with the stunning wolf. He envied her. That was clear from his words.

"You've been helpful to our pack more than once, Zeke. Anytime you need a break from this part of our world, you're welcome in our pack," I said.

Embry coughed. "Umm, shouldn't you ask Roman about that first?"

"Am I not the alpha female? Last I checked, I was, and I'd assume that means I can invite whoever I want into our home as long as they mean no harm to our pack," I replied with a smirk.

"Oh, Cait. Have I told you lately how glad I am that I met you?" Embry laughed, and Zeke just shook his head.

"I won't be making any visits to your pack and upsetting anyone."

I shushed him. "The offer stands. Just give me a heads up before you decide to venture our way."

"That would be safest, wouldn't it?" He stood. "How about we get something to drink and wait for Maciah and Roman to return?"

I glanced at Embry, and she nodded. "Got anything good?" my best friend asked.

Zeke chuckled. "I think our definition of good might differ."

Embry grimaced. "I'm going with you to make sure I know what's in my drink."

I was certain the vampire knew better than to serve us blood, but her distraction gave me the chance to go chat with Vaughn. He was still standing at the window, and I approached him slowly. I'd wanted Roman to have this conversation since they were closer, but it couldn't be postponed any longer.

"How's it looking out there?" I asked Vaughn with my back to the window so I could see his face.

He nodded toward outside without looking at me. "Why don't you look yourself?"

I grabbed his arm, jerking him until he finally focused on my face. "I'm sorry, Vaughn." My words were simple, but my heart filled with emotions I hoped he could sense. I loved Vaughn as a brother I'd never had. I knew he was the glue that had kept all of us sane since my arrival at the pack. I needed him to know he was important to us.

"You have nothing to be sorry for, Cait." He'd used my name and not a nickname. I wasn't okay with that.

"Then, talk to me. *Please.*" I had no problems begging him. We needed him to get whatever was darkening his mood out of his system.

Vaughn sighed, rubbing his hands over his face before roughly shoving his hands into his pockets. "It's been the most stressful day of my life. I can normally deflect better than anyone, but you didn't see him. Roman was going to find a way to die, and then I was going to lose both of you. I know it wasn't either of your faults, but my wolf… he's losing his mind. Something still isn't right for him. He isn't settled. He senses something coming, but he isn't sure what. Like maybe it's something I should be happy about, but at the same time, it's going to change everything. I don't want anything to change."

I wrapped my arms around his waist, locking his arms down as I squeezed tight. "I'm so sorry, Vaughn. Maybe Roman can help you figure out things with your wolf when he's back. I'd try, but I'm new to all this and probably not much help."

Vaughn wiggled until he got his arms loose and hugged me back. "You coming to me and making me talk was more helpful than you realize. I'll be okay, Witchy Wolf. Whatever is coming our way, we can handle it."

"That's right. Remind your wolf that as long as we stick together, everything is going to be okay," I said, hoping like hell I wasn't lying to the beta.

CAIT

Almost thirty minutes had passed, and I still hadn't heard much from Roman other than things were fine. Apparently, Maciah was showing him some boundary lines in case we were around long enough to venture, and the vampire was still asking questions about me and the council.

"How much longer should they be?" Sam asked from the chair she'd taken over near the fireplace.

"I'm not sure," Zeke answered from next to me on the couch.

Embry's legs were propped over mine and nearly kicked me in the face when Vaughn's snarls echoed through the open room.

She was on her feet within a blink of an eye, and I was right behind her. We raced to stand beside Vaughn and found what had his wolf coming out.

Magic swirled in the sky, but there was something familiar about the energy. I closed my eyes and focused, letting Adira guide my thoughts.

Beatrix, we both thought at the same time.

"It's just Beatrix. Apparently, we're not going to her," I said, and the others calmed down only slightly before we made our way outside, just in time to see the portal open all the way and a group of witches stepped out onto the gravel driveway.

Vaughn moved forward, taking his position as leader in Roman's place. Though, as alpha female I was technically above him, I let the beta take control. He needed it more than me. After our conversation, I'd be keeping an extra eye on him to make sure his wolf didn't do anything crazy.

"Why are you here? We're supposed to be meeting at the coven," Vaughn said, voice laced with irritation. I didn't blame him, though. Any change to our plans without notice was cause for concern.

Beatrix flicked magic at him that had Vaughn's jaw locking down and his hands turning into fists. "Don't greet me that way ever again." Beatrix turned to me. "Where is your mate?"

"Right here," Roman's voice sounded from the trees. The sun had already fully set, so I couldn't see him right away, but I knew exactly where he would appear. I watched the shadows until his face came into view. He was still in one piece, and Maciah was right behind him.

"We have a problem," Beatrix said.

The portal closed beside her and the five other witches she arrived with. Some of them might have been warlocks, but I hadn't asked enough about the witches to know the difference. I assumed it was just their power levels that gave them different titles. Or maybe it was women that were only called witches and men were warlocks. Either way, I wasn't sensing any danger from the cloak-covered group.

"What problem would that be?" Roman asked, coming to my side. His hand found mine as we waited for Beatrix to respond.

"We can't break through the blocks on the Supernatural Council location. We've gotten close, but only within a fifty-mile radius. We either need more magic or we need more information."

"Did the location of the prison where Kye and Lillias were kept not help?" Roman asked.

She nodded. "But not enough. They burned the building down, which made it impossible to trace any of the magic used there back to the main structure where we can assume Demi is hiding."

"Can you use my energy to fuel your spell?" I asked.

Roman growled. "Not fucking happening."

"Why? If I can help, then I should."

He turned toward me. "We don't know what your energy will do to them. Not that we can't trust Beatrix, but my wolf doesn't believe it's a good idea and neither do I."

Adira, what do you think? I asked my own wolf.

Roman is probably overreacting, but he's not wrong. There are always risks when mixing magic from different races. Just like when you tried to break through the soul stone to get Sam free. You almost didn't make it back from that.

She was right. There had been a dose of darkness I'd taken on that made me crave power I didn't need. That might not happen to me again, but it could happen to Beatrix, and we didn't need another reckless witch on the loose.

"Okay, so what now?" I asked.

"Now, you hope I don't show you how insulted I felt when I heard there were groups of supernaturals gathering and I wasn't invited," a familiar woman's voice sounded from behind us.

I turned around to see Lucinda and Finn standing there, dressed in armor and ready to battle. The powerful fae sneered at Beatrix and pointed. "I'm still pissed at you."

"I gave you the spell you asked for," the witch replied.

Lucinda's iridescent hair floated around her, showing off the power we were all well aware she had.

"Where's your sidekick?" Beatrix asked Lucinda.

"Not that it's any of your business, but Neva went home to her people. You know, the elves, another race you've failed to include in this little party."

Roman stepped forward. "This isn't a party, Lucinda, and the elves haven't involved themselves in our world in decades. Much like the fae, and we only invited those we knew we could trust."

She smirked, flicking back her long strands. "I'm a changed woman. I saved your friend, didn't I?"

"If you want to help, we'll gladly accept the assistance," I said before Roman could insult the fae further. He might not like her, but I admired her lack of filter. We needed Lucinda, and I trusted Finn would keep her in line for the most part.

Finn grinned at me as if he'd known my thoughts. I smiled back.

"Well, then. Let's get to tracking down some power-hungry rulers. Seems to be what I'm best at," Lucinda said as she and Finn walked toward Beatrix and the group she'd brought with her.

Beatrix turned to Roman. "I'm going to take the offered help, and we'll be back with more information. I've sent some of my most powerful witches to your packs to get them here faster. We're running out of time."

"How do you know?" Roman asked.

"Call it intuition. We'll need to act just as soon as everyone has arrived."

Maciah hissed. "You've invited wolves and witches to my home?"

"Oh, calm down. This isn't your primary home. Don't try and act like this is some inconvenience to you," Beatrix said before turning her back on the vampire.

She was either extremely brave or stupid. Possibly a touch of both.

Maciah sneered at Zeke, who mouthed an apology as his leader stalked back toward the cabin. Something told me that Maciah had been coerced into helping us and was becoming less and less happy about it as time passed.

"How far out did you guys go?" I asked Roman as Lucinda and Finn disappeared with Beatrix and her witches.

"To a mountain top that showed a lot of the valley

around us. After I last checked in with you, he also told me that he doesn't want to fight against our leaders. That he has been tracking a problem within the vampires and doesn't need anything to get in the way of that focus, but Zeke convinced him that if they didn't help, the council issues could be more of a problem than this fight," Roman said.

"So, is he in or not?" Vaughn asked.

"He'll do whatever it takes to set things right in the supernatural world. Even if he complains the whole time. Maybe we're all worried for no reason. Maybe the council is just waiting for help to arrive and stop Demi."

Roman didn't sound convinced of his own words, but it was a nice thought. More likely, there were some council members who didn't need to be magically strong armed into doing what the hybrid wanted. As it had been pointed out several times over, power made people do stupid shit all the time.

Roman's fingers wrapped around my hand, and energy sparked between us.

"The two of you are different. I was going to say something before, but it didn't seem like the time," Zeke said, gesturing between Roman and I.

Neither of us responded to Zeke and he took the hint. "Okay, then. I'll leave you all out here to do whatever it is you'd like to do without my presence."

Nobody objected and I felt somewhat bad. Zeke was only trying to be helpful, but some things needed to stay within our pack for as long as possible.

"Now that he mentioned it, we really should figure

out what the changes between the two of you mean," Vaughn said once it was just the five of us.

"I agree, and it will keep us busy until Beatrix and Lucinda return," Embry said.

Sam eyed the two of us. "Are you sure it's a good idea to do so here?"

"I'd say it's fine, but if anything goes wrong, I don't want to piss off the vampires. We're probably better off somewhere we can't cause damage to someone's home. I saw a spot when I ran up the mountain with Maciah that should work to test things out. We'll head there," Roman answered.

Can we shift? Adira asked.

Of course. Given everything we'd been through in the last day, I wouldn't deny my wolf.

Without telling the others, I transformed into my wolf. It was the first time since I'd come back from wherever the Moon Goddess lived. Shifting had already been easy for me, but the change this time was not only smooth but energizing. My heart pumped faster, and my skin tingled with energy even after we were covered with fur.

Adira stretched out and tilted our head to the bright moon sky. The new moon would have been better for this task, but a full moon would still give us a boost.

Do you feel any different? I asked her since I had experienced differences already.

I'm in more control of our power. We're not purple, and it's not causing me an extra effort to keep the magic contained.

I turned toward Roman who still hadn't shifted to

his wolf form, and we prowled toward him. "Beautiful as ever," he said reverently.

Adira nuzzled him when he lowered to the ground, and then she whimpered. "I know, girl. I'm shifting and you can have your wolf." Roman grinned before standing and stepping back. Within seconds, he was on all four and our wolves practically mauled each other.

We didn't let them run together enough, something that would change just as soon as we got home.

Embry, Sam, and Vaughn took off ahead of us while our wolves took an extra few minutes to solidify their bond. It was amazing the difference in strength we experienced just from spending a moment alone with our mate.

Our muscles hardened, ready for whatever we needed to face. Our vision improved, which seemed impossible because it was already impeccable. Our sense of smell also increased—something I could have done without.

Vampires had an interesting scent I hadn't picked up in my human form. It was dry and stale. Not pungent, but not pleasant either. Nothing like the stench from a dead one.

It's their decaying bodies. If they don't drink blood, they'll slowly and torturously shrivel into nothing, Adira said.

Well, that was disgusting to picture.

Roman's wolf seemed bigger than I was used to as well. I was glad we were taking some time away to figure out what changes we'd both been through. While the events we had to go through to receive said changes weren't pleasant, I was glad they happened before we had to face Demi.

We caught up with the others and he took the lead, showing us the way to the spot he'd seen on the climb up earlier. The steep incline of the mountain had our blood pumping and adrenaline moving by the time we reached the turn-off.

Embry shifted back first as I stood next to Roman in our wolf forms. "Holy hell. You guys are freaky next to each other."

Roman and I turned toward one another. He was glowing a deep purple color with flickers of silver sparking off his now-charcoal coat that used to be more neutral grey. His fur was longer as well. Not like Adira's, but still at least an inch or two longer than before.

Our wolves nodded at each other, and we shifted back. Roman's hands held on to my shoulders once we were both human. "Your ebony wolf is something else."

"What was different besides the color?" I asked.

Sam butted in. "Both of you had power pouring from your wolves, and you're each bigger than you were before, but that's not where I think you're going to find your biggest changes. When Roman was acting like he'd overdosed on steroids at the motel, his half-shift was unlike anything I'd ever seen before. I'd like to see what happens when both of you do that."

Roman grabbed my hand, and we faced each other. I'd done partial shifts before, but they weren't my favorite. I didn't like the extra concentration they took given I already had the excess energy to control, but Adira didn't seem worried about the task at hand.

"Ready?" Roman asked, and I nodded.

I drew on Adira's power, picturing her claws and canines and the physical strength she provided me in our wolf form. I held on to those thoughts until I felt the bite of my teeth elongating and the lengthening of my nails.

Roman did the same, but this time his eyes also changed, and we both appeared to be growing in height. My hips ached from the body changes, but the pain was soon forgotten as Roman's arms started sprouting fur, causing me to see that mine were as well.

"I don't think I'll ever get used to that," Embry muttered, and I turned toward her. She was normally taller than me, but I was now looking down on my best friend.

"I think I could," I replied, then gasped when my voice sounded manly.

"It's your vocal cords being stretched," Roman said in a much deeper tone as well.

I stepped closer to him, drawn to the magic he was emitting. "You're more like me than ever before. Is it weird?"

He shook his head. "Just different. Close your eyes and draw out your power, like when you used to meditate in the fields at the pack."

I did as he suggested. My skin warmed, and sparks of energy pricked at my nerves, but they were full of life and not painful.

My eyes opened to see Roman was emitting the

same friction energy I was. Our hands were still clasped together, so the magic was flowing freely between the two of us and my chest swelled with... I wasn't sure what exactly.

Even though I'd accepted my place within the pack, I'd been the constant source of problems for those around me. I was different from every wolf. While I knew there were enough people that cared about me, being different wasn't always comforting.

But seeing Roman just like me, it filled me with a peace I didn't know I was missing. My hand cupped his cheek as I pulled him closer. Our bond was pulsing through my veins, alive and well and more perfect than ever before.

Love. There was nothing more powerful than what we shared between the two of us.

Roman pressed his lips to mine, and an explosion of power lit up around us as the heat coating our skin intensified.

Vaughn, Embry, and Sam shouted at us, but there was nothing they could do to separate me from Roman in that moment. The closer we got, the more magic began to swirl around us, vibrating with deep purple and silver colors.

"I think we're scaring them," Roman murmured against my lips.

"They'll be fine," I replied as a howl that didn't belong to any of our wolves cut through the night sky.

"Perry and his pack have arrived, which means ours shouldn't be far behind," Roman said, but still didn't pull away from me.

We took another minute, heads pressed together and eyes closed. We might not have done anything overly impressive, but I knew without a doubt that Roman and I were capable of anything as long as we stayed together. Standing with him under the light of the moon with our raw energy binding us together, there was no denying that we were made for each other.

"Let's go greet the new arrivals and hope Lucinda was more helpful than harmful," Roman said as we parted.

The loss of connection hit me square in the chest as we returned to our human forms. I still felt our bond alive and well within, but whatever we'd just done, there was nothing else like it.

"I like Lucinda. You shouldn't assume the worst from her," I said.

Roman grunted in reply as we went to rejoin the others. "Was that what you were hoping for?" I asked Sam.

She grinned at me. "Even better. You nearly burned Embry's hair off with the amount of magic that went flying when the two of you focused on each other."

"I don't see how that will be helpful if we're in the middle of a battle, though," Roman said, making a good point.

Another howl sounded, and Vaughn tensed. I went to him, grabbing on to his arm. "Is your wolf okay?"

Vaughn's head shook, and he started to vibrate. Roman stepped in, nudging me away in case Vaughn lost control.

"Talk to us, Vaughn," Roman said with authority.

Vaughn's head kept shaking, and his face paled. "I don't understand what's happening. My wolf insists we get back to the others, but he's…"

Our beta didn't get to finish his sentence as he stepped away from Roman and lurched forward, shifting into his wolf without warning.

"Is someone here that shouldn't be?" Embry asked.

"I'm not sure, but we're about to find out," Roman answered.

We all shifted, and Vaughn's wolf howled back to the arriving pack. The sound pierced my heart. Something was wrong with our friend, and we needed to sort it out before we left this mountain.

26

ROMAN

Vaughn was rarely the most studious beta, but that made him perfect for our pack; he had great instincts and was never out of control like he'd been since the motel. I'd heard the conversation he had with Cait, but I hadn't gotten a chance to speak with him myself. I had hoped his wolf's concerns were just from stress, but as we raced down the mountain after him, my chest tightened with worry for my friend.

I sped up, having to tap into my new energy in order to pass Vaughn so that I could see what had his wolf going so crazy before he did. Maybe there would be something I could do to calm him.

Cait was right at my side as we arrived at the bottom of the mountain. Perry was standing with his mate and a few others around him. Everything seemed okay with them, so I wasn't sure what all the howling had been about.

Cait and I shifted to our human forms and greeted

Perry. "How was your trip over?" I asked, but before the other alpha could answer, Vaughn's wolf stumbled out of the trees.

His head was lowered, and whimpers sounded from the wolf. I moved toward him, but he snarled at me.

Vaughn, you need to stop right now, I demanded through our pack connection.

I can't. I need her.

Her?

I finally understand why. Vaughn's voice had lost its earlier panic. He was in awe as he passed me and headed for Perry's mate. No, not his mate, the young woman behind them.

She pushed between Perry and Silvie, and I knew with one look at her eyes that she was Perry's daughter. I hadn't seen her in years, and she was no longer the little girl in pigtails that I remembered. Now, she was only a head's length shorter than her father with short coffee-colored hair and deep amber eyes that widened as my beta's wolf prowled toward her.

Everything clicked into place as I continued to glance between the two shifters. I understood why my beta had been so worried about a coming change.

Vaughn changed to his human form when he was several feet away from the crowd, then quickly closed the distance between him and Perry's daughter Kelly.

"Mate," Vaughn purred as he fell to his knees.

"Get up," she hissed as her cheeks turned red.

Vaughn grabbed her hands with both of his. "I've waited so long for you." He bowed his head against her stomach while she continued to try to get him to stand, not at all okay with the scene he was causing.

"She's his mate?" Cait asked in astonishment.

"Appears so," I answered, casting a glance at Perry, who didn't seem pleased that his little girl was no longer his.

"She looks like she wants to kill him," Cait said, worry lacing her words.

I slipped my arm around her. "They'll be just fine."

"Vaughn, please get up," Kelly pleaded once again, and this time my beta finally snapped out of his lovestruck stupor.

Wolves murmured and snickered around them, but Vaughn paid them no attention. He only had eyes for one woman, and she was softening to him by the second. They might be strangers, but the power of a true mate bond between two people who understood the magic was unlike anything else in the world.

I'm sorry you didn't have that moment with me, Cait said through our bond.

I stroked her cheek. *We had it in our own way, when the time was right for both of us.*

She smiled up at me, and it was hard to look away from her eyes so full of love, but we still had business to attend to.

"Perry, Silvie. How about we chat inside?" I said, hoping to give Vaughn and Kelly a minute of privacy while we got caught up.

Perry growled, and Silvie punched his chest. "Our daughter is a grown woman. Get inside. Now."

Silvie's words left no room for debate, and Perry turned for the cabin without another objection.

I passed by Vaughn and placed my hand on his shoulder. "Take all the time you need before you two join us."

He sneered at my closeness to his mate but recovered quickly before nodding in response. Now that the attention was mostly off of them, Kelly was staring at Vaughn as if her world began and ended with him. I didn't expect to see them again until it was time to go.

Embry and Sam were right behind us and followed Cait and me inside. Most of the other wolves that had arrived with Perry dispersed into the trees. I didn't know the exact count, but as we walked closer to the cabin, I saw nearly twenty shifters, which made me happy.

If each alpha brought that many to stand with us, we'd have well over two-hundred wolves, plus the vampires and witches—and possibly fae unless it was just Lucinda and Finn joining us.

The fae had recently been through their own battles, so having just the two of them was more than I expected. Cait was right. I judged Lucinda based on her past behaviors. Given all she'd done for Fae Islands, I could probably lighten up on my view of her. I didn't know her well enough to judge, and Cait had reminded me of that.

When we entered the cabin, the previously open living room seemed much smaller with several vampires and nearly a dozen shifters inside.

Maciah stood uncomfortably near the fireplace with Zeke at his side and a woman I didn't recognize that had long brunette hair with golden highlights. Her skin was fair, making me think she wasn't a mature enough vampire to be in the sun yet, but if she was standing by Maciah's side, maybe that wasn't the case. She held a wine glass filled with crimson liquid I tried to pretend wasn't blood and oddly enough had her pinky out, as if she was British royalty.

"Has Beatrix or Lucinda been back yet?" I asked Maciah.

"No, and a gathering of this many supernaturals isn't going to go unnoticed. If they don't find the location of the council soon, I expect we'll be having visitors of our own before we get the chance to leave," Maciah answered with a bite of annoyance to his words.

He was either very good at pretending not to care, or he'd owed Zeke a big favor that had been cashed in on in order for the vampire to stand with us. Either way, I was annoyed with his attitude toward the situation.

"If you can't handle what you've signed up for, we'll gladly leave," I challenged.

Maciah flashed his fangs at me. "I can handle whatever comes my way. I just wasn't made aware that my home would be the meeting place for your event."

Okay, he had a point. The original plan had been to meet at a coven near here, but Beatrix changed that by showing up.

I nodded in understanding, but I didn't apologize. He still didn't have to be a dick about the unexpected company.

"Did we miss anything good besides the two wolves sucking face outside?" Lucinda said as she stormed through the doorway.

"I told you not to say anything," Finn snapped.

"Yeah, well, you should have known better."

He narrowed his eyes at her. "We had an agreement."

Lucinda's hard eyes softened, something I never would have expected from the obnoxious woman. "I'm sorry, Finnigan."

We all watched in amazement as Lucinda took Finn's hand and quieted. She really had changed from the killer fae I'd heard stories of.

I told you so, Cait said through our bond. She was getting better at picking up my thoughts and emotions, something I thought might bother me, but I'd found I rather enjoyed how much closer it brought us together.

Beatrix entered the cabin. There were dark circles beneath her eyes that hadn't been there before she'd left earlier and deeper wrinkles around her face. Whatever she and Lucinda had done had taken more out of the witch than she'd been prepared for.

"We have the location, but it's likely that they know we broke through the magic concealing the stronghold. This won't be a surprise attack," Beatrix said.

"We're hoping it doesn't come to a full-on attack. If we can stop Demi first, then it should remove the influence she has over the council members," I said.

"That's wishful thinking, Alpha Wolf." Beatrix sighed and headed back outside.

She might be right, but I'd keep hoping for anything other than a battle that could cost any more lives.

"Then, we leave as soon as the other packs get here?" Perry asked.

"Beatrix reached out to her coven retrieving the rest of your wolves. They're arriving about ten miles from the council right about... now," Lucinda said.

"She sent my pack to an unknown location without speaking to me about it?" I asked with a snarl.

Lucinda shrugged. "Seems so."

After Cait was safe, I was never dealing with other supernaturals again.

Cait tugged on my arm. "Let's go outside to get Vaughn and Kelly, so we can leave. Lucinda can transport us to the location, right?"

The fae winked at my mate. "For you? Sure, we can handle that."

I took a deep breath and looked back at Maciah. "You're still coming with us, right?"

He nodded toward the woman, not actually answering my question. "Rachel, go gather the others. We'll be leaving with the witches."

We could easily remove his head from his shoulders, my wolf suggested.

It was a nice thought, but not one we could act on. Maciah was the least of our problems at the moment.

Beatrix was standing in a circle with her witches, their arms draped over each other's shoulders and chanting softly. Beatrix was the only one not wearing a black cloak, and I briefly wondered why before deciding I didn't care.

Vaughn and Kelly walked toward us wearing matching smiles and holding hands. I wanted to be happy for him, but I was too worried about my wolves to do so. "We need to head out. Are you good to come with us?" I asked Vaughn, needing to know that finding his mate hadn't messed with his head.

"I'm good, Alpha. Better than good, in fact," Vaughn replied, the spark back in his eyes that had been missing.

Lucinda and Finn appeared behind us. "Ready, Wolves?"

"We're going with her?" Vaughn asked, astonishment coating his words.

"Beatrix seems a little preoccupied, and we need to move fast," I replied.

Cait grabbed on to Lucinda's outreached arm, and I followed her movements. Finn had Sam and Embry while Vaughn and Kelly seemed torn on what to do.

"Follow with Perry once his pack is ready. We'll see you soon," I said, saving him the choice of leaving his mate, who didn't want to leave her parents. That fact made me realize there was a decent chance that I'd be replacing my beta soon. Something I never wanted to do, but that was a problem we would figure out later.

My eyes met Cait's. It seemed like we'd been waiting months for this moment, and yet everything was happening so fast.

Are you okay? she asked.

I squeezed her hand with the one not holding on to Lucinda. *I'm fine.*

"Whatever you do, don't throw up on me," Lucinda

warned just before the ground disappeared from underneath my feet.

Within two seconds, we were surrounded by different trees and early snowfall that was already on the ground in this part of Washington.

"Welcome to the Canadian border," Lucinda announced as Finn appeared with Embry and Sam.

Cait went to them, a little unsteady on her feet, but overall, she seemed fine.

Murmurs sounded beyond the trees. "We need to go check on the others," I said.

Without hesitation, Cait, Sam, and Embry followed the direction of the voices while Lucinda and Finn stayed behind, which was fine by me. Flakes of snow began to fall around us, but thanks to my wolf, my body acclimated to the low temperatures.

The night sky was covered in clouds and the wind was blowing, but the tall evergreen trees kept the impact from cutting through us as we walked through the darkened forest.

The other packs came into view finally and my stress levels spiked. There were dozens of shifters standing around, laughing and chatting freely. These wolves were happy and content, and nothing in their packs had been going wrong until we asked for their help.

They had a choice. They know the risks of being here, Cait said through our bond.

But we convinced them, I replied.

We merely warned them of a future nobody wants. One

where a powerful hybrid could rain havoc on the other packs if she isn't stopped.

Cait was right, but so was I. We'd practically begged the other packs for help, knowing that our pack would have never stood a chance against the Supernatural Council guards and hunters along with Demi.

We'd needed these wolves, and not all of them would be making it home after tonight.

I shook off the guilt as Collin approached me. He was one of the higher-ranking shifters in Vaughn's Super Squad.

"Was the trip over okay?" I asked him as we shook hands.

His grey eyes met mine as he nodded. "Everything went just as planned besides where we arrived at. Where is Vaughn?"

"He's coming with the others that were at the vampire house with us. He finally met his match," I said, unable to hold my grin back. I really was happy for my beta.

"A mate for Vaughn, huh? Is it wrong that I feel slightly bad for her?" Collin laughed.

"Not in the least." I wanted to ask him how he felt about taking over as beta for Vaughn, but I wouldn't know if Collin had the beta gene in him until Vaughn made his decision. Only then would our wolf magic show who would make good candidates for a replacement. A wolf was either born to lead, or they weren't. Only time would tell if Collin was.

Lucinda and Finn broke through the tree lines with dozens more wolves behind them. The others had finally shown up, and there was no more time to wait around. The council would know we were there, and I'd rather be making the first move in this unknown territory.

I looked for my mother who would have arrived when Collin did. I didn't see her until I turned around. She was already with Cait, Sam, and Embry, along with Embry's parents. I went to Cait's side and took her hand. Our bond flared to life without notice, causing my chest to swell and energy to race along my skin.

Looking down at my mate, her eyes glowed with raw power, and she was growing taller by the second. I pulled her closer to me, holding her face between my hands. "Are you ready for this?"

She nodded. "As long as we're together, nothing can stop us."

Gods, I hoped her words were true. I pressed my lips to Cait's as her arms wrapped around my neck tightly. Strength filled me as we took a moment to ourselves, and she stayed with me even after we pulled apart.

Beatrix approached us. The dark circles under her eyes were gone, along with most of the wrinkles I was used to seeing on her aging face. "I don't usually like to be wrong about things, but I'm glad I was wrong about the two of you. Everyone is here and ready to follow you. The stronghold is only a few more miles east of us."

Vaughn also joined us with Kelly at his side. "We're ready to stand by your side."

"Then, let's go," I said.

There was nothing else holding us back. We'd done everything we could to prepare for whatever came next. Everything else was left to fate. Normally, that would leave me with a sense of peace, but nothing of the sort filtered through me as we took the first steps toward the Supernatural Council fortress.

27

CAIT

Magic flowed through me as we raced through the forest with our pack and the others at our side. The more connected to Roman I became, the clearer I saw my path.

We had to find Demi first. I had to be the one to stop her with Roman at my side. This was something we'd do together. That much was clear from my visit with the Moon Goddess.

I know what we have to do, Adira said.

And that is?

With memories back that I didn't know were missing, I've seen war unlike anything you could comprehend. Our supernatural world has existed for centuries, and there were times when every creature was out for themselves. Races didn't stick together. Individuals only looked out for themselves.

What does that have to do with the now? I asked.

I'm not positive. All I have is my instinct to go by, but we're going to have to do something Roman won't like.

Should I know what this something is now, or wait for later?

She sighed. *With how close you and Roman have bonded since you've come back to life again, I would say the plan is more likely to succeed if you don't know it ahead of time.*

As much as that worried me, I trusted Adira with my life, because it was hers as well. We were one, and she'd lived many more lives than me. Whatever we needed to do—no matter the cost—we'd find a way.

Will Roman be part of the plan? I asked her.

He'll be the most important piece.

Something twisted in my heart. I wanted to ask more, but as the stone walls of the council stronghold came into view, I sensed Adira's presence slip away.

"Is everything okay? Adira blocked me out," Roman said once my conversation ended.

"Yep. She was just giving me an unnecessary pep talk."

Roman's blue eyes appraised me. He wasn't buying my words, but he also didn't push as we slowed.

"Look," Embry said from my other side.

Guards were posted along the top of the stone walls surrounding the structure we needed to get to. I closed my eyes, trying to get a feel for what kind of barriers we might be up against, but there was no resistance as I sent a wave of my energy out into the open.

When I reopened my eyes, the guards were jumping from their positions, landing inside the compound instead of coming toward us.

"They had the perfect vantage point. Why would they jump down?" I asked.

"They either want us to think they're scared by the amount of people with us, or what lies behind those walls is more powerful than whatever they could attack us with from above," Roman answered.

His words didn't make me feel any better, but I also refused to feel doubt. We had to remain positive for as long as possible. The moment we had no faith in ourselves would be the moment we lost.

Lucinda and Finn appeared in front of us. "The thing I've learned about going into battle is you can't be afraid to just charge in. The longer you wait, the more time your enemy has to prepare for your death," Lucinda said.

"She's not wrong, but we'll follow your lead. This is your fight. We're only here to make sure we don't have another tyrant succeed at taking power that doesn't belong to them," Finn added.

Roman and I shared a glance before turning to take in the waiting group behind us. "Nobody has come out to talk to us. I don't think they're going to," he said.

"No, probably not," I replied. Believing in that scenario had only been wishful thinking.

We were both pulsing with a power that was begging to be released. I wasn't afraid of attacking instead of waiting anything else out.

"Kelly, can you send word to your father asking him to pass along a message to the other alphas?" Roman asked.

She nodded. "Of course."

"Tell him that we are going to enter the stronghold. We're not waiting for the council to come to us. Cait isn't handing herself over to them. We're prepared for a fight. The others can follow us if they choose," Roman said.

Beatrix pushed through the shifters around us. "The witches won't be retreating, no matter which way this goes."

Her words didn't surprise me. They'd be wanting the magic that was about to be released into the world. Though, the other packs didn't have the same motivation. Sure, they'd come this far with us, but we'd said all along that we hoped there wouldn't be a fight.

Given the guards disappeared and nobody had come out, there was no denying what was coming next.

"Message sent. Dad will tell the other alphas. He said our pack isn't going anywhere until you do," Kelly replied.

Roman nodded and squeezed my hand before meeting my eyes. *I love you.*

Forever and always, I replied.

With those final words, we took the first steps toward the stronghold.

Every foot forward had our speed increasing until we were running at full speed. I watched the walls for any sign of attack, but nothing happened.

We were headed straight for two twenty-foot-tall wooden doors that were already cracked open.

Are you sure we're doing the right thing? I asked Adira.

Absolutely.

Damn, I sure hoped so.

Sam, Embry, Vaughn, and Kelly moved around the rest of us to push open the doors all the way. I tensed, hoping there wasn't a trap right at the entrance, but it wasn't until the doors were shoved aside that we saw what was waiting for us.

I didn't think the council had this many guards, I said to Roman.

They didn't.

Row after row of supernaturals waited for us, each of them with the same glazed look in their eyes. They either held weapons or were already shifted into their predator forms. They also seemed frozen in place, waiting to be woken up from whatever stupor they'd been stuck in.

The stronghold was probably a mile wide and went beyond what I could see from where we stood. They'd been building this mini city for decades, from what I'd learned before arriving. There were streets made from cobblestone clearly marked with aging signs I couldn't read clearly and buildings running along them. Old metal lamp posts provided the only light down the roads, and I followed them until setting my sights on the tallest structure around. There was a large bell in a tower at the center, along with several more towers where I could see guards posted.

"That's where Demi is going to be," I said as I recalled the image of the hybrid Kye and Lillias had drawn for us before we left that I'd made sure was etched into my memory.

Long auburn hair, black-as-night eyes, tall slender body, and crimson lips. As long as she hadn't glamoured herself, the hybrid should stand out among the mindless guards we were facing.

The bell I had seen chimed, the sound growing in volume as it continued to swing back and forth.

"Attack!" a guard shouted from the opposing crowd, and the others began to move forward. The haze over their eyes was still present, and each incoming supernatural was emitting hate like nothing I'd ever seen before.

"Try not to kill them all. They're under *her* influence," I yelled as I raised my hands toward an incoming attacker that Roman got to first, shoving him a good twenty-feet back. The fact that Roman hadn't ripped the guy's head off told me he agreed with my previous words. These people didn't know what they were doing. They didn't deserve to die if there was any other choice.

Ramona, Sam, and Embry shifted next, biting legs and tearing out muscles of the mindless guards. Even though the attackers weren't in control of their thoughts, they still moved with precision, and I was glad to see three of the women I loved most in this world sticking together, watching each other's backs.

Adira's presence pushed to the surface, but she didn't want full control. We completed the half-shift we'd practiced before, and Roman did the same thing. Our energy grew into a wall around us that guards tried to break through, but they yelped in pain as they made contact with the barrier.

"We need to find Demi," Roman said, his voice rough. "If we don't soon, I'm going to start killing people."

"Go. We can handle this group," Vaughn said from

next to us, and I was surprised to see Kelly slamming a witch onto her back with what seemed like little effort.

I glanced back and not as many wolves as we'd arrived with were present, but there were still enough. The vampires were just coming in and disappeared before my eyes, moving too fast to be seen. I hoped they'd gotten the memo we weren't here to murder every guard...

Roman grabbed my hand, pulling me toward the main building with the echoing bell. "You're right. Demi's going to be waiting for us there. We need to hurry."

We pushed through the fighting crowds, surprised that more of the guards didn't try to attack us.

There is probably a reason for that, Adira said.

Demi wants us to find her.

That's most likely.

"She has been luring me in from the beginning. We're walking right into whatever she has waiting for us," I said to Roman as our destination came into view.

"Do you want to go back?" he asked with no judgement in his tone.

"Absolutely not."

"Then, what does it matter?"

He was right. It didn't matter what we knew or what Demi had planned. We were here to stop her. We'd either succeed or we wouldn't. There were no other options—no running from the dark magic I could now sense pulsing from the structure before us.

The energy reminded me of the soul stone in

Australia. Goosebumps crawled along my arms, and I wanted to reach out and take the magic for myself.

A group of wolves howled from behind us. I recognized Collin and some of the other Super Squad members. They'd followed us, probably at the insistence of Vaughn. I wanted to tell them to go back, that this wasn't their fight, but we were pack. When one of us was threatened, we all were. I understood that better than ever as their unified emotions flooded into me, offering me their support.

"You took long enough to get here," Demi's voice resounded around us, one I recognized from the conversation I'd overheard in West Texas. She really had been pulling the strings all this time.

I turned toward the sound, but I didn't see her.

"I made you who you are, Cait. Yet, you've brought an army to harm me. Where's the gratitude for my efforts?" she asked, her voice moving around us instead of staying in one spot.

"Oh, I have plenty of gratitude. Why don't you quit hiding so I can show you?" I replied.

She hummed, being overly dramatic. She was procrastinating and I wanted to know why.

Roman's grip on my hand tightened. *She's up to something,* he said through our bond.

I agreed with him, but there wasn't anything we could do that didn't put us at a disadvantage.

Remember, it's always best to let your opponent show their hand first. Even if that means taking a couple painful hits, Adira said.

I grimaced. A couple hits from a powerful hybrid didn't sound the same as all the times before.

A wave of dark magic blasted over us. Our pack wolves whimpered under the pressure of the unknown magic but stayed their ground.

I did the first thing I could think of, even if it was a terrible idea, and absorbed the energy that clung to my skin. In small amounts, I could handle foreign magic, but there was nothing minuscule about the power I was taking in.

Careful, Roman warned me.

I just wanted a taste in hopes of figuring out what we were really up against.

"You know if I thought I could trust you, I'd share the powers I've acquired over the years with you, Cait. But I doubt that you'd return the favor and that's just selfish behavior that I won't put up with," Demi called out.

"And here I thought we could be friends," I retorted with a roll of my eyes, adjusting to the foreign magic I'd taken in until I felt like I was going to vomit.

Expel the energy, Adira demanded, and I did so without question, pushing the unwanted force out from my palms and letting it wander into the sky. Nothing about Demi's power made me stronger, and I'd need to avoid it as best I could.

Doors banged against the brick of the main building and a shadowy form exited onto the stairs. Flares of red peeked through the swirls, climbing higher into the sky, and more guards trickled out behind what I could only assume was Demi.

Roman and I stood on the cobbled road with our wolves behind us, facing the wide stairs, waiting for Demi's next move. One that was sure to hurt, but Adira was right. We needed to know how she fought before we could best her.

We stood our ground, waiting out the theatrics of the hybrid. The shadows around her calmed and began growing smaller, as if she was sucking them back into herself. Her auburn hair appeared first, followed by blood-stained lips.

She drinks the blood of those she draws power from. I can smell it on her, Adira said.

The hell? That was… disturbing to say the least.

Demi wore a one-piece dark-red suit that matched her hair perfectly. Her hair fell in waves around her shoulders, and her black eyes glinted under the light of the moon.

Not moving to act against her was painful, but not nearly as much as the dark magic that unexpectedly shot from her hands at me and Roman.

My muscles seized as we fought off her power and she stalked closer, a smirk plastered to her face and claws out as she reached for me.

"I will get what I want," she taunted before gripping my neck, cutting off my air supply.

Okay, this wasn't what I had in mind when I agreed to let Demi get the first couple of strikes in before I made my move. She was literally sucking the life out of me, and Roman was paralyzed beside me. The barriers around us that normally burned our opponents didn't seem to bother Demi in the least.

Our wolves attacked then, but Demi snapped two fingers on her free hand, and an opaque shield appeared around us, blocking anyone else from interfering.

My mark pulsed along my wrist, burning my forearm like never before. No matter how it hurt, I drew on the energy growing up my arm. My core filled with heat, and I pushed back on the dark magic pressing down on me.

Smoke rose around my neck and Demi hissed. I was finally hurting her, but she wasn't letting up. The harder I fought back, the less her initial hit held me back. My arms could move, and my nails were already claws that I used to dig into her ribs.

Demi punched me in the stomach, causing even more breath to escape me—breath I didn't have to lose.

I struggled to take in air as she kept her hold on me. I could hear the howl of wolves all around us, but they weren't getting through.

A snarling growl echoed within the barrier—one I was intimately familiar with.

Roman had shifted to his wolf form and launched himself at Demi. She easily backhanded him, sending my mate crashing to the ground.

"Nobody is going to save you."

My eyes moved beyond Demi's face and toward Roman's wolf. He wasn't moving and wasn't responding to my pleas through our bond.

"You hurt my mate." The words left my mouth with no emotion as I did exactly what Roman wouldn't want me to do, and something I'd just told myself I shouldn't do.

I opened myself up to the dark magic Demi was wielding. I called the power to me, reversing the energy she was taking from me. I couldn't see any other way to get her off me.

Her soulless eyes widened as she realized what I was doing. She fought back, and the tug for power began. A war I didn't intend on losing.

I called on my pack. The barrier around us might not be allowing anyone in, but it didn't stop the connection I had to the wolves around us. I took what I could from the shifters I made a vow to protect. Not enough that their energy would be too drained to keep fighting, but a little from each one was more than enough.

Demi's hold loosened on me as I grew stronger while doing my best to ignore the underlying nausea. With renewed strength, I shoved her back and she stumbled to the ground just a few feet from me. I glanced at Roman's wolf again. I could see the rise and fall of his chest, which was enough for the moment, even if I couldn't hear him through our bond.

My eyes went back to Demi. Her head was down, and her hair created a curtain over her face. I reached down and grabbed her shoulders, hauling her up until our faces were level.

I slammed my head into hers, soaking up the support of the pack as I began to let go of the dark magic before it weakened me. My skin hummed with power that needed to be let loose, and I knew exactly where I was going to send the energy.

Grabbing the front of Demi's outfit, I punched her with my glowing fist, leaving burn marks on her face with every hit I made. She didn't fight back, which began to worry me. Instead of continuing to pummel her, I tilted her head up, moving it side-to-side until I could see her eyes.

There was a grin on her face that shouldn't have been there, considering how many times I'd hit her. "Thank you for doing exactly what I wanted." Demi's arms came up before crashing down onto mine and breaking the hold I'd had on her. She grabbed hold of both my shoulders, claws locking her grip down and sending magic into my body that had black spots appearing in my vision.

Cait! Roman's voice echoed through my head, but I couldn't lose focus. I had to fight back and get free of her hold.

She's taking the pack power. You have to let them go, Adira said with panicked words.

I tried to do as she asked, but the harder I pictured cutting my ties to the individual wolves, the more darkness swarmed my connection to them, wrapping around the threads of each wolf in our pack and pulling on their strength.

What had I done?

28

CAIT

Roman was coming toward us again, and he was back on two feet, growing in size with every step he took. Energy like never before exuded from him as his love for me provided the only strength I could still latch on to myself.

He's going to be the distraction while I break the connection to the pack, and you need to do something you don't want to, Adira said.

Is this the part of the plan you wouldn't tell me earlier?
It is.

The growls escaping from my mate gave Demi the slightest pause as she turned her head to the incoming threat.

A sigh left her lips, as if Roman was nothing more than a bug that she needed to flick away. I watched helplessly as she sent a stream of ebony-colored magic into Roman's chest. The glow of energy around him took in her power, and a smile spread across Roman's face.

We need to give Demi all of your power, Adira said while the hybrid was preoccupied.

Why? Roman seems to be doing what you wanted. I can get free, and we can finish this together, I argued.

No, Cait. That's not how this *ends.*

The tone of her voice told me there was a very good chance I was going to die again. Something I absolutely was not okay with.

My plan is the only way to save Roman and the rest of the pack. The only way. I'm sorry.

Damn it all to hell.

As Roman closed in on Demi again, she released me, and I fell to the ground like a sack of rocks. I was weak from her trying to take from the pack through me, but as I focused on the growing tattoo from my Luna Mark, I drew on the pure power I was gifted by our Moon Goddess.

The intertwining spirals darkened from silver to a charcoal color. I growled as my muscles ached from the draw of energy that was rapidly recharging me.

I was stronger in that moment than I'd ever been. Demi had her back to me. All I had to do was reach up and rip her heart from her chest. I could kill her. I knew it.

Trust me, Cait. We can't stop her that way, Adira said in response to my thoughts.

I trusted my wolf. We were one, but what she was suggesting didn't make any sense. If I gave Demi what she wanted, how could we possibly still win?

She thinks she's strong enough to wield your power for herself. We need to show her she's not. No matter the cost,

Adira said, but her words didn't make me feel any better.

I didn't want to die.

I didn't want to give that bitch everything that I was, even if it was what ruined her.

Most importantly, I didn't want to break Roman's heart all over again.

Fuck! I screamed inside my head. I already knew what I would do. It didn't matter what I wanted. Not anymore.

With shaking legs, I stood back up. Crackles of energy sounded around my glowing form. Demi was hitting Roman with waves of dark magic. Even though he was still standing, blood was dripping from his nose and ears, and open wounds had formed on his chest. He wasn't going to last much longer.

His eyes brightened when I joined the fight, but I'd already shut him out the moment Adira told me it was time.

I spun Demi toward me. "You wanted me. You can have me." My fingers tightened around her wrists as I pushed everything that I was into the hybrid I hoped was about to die alongside me.

Otherwise, I was going to torture Adira in our next life until we found Roman again. Maybe even long after that.

Demi's smile grew as darkness swelled inside me. She was pulling just as fast as I was pushing my energy into her. Everything about what I was doing felt like the right move when I had hoped it would be wrong.

My eyes met Roman's as he realized I wasn't

fighting back anymore. The silver specks disappeared as a storm built within him and he snarled, leaping onto Demi's back.

She paid him no attention, and I could feel him pressing in on the walls I'd created between us.

"Cait, don't do whatever it is you think you're doing," he demanded before starting to shift into his wolf form, likely so he could rip the hybrid's head from her shoulders.

Demi cackled before blasting him off her, interrupting his shift and causing my mate to groan in pain—a sound that only fueled my drive to see my task through. I wouldn't let him get hurt anymore.

I expelled my energy with more force than ever before. As I did so, the previously glowing tattoo began to fade, which I took to mean that whatever I was doing was working. Only, Demi didn't seem to be overwhelmed in the slightest.

Just a little bit more, Adira encouraged.

Greedy wolf, I thought.

My vision waned, and Demi began to sway before me, pulling away, but my grip tightened as my claws dug into her wrists.

She snarled at me, fighting to get free, but the remainder of my strength was focused on doing whatever it took to keep a hold of the hybrid.

"That's enough," she screeched, her voice cracking as wrinkles formed around her eyes.

I tried to reply, to say something witty that would hold her attention, but I couldn't make any words leave my mouth.

The cloudy shield around us began to shimmer, and fissures formed along the edges. Dozens of witches were surrounding us now, doing whatever they could to get in. I had to hurry and finish what I'd started before they interrupted us.

With one final push, I lost the hold I'd held to keep Roman out of my mind and gave the last of my energy to Demi. She screamed out at the same time I did, but my grip never broke.

Roman's energy filtered through me, and I tried to fight him off. I didn't want him to get hurt in whatever was about to happen.

Shadows escaped from beneath Demi's crimson clothes, darkening the outfit and turning on her. Her cries grew louder, and I could no longer hold on to her as my strength faded.

I fell backward, but Roman caught me before my head could even touch the ground. "I have you, Mate."

My heart was slowing just like before when I died in the motel room. I tried reaching for him, but I had no energy left in me to do so.

I love you, Roman, I said with acceptance through our bond.

Don't talk like that. I'm going to save you.

I wanted to tell him his efforts were wasted. That Adira had told me I needed to give all I had left, but I couldn't do it. I wasn't strong enough.

Roman laid me gently on the ground behind a row of witches and turned my head so I could see the finale. I blinked several times, but nothing would come into focus as my chest began to burn from lack of air.

My body was shutting down on me.

"I know what you did. I'm going to fix it, and then me and your wolf are going to have a long talk," Roman said as he walked away from me.

Embry and Sam's wolves appeared in my vision, blood coating their chests and muzzles. I wanted to reach out to them, but even that seemed like too much effort. They each took position beside me, and that was comfort enough.

Roman was standing next to a circle of witches, possibly yelling if the flailing of his hands meant anything. Though, I couldn't hear anything going on and I wasn't even sure I could trust what I was seeing.

Hang in there a little bit longer, Adira said.

So, now we're into prolonged torture? I countered.

I'm not the one who said you had to die. That was all you.

Rage filled me as my wolf's presence pushed forward. *Just keep watching and I'll fill you in after,* she added.

I no longer had any idea why I trusted her so much. I wanted to yell at the beast, but even that was a feat too big, so I settled on doing the only thing that didn't seem like it would cause any added pain.

My gaze focused on Demi as best I could. She was on her knees almost fully engulfed in the shadows. I couldn't see any details beyond that, but I could finally hear shouts that I assumed were coming from the witches.

A high-pitched scream sounded above any other noises, one that had Embry and Sam whimpering next to me. My eyes stayed on Demi as a new shield enclosed around the hybrid.

She shifted to a wolf form that glowed just like mine, but instead of purple, the color was the same auburn as her hair.

The wolf's head angled back, and I assumed she was howling, but no other sounds escaped the barrier she was cocooned within. The witches' chants grew louder, and the wolf began to shake. Slowly, fur began to fall from the beast. No, not fur. Demi was turning to ash as shadowy smoke rose from her wolf until the fumes circled at the top of the shield. The witches moved and surrounded the barrier, placing their hands on it.

I had no idea what they were doing. All I knew was that there were no more screams, and I hoped that meant everyone was okay.

I closed my eyes and Embry's wolf nudged me, but I had nothing left in me to respond with. Adira might not have thought I was going to die, but I wasn't regaining my strength. There was no light left within me.

As long as I'm here, you're not dying, Adira said, but even her voice sounded farther away than normal.

My next breath was more of a shudder as the muscles in my body gave in to the weariness.

A growl sounded just before someone—likely Sam— bit my leg. I didn't even have the desire to kick them back.

"Now, Beatrix!" Roman's voice snarled, jolting me from the final sleep I'd been so close to.

Just as cold hands slammed into my chest, Adira

and the pack's presence filled me with an overwhelming vengeance. Energy was coming at me from all directions, and I couldn't catch my breath as I continued gasping for air.

When my eyes finally opened again, Beatrix was kneeling over me with purple eyes and violet smoke encompassing the both of us.

"You did it, Cait. Your power killed her," Beatrix said.

"The witches…" I groaned. I hadn't lasted until the end. I didn't understand how I could have killed Demi.

"No, we only kept the energy contained that you forced into her. Everything else was all you."

I tried to be happy about that, but then I noticed Roman's hands were on Beatrix's shoulders, blood dripping from his fingertips. As my gaze met his determined one, I tried reaching out through our bond, but Beatrix decided to press harder against my chest, sending a wave of agony through me.

I had to clench my teeth to keep from screaming out as my hands fisted at my sides and my body convulsed against the hard ground.

What is happening? I asked, but I had no idea who would hear me.

Roman and Beatrix are saving you, Adira said.

How? I knew she'd said I wasn't going to die, but I'd been certain my wolf was wrong just minutes ago.

You gave your life to Demi, but when Roman distracted her, I took over the connection to the pack, blocking it from the hybrid, so that I could use their energy to keep you alive when you should have died. Now, Beatrix is giving back to you what she took from the hybrid.

Why the hell didn't you tell me the whole plan? I seriously wanted to murder my wolf as my strength agonizingly rebuilt.

Because you needed to be willing to give all of you. If you had any hope of surviving, you would have held back. I shared what needed to be known with Roman's wolf at the last minute. He passed along what Roman needed to do.

Just as I wanted to scream at my wolf, power stopped rocking my core and Beatrix's cold hands were replaced by Roman's warm ones, distracting me from my murderous thoughts. "Cait?"

"I'm still here," I croaked, relaxing under his touch as our bond began to heal both of us.

"I'm going to kill our wolves," he said as he gathered my battered body into his arms.

As much as I wanted to agree with him, I couldn't think of anything else with him being so close other than being grateful that I could still feel the power of his touch and hear the beat of his heart.

Vaughn spoke from somewhere behind us. "Sorry to ruin the reunion, but our fight isn't over. Most of the guards have stopped fighting, but they're in a useless daze as the spell wears off, and there are more than a handful who were fighting against us voluntarily."

"You've got to be kidding me," Roman groaned. "Embry, stay here with Cait. The rest of us will finish this."

Embry's wolf nodded, and Sam was already racing back toward the other fight with Vaughn and Kelly on her heels. Roman sat me on the ground and kissed my forehead. "I'll be back just as soon as I can. Stay here with Embry and the witches."

"Hurry back," I said with a faked groan.

He nodded and shifted to his wolf form after taking a step back from me. I rolled over, watching him disappear around one of the other buildings, then started to call my own shift forward, even though I wasn't back to one hundred percent yet.

He's going to kill you, Embry's voice said as her wolf stared at me.

Yeah, well, he'll get over it. I need to be there with him. I felt that need deep in my soul.

Beatrix sighed just as I finished the change to my wolf form. Relief rolled through my muscles as the energy of my wolf took over. We turned toward Beatrix, waiting to hear what else she had to say before taking off. It was the least she deserved after helping save my life.

"Your energy is unlike anything I've ever known. I can still feel its power pulsing through me, even though I tried to give it all back."

I wasn't worried about Beatrix having access to my energy. She deserved a reward after what she'd done. I closed the distance between us and pressed my wolf head against her stomach. She tensed and patted me awkwardly. It probably wasn't often she was this up close and personal with a wolf.

"Thank you, Cait." Beatrix turned away and went back to her coven while Embry waited for me.

We shouldn't be fighting again so soon, Adira said

when we started running with Embry in the direction of the others.

What if Roman needs us? This fight isn't over.

Let's finish this, then.

If the others had everything under control, then I'd stay out of the ongoing battle, but I wanted to at least be close enough to help however I could if needed.

We ran through the streets, and I already knew I wasn't as powerful as I was before. Even if Beatrix had only kept a fraction of my energy, I was still missing plenty more of it. I had a feeling the Luna Mark was a gift I'd received for a purpose and now that the purpose was fulfilled, a few things were going to change, which was more than okay with me. I had no desire to be a beacon of power for the rest of my life.

A warmth filled my chest as the wind brushed across my fur. I looked up into the full moon, which was tinted pink just like the color of Luna's aura, and I knew my thoughts were accurate.

Are you good back there? Embry asked when I slowed.

I'm more than good, I replied and truly meant it.

29

ROMAN

Walking away from Cait to help finish this fight was not something I'd wanted to do, but I'd had to do it. Once I knew she was okay, I needed to be there for my pack. I'd already sensed the lives lost as they'd been picked off one-by-one. Nine in total. At least, so far.

Ramona is down. I'm diverting to her, Sam's voice sounded through my mind.

They need help near the black stucco building over there. I'm pretty sure it's one of the council prisons and those still fighting against us are guarding it for some reason, Vaughn said after her.

As much as I wanted to check on my mother, I trusted Sam to take care of her, because if Vaughn was asking for help, then there was a serious problem.

My wolf's paws pounded against the ground, harder and faster than ever before, kicking up loose cobble as we went. While I was more than furious with him for keeping Adira's plan from me, I understood why they'd done it. Cait might have still gone along with the strategy, but I wouldn't have.

It was the best way to keep her alive. Now focus, so we can stay alive, too, my wolf said as we arrived at the battle still going strong.

Knowing that the remaining threats were here voluntarily made things easier. If these supernaturals were trying to kill us all on their own, they didn't need to be fought with caution. Instead, throats were about to be torn out.

We crashed into a group of shifters, breaking up a good portion of the fight before whipping around and clamping down on one of their necks. Once I heard bones break, I moved on. The shifter might not have been dead, but he would be soon. He could suffer the last few moments of his life. That wasn't my problem.

A vampire slammed into the side of my wolf, sending me sailing in the opposite direction I'd been headed. I'd never even seen the bloodsucker coming, but I was quick to get up. Bones were definitely fractured in my ribs, but I'd pushed through worse pain, and they'd heal soon enough.

The vamp disappeared, then reappeared right next to me, grabbing on to the back of my neck with his fangs extended. A vampire bite could be lethal to shifters. If he pumped enough of his venom into me, my own body would turn on me. That wasn't going to happen.

My claws extended, swiping at my attacker as I called on the energy I'd newly acquired. Something about it didn't feel the same, but there was still enough strength there that I could draw on.

I hit my mark, leaving deep gouges down the left side of the vampire's face, ripping half his mouth out. He hissed at me, still capable of using his fangs, and moved to bite me again.

I bucked beneath his hold, but I already knew I wasn't going to get out of the way in time.

Another force slammed into us, sending both the bloodsucker and me tumbling ten feet to the right. Maciah stood above us and sighed before leaning down to grab the vampire by the neck.

Without hesitation, Maciah ripped the guy's head right from his neck, causing blood to splatter across my wolf's face. Maciah nodded at me as he dropped the body to the ground, then took off to help others.

"Roman!" the sound of Perry's voice hit me right in my gut.

My wolf's ears picked up on the painful call, and I turned to the left only to find Perry battling against three warlocks. I took several steps toward him, then paused as the ground began to shake.

I heard Cait's wolf howl before her voice sounded in my head. *Are you okay?*

Stay away from here, Cait.

I could sense her getting close and not listening to me. Stubborn woman was going to be the death of me.

The dirt beneath my paws started to crack, and the building we were all fighting near began to crumble as its foundation was rocked.

I leaped over a fissure in the ground, intent to get to

Perry before something worse happened. Fog rose from the opening in the dirt and roars were sounding from below.

Whatever was down there was furious, and I wasn't sure if that was going to be a good or bad thing for us. Either way, I still had a task to complete.

Dodging falling debris, I was only a few feet from Perry when I noticed the puncture wounds in his calf where a yellow poison was oozing from. Damn it. He'd been bitten, and that was the only reason these worthless warlocks had the upper hand against my father's best friend.

Just as I leapt toward the magic-users, Cait's wolf appeared in my peripheral, copying my actions. We landed just moments apart, and I wanted to demand she leave, especially with whatever was coming out of the ground, but I knew it would be a wasted effort.

My wolf's teeth sank into the ribs of the nearest attacker, biting down until our hold was good enough to tear out bones. Just as our head jerked back, the warlock grabbed on to our head and sent a stream of magic that had my bite locking down tight and the rest of my body seizing.

I couldn't let go to back up and regain my composure. The electrical current coursing through my veins kept me from moving any part of my body.

Cait was right behind us, fighting as if she hadn't almost died a short time before. My mate was a warrior. There was no doubt about that, even though I wished it wasn't true because of the danger it kept putting her in.

Her claws sank into the stomach of the warlock she

was battling, and it wasn't until then that I noticed she wasn't glowing like I was used to, either. Something had changed when Cait gave Demi all of her energy. I didn't like it.

Cait didn't slow down though. She ripped out the magic user's guts without a care in the world, then her wolf jumped up and bit into his neck, whipping her head back and forth until the warlock went limp beneath her hold.

My heart was racing from the shockwaves still tearing through my body. The one I was still latched onto snickered above me. "I can heal myself from some broken bones and shredded skin, but can you replace your heart once it gives out?"

No, I couldn't, but while the warlock had been focusing on me, he hadn't noticed that my mate and Perry had killed his friends. They moved together toward me, slower than I would have liked, but there was a gleam of murder in Cait's wolf's eyes that told me she had a plan that wouldn't be rushed.

Her wolf lowered to the ground as I stayed put, trying not to draw attention away from myself. A light shimmer pulsed around Cait, and then she pushed off the ground in one smooth motion, practically flying toward us with her jaws open as wide as they would go.

Her snarls finally alerted the warlock holding on to me that he wasn't as safe as he thought, but it was too late. Cait's wolf hit her mark, devouring the head of the magic user and tearing it clean off.

My wolf collapsed to the ground once the electrical

current ceased, and I needed an extra moment before we could get up. Perry was right beside me and let out a strangled noise as he grabbed on to my front paws, tossing me behind him in the most ungraceful way.

I landed on my back and groaned as Cait knelt beside me, already back in her human form. She glanced up at Perry with glossy eyes. "Thank you."

I shifted back as well. My wolf needed a break and I wanted to know just how bad Perry's injury was. When I was on my knees, still recovering and in my human form, I saw the mountain of rubble laying where I'd just been, and Cait's thanks made more sense to me. Perry had saved me from being crushed by one of the walls to the building next to us.

Perry leaned against a post, sweat beading along his forehead. "Poison. Vampire bite," he heaved.

No, we would not lose this man. I couldn't let it happen, but as far as I was aware, the spell to stop the venom from traveling to his heart and taking his life required time Perry didn't have.

Silvie, Vaughn, and Kelly raced toward us, all of them already shifted back to their human forms as well. Kelly had fresh tears falling down her cheeks, but not Silvie. She charged in, and it wasn't until her arm swung back that I noticed the glint of a blade in her hand.

Kelly cried out, none of us expecting what her mother was about to do.

Using two hands, Silvie swung a sword at her mate. The metal was razor sharp and cut through Perry's leg in one cut. He fell to the ground as a witch joined Silvie.

"Hold still, Mate. You might not walk right again, but I'm not letting you die on me just yet. I haven't had enough of you. Just hope the venom didn't travel beyond your leg and I don't have to cut anything else off," Silvie said with a wink as she grabbed onto his hands.

A witch I recognized from when we were fighting Demi coated her hands in a turquoise magic before pressing them over Perry's stump of a leg. I cringed as he roared, but I didn't look away until I could be sure he was safe.

Seconds turned to minutes as we waited. Perry's face was ashen, but he was still breathing and that was most important.

Finally, the witch released him. "There's no trace of venom in the rest of his body. He'll be okay." She glanced down at his missing leg. "Well, he'll live anyway."

Her last comment wasn't necessary, and I was about to tell the witch just that in my own words, but Cait tugged on my arm.

"Uh, should we be worried about that?" she asked, pointing behind us.

Eight supernaturals in blue robes stood together, emanating power like I'd never felt before. Anyone who was fighting against us before was now laying on the ground, twitching like dying snakes.

I focused back on the eight individuals, and the instinct to bow before them surged through me, but I fought against it, staying upright until we knew if the new arrivals were another danger to us.

Their hoods were up, and a shadow kept me from identifying anything about them. One stepped forward from the group, walking toward us in slow steady movements, almost as if they were floating above the destroyed ground.

"You have done us a great service today, and we won't soon forget that," a voice echoed that was so even-toned that I couldn't be sure if there was a man or woman behind the darkness hiding their identity.

The being I assumed to be a council member continued, "Demi came to us long ago, asking to join our group of hunters and offering her allegiance. We denied her request, because she wasn't the kind of supernatural that we wanted representing us. What we didn't know was that she would spend the next decade gathering all the dark power and information that she could against us. When she asked for a meeting again, stating she had information we needed to know, we fell into a trap, something I can assure you will never happen again.

"For months, Demi used her power to control us, making us ask for things we had no business asking for. When we finally found a way to break through her hold over us, she was prepared and banished us to the lowest level of our prison here. We've spent the last three months trapped below ground while she took over the Supernatural Council. Our powers were suppressed by our own safeguards until you killed her and we were able to break free."

There was a wave of relief that went through me at knowing the council we were supposed to trust hadn't been compromised. At least, not in the ways I'd been assuming.

"So, what now?" Cait asked.

The cloaked being turned toward my mate. "Now, you can go home, and we will clean up this mess before starting over. Once we have rebuilt our foundations, we would like to properly thank you and the others who showed up today."

"No thanks necessary," I said. Even if the council hadn't been as shady as we believed, I still didn't want anything to do with them. More than anything, I just wanted to start a life with my mate that she deserved.

The council member nodded. "I understand. Maybe one day you'll change your minds. The offer will always be there. For now, our guards will help gather your fallen and get you home."

We watched the cloaked figure make its way back to the others who'd stayed behind. Fog came up from the ground, engulfing the eight council members until we could no longer see them. With a single gust of wind, the fog disappeared along with the council.

"I don't know about the rest of you, but I'd like to get the hell out of here," Perry said with a groan from the ground.

I moved to help him up, but Silvie wrapped her arm around him and had the task handled. "Then, let's get going, my love," she said.

Vaughn looked at me. "Do you mind…"

I waved a hand. "Help them. They're your family now, too."

He grinned like a fool in love, and I tried not to let

my sadness show at the thought of him leaving us. I turned away with Cait and took slow steps toward where Sam had run off to get to my mother.

I held on to Cait, looking down at her. "Thanks for coming, even when I specifically asked you not to."

She grinned. "Anytime."

I had no doubt she meant that.

We passed by Lucinda and Finn just in time to see them wave and teleport to wherever they were headed next. I couldn't deny Cait had been right to trust the fae, and I was thankful for their help.

I searched for Maciah and the other vampires, but they were nowhere to be seen, which didn't surprise me. Though, I had a feeling this wouldn't be the last time we saw them. Zeke seemed too interested in our pack to stay away forever.

Beatrix and a group of her witches were moving through the bodies scattered on the ground. Cries from the magic users could be heard as they gathered their fallen witches and warlocks. Plenty of lives were lost, but they were not in vain. We did what we came here to do and restored the order of our world. Or at least, hit the reset button.

Cait sniffled next to me as she saw the lost members of our pack I'd already sensed. I held her tighter against me as Sam and my mother came into view. No words would make the losses hurt any less.

Embry was already with them and moved to help Sam lift my mom from the ground. She had a large cut in her upper thigh and a head wound that hopefully looked worse than it really was from all the blood I could see crusted in her hair.

"Is it over?" my mother asked.

I nodded. "We can go home now."

Portals were being opened around us that would lead those of us left back to where we wanted to be most. We all had people to bury, but our lives were safer because of what we did here.

The entire supernatural world was safer.

EPILOGUE

CAIT

Two Months Later

I n the weeks since our fight against Demi and those who stood with her, it seemed like everything had changed. Normally, change wasn't something I was fond of, but in this case, I'd accepted there was no point in fighting against any of it.

We'd lost eleven pack members by the time we got home. Brothers and sisters who wouldn't soon be forgotten. After getting all the other wolves back to the pack and giving the fallen shifters a proper send-off, we'd had another goodbye to get through. One I took harder than I'd expected.

Vaughn had found his mate, and it was time for him to move on. Kelly's family needed her more than we needed him, even if his departure left a hole in my heart. When Roman had released him from the pack, an ache formed in my chest at the loss of our beta.

He was the glue that had kept this pack together the last several months, and there wasn't a dry eye for miles when we'd said our goodbyes to the humorous wolf. He promised to visit, but we all knew nothing would be the same and that was okay.

What surprised me the most was when Sam's wolf presented herself as a beta candidate with the power inside her to do so. It wasn't something we ever saw coming—we'd assumed Collin would be next in line—but she was the perfect fit, and we trusted her with our lives, which was most important.

So, with the pack back at home and our lives no longer in danger, I'd focused on all of the good in my life and the reasons I had to be grateful for having my world turned upside down all those months ago.

Roman's presence broke me from my inner thoughts, and I looked up from the book I was currently reading in the library to find he wasn't alone.

"We have a visitor," Roman said before gesturing toward the shifter at his side. "This is Mateo. He said he has business here, but he isn't sure what it is."

My chest tightened. Unknown wolves didn't just randomly show up and have no clue as to why. We didn't need any more drama in our lives. Things had finally settled. I badly wanted to tell the new arrival that he could just give us a call once he figured out what his business was, and be on his way.

Instead, I set my book down on the table, stood up

like the alpha female I was, and smiled at our guest. "Then, I guess we better figure it out."

Mateo had dark-chocolate eyes and matching hair he kept shaved short. There was a deep scar over his left cheek that told me he'd lived a rough life. His dark-wash jeans and black t-shirt were clean but wrinkled, as if he'd been wearing them for several days now. That made me wonder where he'd come from and why he wasn't with a pack.

"I think I found something about your mark that you'll find—" Embry's voice cut off as she noticed our guest. She'd become obsessed about figuring out why the Luna Mark I'd received had faded into nothing more than what appeared to be a birthmark and why I hadn't gotten all of my energy and abilities back after the fight.

I'd been concerned at first as well when she made some valid points, wondering if it would affect me in ways that would leave our pack vulnerable, but Adira still shimmered purple when we wanted, and I could still kick Embry's ass during training. I stopped wasting my time with worry after that. I had better ways to spend my days. Much better.

"Holy-mother-freaking-hell," she muttered, frozen on the staircase with the book hanging precariously from her fingers.

I went to my best friend, worried that we now had more than one problem on our hands. "What is it?" I asked, but she wouldn't look at me.

Embry's gaze was locked on our guest. When I

glanced back at Roman and Mateo, Roman had moved away from him and was smiling.

It took me a moment longer than I'd have liked to realize what was happening. I removed the book from Embry's hands and gave her a shove off the stairs. "Well, don't just stand there with your mouth hanging open. Go get him."

She sneered at me before taking cautious steps toward her mate. Once the initial shock wore off him, there was nothing slow about either of their movements.

Mateo scooped Embry up into his arms, and she wrapped her legs around his waist. "*Mi tesoro*," he whispered, and that was our cue to leave.

I gave the two wolves a wide berth as I made my way to Roman. We closed the door on our way out of the library and found Sam and Ramona coming toward us.

"Where's the rogue shifter?" Sam asked.

I grinned. "He's not rogue. He's in love."

Sam's brow furrowed, and Ramona matched my smile. "Is that Embry in there with him?"

"Yep," I answered.

Sam groaned. "Just when I was starting to like her."

"It's okay, Sammy. We'll find you a mate soon enough," Roman said. She growled at him.

"No, thanks," Sam muttered before heading toward the front door. She was still just as rough around the edges as when I'd met her, and I couldn't wait for the day someone knocked the breath from her lungs.

Roman went to his mom, cupping her elbow. "How are you doing today?"

"Better. I went for a run with Sam and was faster than the day before."

Her femoral artery had been damaged during the battle, and it was weeks before she was even able to walk without assistance, so to hear she was continuing to increase her speed made my heart happy. Ramona missed Jack with a fierceness, but her time in this life wasn't over yet.

"Now that I'm feeling as good as I'll probably get, I'll be headed out to West Texas soon. I'd like to meet Moira," Ramona said, surprising me.

I'd almost forgotten about the new alpha who was also Ramona's aunt. We hadn't heard anything from them, but we considered that a good thing.

"I think if you're comfortable with it, then that's a great idea, but I'll be sending at least two other wolves with you," Roman said, always the overprotective alpha.

Ramona sighed. "We'll talk about that later. I'm going to go rest for a bit, now that we know nothing is wrong. Let's plan for dinner with our new guest. If he arrived alone and lost, let's hope he's here to stay instead of planning to whisk our Embry away from us," Ramona said before walking away from the two of us.

Her words had a sharp pain burrowing into my chest. No, Embry couldn't leave me. She was my best friend. The thought hadn't even occurred to me when I realized her mate had found her. We'd just said our goodbyes to Vaughn. I couldn't handle letting her go as well. Not if there were any other options.

Roman grabbed my hand and pulled me into his arms. "Easy, Kitten. He left his pack. His wolf was restless, and he took a chance. One that worked out in his favor, considering there is no yelling coming from the library. Embry is staying here. I'll make Mateo a pack member tonight if I have to."

As selfish as I knew my freak-out was, I nearly cried tears of joy when Roman finished speaking. There might not have been an official bond between me and my best friend, but I couldn't fathom life without her at my side.

I looked up at him. "Thank you."

His lips came down on mine. "Anything for you, Mate."

I raised a brow. "Anything, anything?"

He laughed, pulling me flush against him. "You already have all of me. What more could you want?"

"Just a lifetime of forevers with you," I answered, even though he was right.

I had everything I didn't know I needed before arriving here. I had a family, a home, and my mate.

A rumble built in his chest as he picked me up, carrying me toward the stairs and hopefully to our bedroom, so I could properly show him just how much I appreciated having all of him.

As his steps quickened, I knew then, without a doubt in my soul, that everything would be okay. No matter what came our way, we'd find a way through it, because together… we were unstoppable.

The end has arrived, but that doesn't mean the party is over! Luna Marked is part of a much bigger world I will continue to build on for at least a couple more series. If you follow Mystics and Mayhem on Amazon, you'll see all the books included in this world.
Each series can be read on its own and in any order. There are no spoilers to be worried about! Only fun cameos from some of your favorite characters!

Next up in this world is Vampire Heir! This series features a snarky huntress and the sexy vampire bound to protect her. Releasing November 4th, 2021! You can preorder your copy HERE!
While you wait for the next series, make sure to read Lucinda and Finn's story in Broken Court! Now complete in ebook, audio, and paperback!

STAY IN TOUCH

Find Heather on Facebook:
Reader Group:
Want to talk all things books and get updates before anyone else? Come hang with me in my reader group!
Heather Renee's Book Warriors

Author Page:
Teaser and big updates are also posted here!
Heather Renee Author

Newsletter:
I sent this out sporadically. Don't worry. You won't ever be spammed by me and you get a couple goodies when you sign up!
http://smarturl.it/HeatherReneeNL

Blood of the Sea Series

A complete Young Adult Paranormal Romance series featuring vampires, open seas adventures, and the occasional pirate.

Standalone

Marked Paradox - A complete Young Adult Fantasy fae story about a realm divided and one fae to bring them back together.

ACKNOWLEDGMENTS

It's hard to know where to start with this series. Luna Marked has changed my world in all the best ways. This series has brought me so much joy and I'm so thankful for all of you that have embraced Cait, Roman, and crew!

A huge thank you to my very own Asstie Jamie. She not only is the bestest friend and editor, but she also created the word Asstie and deserves all the wonderful things!

Love and hugs to my assistant Michelle who this book is also dedicated to. No words can describe her awesomeness. She is my perfect sidekick. For this reason, I gift her Zeke!

Big thanks to my cover designer Jay with Covers by Juan. You've been a huge part in my author world and I look forward to another 20 covers with you!

And the biggest of big thanks to my readers. Without your support, I wouldn't be the author I am today. You have allowed me to do a job that I love and that can offer an escape to people all over the world. From the bottom of my heart, I thank you for your continued support! Here's to another 25 books!

ABOUT THE AUTHOR

Heather Renee is a *USA Today* bestselling author who lives in Oregon. She writes urban fantasy and paranormal romance novels with a mixture of adventure, humor, and sass. Her love of reading eventually led to her passion for writing and giving the gift of escapism.

When Heather's not writing, she is spending time with her loving husband and beautiful daughter, going on their own adventures. For more ways to connect with her, visit www.HeatherReneeAuthor.com.

Ingram Content Group UK Ltd.
Milton Keynes UK
UKHW052235060623
422929UK00021BA/798/J

9 781735 474656